The Beauty of You

by

Jennifer Wenn

The Royal Family, Book Three

The Beauty of You

Cover Art by *Debbie Taylor*

The Wild Rose Press, Inc.
PO Box 708
Adams Basin, NY 14410-0708
Visit us at www.thewildrosepress.com

Publishing History
First Tea Rose Edition, 2015
Print ISBN 978-1-62830-707-8
Digital ISBN 978-1-62830-708-5

The Royal Family, Book Three
Published in the United States of America

Dedication

To Louise—sister and fellow writer,
a kindred spirit in every way...biatch...

Chapter One

Chester Park, Berkshire, October 1814

"You are despicable!"

Sitting on the bed she now was to call her own, Charmaine looked up into her new husband's furious face hovering above her.

"I know." Her clipped voice echoed in the silent chamber, and Sinclair Darling, Earl of Chilton, sneered in disgust.

"How can you sit there without even pretending to be sorry? *You* were the one who made sure we had to marry, not I. What I don't understand is *why*. Why on earth did *you* want to marry *me*?"

She wished she could offer him an easy answer to his question, but how could she? She didn't know what had possessed her to act as she had, and now it was too late for regrets. What was done was done; all she could do now was to see it through.

"I don't know."

"You don't know?" His scowl intensified until his dark eyes looked like two pieces of hard coal. "How could you not know? We are husband and wife now—married! Not because I wanted you, courted you, and in the end proposed to you—you know, how normal people commit to each other. No, we are married because you tricked me!"

"I did not trick you..."

"Yes, you did."

It was no use arguing with him. He was simply too angry with her. Instead of listening to her, he would more likely jump on every possibility to fight verbally with her. He would use that crazy, illogical logic most of the Darlings possessed, and in the end she wouldn't know what had been said, or why. So, in a desperate attempt to save what was left of her wounded pride, she forced herself to stay quiet.

Growling in frustration over her lack of response, Sin started to stalk across the floor, sending brooding gazes at her every time he passed her. One part of her wished she could give him what he so desperately needed—the truth. But would he listen to her? And more importantly, would he believe her?

"I'm sorry," she said for the hundredth-plus-one time, and for the hundredth-plus-one time he sneered at her.

"How can you be? You got what you wanted."

"I didn't want this."

He shook his head. "Of course you did. Why else would you have forced a marriage between us? For some strange, inexplicable reason, you wanted *me*."

"I didn't want you."

That took him by surprise. "You didn't want me?"

"No."

"But why…?" His voice trailed off as he tried to make sense of what she was telling him. Or rather, what she wasn't telling him.

She watched him pace restlessly all over the polished wooden floor, pulling his fingers harshly through his thick brown hair. Overwhelming guilt made her heart ache with compassion for him, too aware of how this was all her fault, not his. Again she repeated how sorry she was, and he sent her another disgusted look.

"Stop telling me you are sorry, because I don't believe you truly are. You insist you didn't want this, yet you still remain the sole reason why I stand here before you and have the doubtful pleasure of calling you my wife."

"I had no choice." A lump started to build in her throat when he shook his head in disbelief.

"There is always a choice."

"Not for me."

Surprising her, he stopped charging around and instead knelt in front of her, enclosing her cold hands in his large warm ones. "Then humor me. Please try to make me understand. Why did you make sure we would be found in bed together by my parents? You knew they would never settle for anything less than marriage, so please don't say you didn't plan it."

It was evident he worked hard to restrain his anger, softening his voice on her behalf. For a moment she wanted to let him lure her into a false sense of security, because it felt good to not live in fear, if only for a second or two.

She had known Sin her whole life, as they had grown up in the same county. Harveyfield, her childhood home, was situated only a short walk down the winding road from Chester Park, the enormous, ancient castle the Darling family—and now she—called home.

They had never interacted before, as he was six years her senior and they had spent their childhood years in different types of schooling, he getting the education the heir to a duke deserved. But as her one-year-younger sister Penelope and his little sister Francesca were close friends, she knew everything there was to know about him anyhow.

Sinclair Darling was a good, decent man and a devoted, trustworthy brother who spent most of his time trying not to crumble under the heavy weight of being the heir to the Dukedom of Berkeley. Maybe that was why she thoughtlessly had put her foot in front of him, forcing him to stumble and helplessly fall down on the bed, landing heavily upon her just as his parents walked through the door.

It was rather odd, though, that marrying him had never been an option to her before. To be completely honest, she had never considered him a possible husband at all. Especially not someone to fall in love with.

Her sister Penelope had once mentioned how Sin had admitted he found Charmaine's beauty astounding. But she had never thought twice about it. That is, not until the fateful moment when she heard his parents' voices outside the guest room as he helped her toward the bed. When she'd looked up into his strong, anxious face, she had realized for the first time that she carried her own destiny in her two hands. Or rather her feet.

If she dared…

"Do you know what really baffles me?" Sin continued. "You could have had any man you fancied. You are the bloody Incomparable Queen of the *ton*, for goodness' sake! The ballrooms of England are filled with men who would have been more than ecstatic if you had accepted their proposals."

4

She tried to look away in a desperate attempt to ignore him, but he grabbed her chin lightly, forcing her to look straight at him. The pain and confusion in his dark eyes overwhelmed her, tormenting her already guilt-stricken heart. But she forced herself to stay serene, coldly meeting his gaze.

"So why choose me?" he continued harshly. "The one man in England who doesn't want you?"

"I didn't choose you."

"So you keep saying, and yet I don't believe you." He let her go and stood to continue his restless pacing in front of her. His body seemed filled with an angry energy that desperately needed to come out.

"Then don't." She forced her voice to sound as bland as possible and felt almost sorry for him as he rolled his eyes in frustration.

"How can you be this cold? Doesn't it mean anything to you that the man you now call husband can hardly stand the sight of you?"

Every last part of her wanted to slide into his arms and cry out the truth. She desperately wanted to wipe away every last shred of contempt he felt against her, but she couldn't. It pained her, but she had to play the part she had played most of her life, The Incomparable Queen of the *ton*—a selfish and inconsiderate beauty who was too spoiled for her own good.

She needed space and time to think. And the only way to get that was to make him loathe her even more so he would choose to stay out of her way. Seeing this through wouldn't be easy, but she hoped it would be worth it.

It had to be.

With a quiet sigh, she squared her shoulders and

drained her face of all feelings before meeting his dark eyes.

"No, why should I?" She made sure to shrug daintily, seemingly disinterested. "It's not as if I am the one of us who should be grateful for the gift he has been bestowed."

He stared at her, openmouthed, clearly not believing his ears. "Are you telling me I should rejoice in the fact that I'm now married to you?"

She yawned in a bored fashion behind her hand. "Yes."

"Why?"

"Why?" She made sure to look utterly confused, with a little pinch of outrage. "Because I'm the most sought-after woman in England."

The look of shock on his face was almost funny, and she bit her lower lip lightly to stop herself from giggling like a mad woman, due to the stress.

"I can hardly believe I have to tell you this," she continued instead, looking down at her perfectly cut nails. "You said it yourself. Every man who ever met me yearns for me. You should be grateful, not upset."

"You don't think I have the right to be upset?"

"No. Why should you? You are married to me."

Sin shook his head in disbelief. "You forced me into this marriage…"

"I did not force you into anything. It was you who had the bad manners to place yourself on top of me so I could hardly breathe. You are quite heavy, you know. As I see it, it is you who should apologize to me, not I to you."

"I don't want an apology. All I want is the truth."

She ignored his pleading eyes and her aching

heart's response. Instead, she straightened her skirt carefully, just to have something else to focus on.

"I have told you the truth."

"No, you haven't."

"Yes, I have."

"No, you..." He interrupted himself, stopping the childish discussion with a heavy sigh. "This is going nowhere. Talking to you is like hitting my head against a wall. I always thought Fanny was wrong, that there was more to you than a pretty face. But I guess she was right all along—inside your beautiful exterior there is only blood, bone, and selfishness."

She dug her nails into her palms to stop the urgent wish to redeem herself in his eyes. Instead she snorted with all the contempt she could muster. "Of course Fanny says my beauty is only skin deep. I would too, if I were as homely and unattractive as she is."

She watched his nostrils flare angrily as she insulted his beloved little sister. She knew she was at the point of no return, and her whole being desperately wanted to stop this verbal suicide, but she hardened herself. This was not the time to save herself from his wrath. She was doing it for Penelope's best, but she couldn't tell him that.

He would never understand.

"I have always pitied your poor parents, to be stuck with such an unattractive daughter. It's just as my parents, who thought they could do better after having me, only to find themselves burdened with Penny instead."

Ignoring his seething anger, she continued brutally, making sure not to soften her words. "I must admit the thought of Fanny's homeliness scares me a bit. What if we would have a daughter like her? Someone who isn't beautiful?"

"Are you out of your mind?" Sin yelled at her, finally losing his temper. "It is my sister you talk about, someone I hold most dear. If I were to have a child like her I would be overjoyed. I love her with all my heart, something you obviously never will understand, as you just made it quite clear that you don't care about anyone, not even your own sister."

He charged toward the door which connected their bedrooms, but stopped halfway. Hesitantly he turned to look at her, as if he wanted to give her one more chance to redeem herself before it was too late.

"How can you be this cold?" he whispered hoarsely, his voice strained with emotion.

Because I have to.

"Please," she sighed, as if she found him extremely tedious. "Love means nothing in the end. Only beauty prevails. Fanny should be thankful for being an heiress. She would never have caught the eye of a man like the Duke of Hereford otherwise."

It was saddening to see how the last little warmth toward her disappeared from his eyes, leaving only a cold wall of disgust. He was her husband, the man she was supposed to spend the rest of her life with. And yet here she was, saying everything she could think of to make sure he would hate her.

She wanted nothing more than to explain herself, but she knew she couldn't. So instead she kept quiet, fussing over one of her perfect nails, making sure he got an impression of exactly how unimportant she found his rightful anger.

"You are awful."

She looked up and met his eyes, so he could see how untouched she was. With a staggering breath, he stumbled backwards toward the connecting door, and she winced as it crashed shut behind him.

Breathing deeply, she leaned back until she lay on the bed, her eyes aching with unshed tears. *Damn you*, she thought with raw hatred. *Damn you for forcing me to destroy my own life.*

Chapter Two

"You look like hell."

Sin looked up from the swirling glass of wine, frowning slightly toward his younger brother Sebastian, who sat down in the other armchair with an annoying grin.

Bloody hell.

"Go away."

Ignoring his older brother, Sebastian reached for the bottle and filled an empty glass to its brim, showing no inclination of going anywhere.

Bloody hell and back.

"And here I thought you would be dancing with happiness over being married to the woman you have been desperately in love with for the last decade."

"I'm not in love with her."

"Yes, you are."

"I am *not* in love with her."

Still grinning that annoying, omniscient grin as only he could, Sebastian raised his glass cheerfully with every word. "Yes. You. Are."

Sin closed his eyes, hoping his brother would be long gone when he opened them again, but to no use. The imp still sat in the other chair, his green eyes shining with mirth and his red hair sparkling in the light from the fireplace.

It was amazing that two brothers could be as

different as he and Sebastian, both in looks and in personality. Sin was a typical Darling when it came to his looks, brown-haired and gray-eyed. Tall and broad shouldered. He had a tendency to brood and act with too much seriousness, but it all came from feeling the weight of being *the* heir and all the responsibility that brought. He usually didn't talk too much, which was somewhat odd, as he happened to be part of a family that never stayed silent, not even if their lives depended upon it.

Sebastian, on the other hand, was the worriless imp, always full of mirth, driving everyone crazy with his pranks and smooth tongue. He had inherited their mother's Irish looks, with his red hair and green eyes. Their father insisted he also had inherited their mother's Irish temper—but only when she didn't overhear, of course.

Their sister Francesca—the youngest of the three siblings—was a perfect mix of them both, with the Darling coloring and the Irish mirth.

"Come on, Sin, everyone knows you have been yearning for her ever since you came to the age when girls suddenly weren't as awful as you first thought."

"Everyone?"

"Everyone but Fanny. Our dear sister is not very sensitive when it comes to feelings. She wouldn't recognize a feeling if she were hit in the face with it. When you come to think about it, it's amazing she succeeded in getting married at all, and that to a man who actually loves her."

Sin sighed again, defeated. Who was he kidding? He *had* been in love with Charmaine ever since she turned into a young woman, desperately so. But she had never looked at him twice, which probably was the sole reason he hadn't joined her constant crowd of admirers.

Or maybe it was his fear of having to converse with her. He was not as smooth when it came to the ladies as most of his male relatives were. His uncle Rake was an infamous libertine who left piles of crushed hearts behind him, and even his own father had been quite the rogue in his day, not once stumbling upon words.

Sin knew he was a somewhat attractive man, the number of starry-eyed young misses surrounding him at parties and assemblies told him as much. But he usually pretended not to notice them and escaped their clutches as soon as he could.

This had of course created a reputation for him of being elusive, but it didn't seem to stop the misses' eagerness to become Lady Chilton. Instead he had his own entourage wherever he went, a frustrating mix of determined mamas and their eyelash-batting offspring. He had more than once told Francesca that if he ever found her batting her eyelashes at a man he would grab a pair of scissors and cut them off.

"What's wrong?" For once Sebastian lost his usual mirth and looked as sober as his brother, and Sin sighed heavily.

"I wouldn't know where to start."

"It can't be that bad."

"Trust me, it is. She's not what I thought her to be. I always believed Fanny to be wrong when she ranted on about how awful Charmaine really was, and that under the beautiful exterior only rotten eggs remained. But now…"

Tasting the delicious wine, he braced himself,

aware that he couldn't hide the truth from his brother. It was just that somehow it felt as if saying it out loud made it true, and for some strange reason he was stupid enough to still nurse a pathetic hope about her being better than she seemed.

But she wasn't.

"She is the most shallow, selfish, coldhearted person I've ever encountered, and I can't believe I have thought so highly of her for such a long time."

"Come on, Sin, it's Charmaine we're talking about. Our neighbor. The one we have known most of our lives and who might not have behaved with warmth toward us—or anyone else for that matter—but who we know loves her sister very much."

"No, she doesn't."

Sebastian looked genuinely surprised over Sin's harsh honesty. "She doesn't?"

"No."

"And how would you know this?"

"She just told me."

"She said she didn't love her sister?"

Sin felt like growling. "Not straight out, but she made it perfectly clear, and when I questioned her about it she didn't deny it."

"Bloody hell."

"My sentiment exactly." Sin sighed, with a compassionate look toward his confused brother. "And now I don't know what to do. At first I could hardly believe my luck. By some strange twist of fate I was able to marry the only woman I ever considered for my wife. But then I started to wonder why. *Why* did she want to marry me? She has never shown any interest in my person before, hardly greeted me when we happened to meet…"

"I thought it was you who took the chance when it was presented to you and made sure you two had to become husband and wife."

Sin shook his head again. "No. That was all her doing. She tripped me, and I fell down on top of her just as Mother and Father walked through the door."

"Interesting."

Sebastian wiggled his eyebrows impishly, not taking the situation as seriously as he should, but Sin didn't take him to task for it. This was his brother, after all, and Sebastian never stayed serious for more than a few minutes at time.

"I have asked her over and over again why, but she refuses to answer me. Instead she tells me to stop questioning her and be grateful for having her as my wife. That's the word she used—grateful."

"Well, you should be. Now you have every right to do whatever you want with her. She is yours and yours only. When it comes to her, no one can deny you anything, not even she. So stop fretting over her turning out worse than you thought and instead get to know the true her. She is your wife now, for life."

"Are you telling me to bed her?"

"Yes."

"It is my right..."

"It is."

"She can't deny me."

"No, she can't."

An image of a naked Charmaine waiting for him in his bed crossed his mind, and his heart started to pound heavily. The mere thought of being able to kiss those luscious lips and caress her soft skin made him weak with lust, and he knew he couldn't go through with it.

He loved her.

It might be naïve and stupid, but he couldn't act as cold toward her as she did to him. This one week of unhappy marriage didn't erase all the years of longing he had lived through, all those horrible times when he had thought she was on the verge of getting married to someone else.

His heart still ached when he thought about the time she had been courted by Lord Dane, a goodhearted fellow who Sin had liked immensely before he made Charmaine blush prettily every time he looked at her.

He had died a thousand deaths during those months, as the happy couple came closer and closer to a wedding, not knowing how to continue with life if she married her beau but too unsure to do anything about it. And then Lord Dane suddenly left London, marrying another woman within a month's time.

Charmaine, Francesca had told him, didn't even blink when she heard about it. Unaffected by what should have been devastating news for her, she didn't seem to notice Lord Dane's disappearance from her side, instead focusing on—or ignoring—the next beau in line.

But she didn't blush anymore.

"I must confess I do wonder why she never accepted a proposal," Sebastian interrupted Sin's tormenting thoughts. "She must have received hundreds of them since her debut two years ago. One would think that at least one of those men should have made her heart flutter a little."

"But she didn't accept anyone, and I can't help feeling sorry for poor Lord Nester, who had to listen to all these men spilling their hearts out, unable to give a suitor a favorable answer. If anyone is happy over this marriage, it must be him."

"Are you feeling sorry for that awful man? Have you already forgotten what he did to our dear Penny?"

Sin shook his head. "No, I haven't. And for what it's worth, Charmaine made a heroic effort when she ran the whole way here in the middle of the night to tell us about her father taking Penny to London, ready again to give his own daughter to the sadistic Lord Bolton, the sick bastard."

"I still find it hard to believe a father can do something so evil against his own child. Without remorse to give away one daughter to save the other. Love is strange."

Sin couldn't help but laugh.

Sebastian sure was right about that. Of all strange things, love was the strangest. Charmaine's odd family situation was evidence of that.

All her life she had been spoiled rotten by her devoted parents, who at the same time had ignored her younger sister. For as long as Sin could remember, Lord Nester had always bragged about his older daughter, puffing about how proud he was of her, and kept informing anyone who happened to listen about her popularity.

Not once did he mention the daughter just one year younger, who also was a very beautiful young woman only not as astounding as the magnificent Charmaine. His lack of feelings for Penelope couldn't have been clearer than when his old friend Lord Bolton had demanded Charmaine as wife and Nester coldheartedly had given him Penelope instead, to use in any way the man liked.

Penelope had managed to escape and had found a refuge with the Darling family, forever cut off from her own family. Charmaine had never said a word about it, continuing with her life as she always had, still letting her father spoil her despite what he had done to her sister.

"How is Penny, by the way? I haven't seen her for a while, not since Uncle Rake rescued her from Bolton's townhouse."

Sin made a sad face. "Neither have I, but Mother says she's still in shock, although it's hard to tell if it is because of her experience in London or because of Uncle Rake leaving her."

"Poor Penny."

"Indeed. I hope she will find her way back to happiness soon and that Uncle Rake will change his mind and realize how much he needs her."

Sebastian snorted with disbelief. "I can't believe how idiotically you men in love behave. I hope I'll never fall in love with someone. If I ever turn into such an ass because of fancying myself in love, I promise you I'm going to kill myself."

With those last words Sebastian stood up, leaving his brother to broodingly stare into the crackling fire, still angry and confused but not as seething as earlier.

Why had she tripped him?

It didn't matter how much she denied the fact, she still was the cause to their forced marriage. It frustrated the hell out of him, not knowing what lay behind such odd behavior. He knew without a doubt she didn't love him, and he couldn't think of one thing she had to gain by marrying him instead of someone else. So perhaps the tripping hadn't been planned.

But the question still remained—why had she not protested the marriage when the opportunity presented itself?

He knew he was one of the most sought-after bachelors of the *ton,* being the heir to one of the richest families in England. But he didn't think it mattered to her. Or at least he used to think so, before she became his wife and turned his whole image of her upside down.

"So what *are* you going to do about Charmaine?"

He looked up into the worried face of his grandmother, the Duchess of Berkeley, who seemed to have emerged out of nowhere to stand beside the chair Sebastian had just left. It was obvious she had overheard their conversation, and he couldn't help feeling a bit embarrassed when he thought about how openly emotional he had been, admitting loving the minx and all.

"I honestly don't know." He took a deep sip of the wine to settle his roaming emotions. "I seem to get nowhere with her. Every time I try to talk to her it ends with me leaving, even angrier than before. She's just too stubborn."

He took a calming breath as he felt anger rise inside him again at the mere thought of her cold selfishness.

The duchess sat down in Sebastian's abandoned armchair and reached for the wineglass he unbeknownst had left for her.

"I think there is more to Charmaine than you see, my dear Sinclair."

"I used to think so too, but during this week of

marriage she has proven me wrong over and over again. There is no goodness inside her. She doesn't care about anyone or anything but herself, and then especially her beauty. It sickens me to think how I've been defending her against Fanny all these years and it turns out my sister was right all along."

"It's not the poor girl's fault you put a halo over her head and called her a goddess and are now unable to stand her turning out to be a mere human."

He hated to admit his grandmother had a point there. He had glorified Charmaine over the years, secretly admiring her from afar. Of course he didn't know what she really was like; he had never been closer to her than dancing with her now and then, and that only when he had mustered enough courage to ask. Shallowly, he had fallen in love with her astounding beauty, and now he had to live with the fact that she was a magnificent but empty shell.

"You have to give her a chance to explain herself, as I still think there is more to this than meets the eye. Am I wrong if I assume she's behind the whole getting-caught-in-bed happening?"

"Of course she is. I would never…"

"Of course you wouldn't, my dear," the duchess interrupted him politely. "I know you would never do something as spontaneous as letting your feelings rule your actions."

"Thank you. I think."

"You are welcome, my dear."

They sat silent for a while, sipping their wine while enjoying the crackling fire. Sin loved his grandmother dearly, and his wish was to find a woman as courageous and loyal as she. Anna Darling was not his relative through blood, as she was his grandfather's second wife. Sin's father, George Darling, the Marquis of Newbury, was the firstborn son in the first marriage, but that didn't matter in anyone's eyes.

Many years ago Anna had visited George at Chester Park, together with some mutual friends, and had fallen helplessly in love with his father, the much older Hannibal Darling, the Duke of Berkeley.

It had taken her a long time to make him realize, first of all, she wasn't too young for him, and, secondly, he couldn't live without her. Such courage amazed Sin. The couple still were happily in love with each other after all these years, and the duchess had more than once confessed she wouldn't know how to live without his grandfather.

"You say she doesn't love her sister, which I find quite strange. Charmaine might be a bit spoiled…"

"A bit?"

"Yes, dear. A bit."

"She's spoiled rotten, that's what she is. Do you remember how her parents denied Penny new clothes for her debutant season, all because Charmaine needed more outfits? That's not *a bit* spoiled in my book."

"I know what Lord and Lady Nester did, but I don't think it was Charmaine's fault. She never asked for more clothes. It was her parents' decision, not hers."

"She could have refused."

The duchess looked at him with her intelligent eyes, smiling secretively as if she knew something he didn't. "Could she, now?"

He frowned, not liking where she was taking this. "Yes, she could have. It's not so hard to say the word 'no.' Hell knows she's said it enough to her suitors."

"Did she, now?"

"Grandmother, stop this! You can't possibly make Charmaine into something better than she is. You can't turn night into day. It's impossible."

The duchess leaned back into the chair, glaring patronizingly at him. "And yet you did. You made her into something she isn't, and now you're furious with her because she isn't what you supposed her to be. Have you ever considered it's not so easy being the Incomparable Queen with two doting parents surrounding you? You just said it yourself while speaking to Sebastian—they never cared for Penny, only for Charmaine."

"That was a private conversation."

Ignoring his silent reprimand, the duchess continued stubbornly. "It wasn't Charmaine's fault."

"Maybe not. But it still doesn't mean she cared about Penny being left out."

"And yet Penny still claims her sister loves her, something Charmaine has proven more than once since arriving the night Penny was abducted."

Sin slumped deeper into his chair, broodingly crossing his arms over his chest in a quiet rebellion against her logic. He really didn't need to hear this right now. All he wanted was to get drunk and fall asleep and hopefully spend a night without hot dreams about the woman sleeping in the connecting bedroom.

"She hasn't left Penny's side during the last week. Is that something a selfish and unloving sister would do?"

"She has nothing else to do here but sit at Penny's side. The façade is everything, after all."

The duchess sighed ruefully, for now giving up her

quest to make him more favorable toward his wife. "You are an impossible and stubborn man, and I feel sorry for poor Charmaine, who doesn't stand a chance against your prejudice."

He resisted a childish need to stick his tongue out at her retiring back. Instead, he emptied his wineglass before refilling it again. His mission had been to get drunk, and he was behind schedule.

As he downed his fourth glass in a row, a welcoming numbness settled in his mind and, relieved to be so near his ultimate goal, he filled another glass. And then another.

It didn't help, though; he still dreamt about her.

Chapter Three

"What's wrong with you?"

Charmaine closed her eyes for a disappointed second before straightening her face into perfect blandness, looking up from her embroidery with a polite smile.

"I beg your pardon?"

The duchess ignored the gracious retort, instead closing the door to the small salon before turning around, determination written all over her ageless face.

"At first I thought it was because you were too affected by what had happened to your sister, and being the considerate person I am, I held my tongue. But then days turned into weeks and I started to wonder if maybe it was your nerves. It couldn't have been easy for you, leaving everyone and everything you were used to and moving into an unknown home with people you've barely met before. But now it's been two whole months, and I can't keep making excuses for you. Something is definitely wrong with you, and I want to know what."

Charmaine folded her needlework neatly into a perfect square, placing it beside her on the sofa. Desperately she collected every ounce of strength she could muster to hold on to her indifference in front of the duchess.

She should have seen this coming, but she had

been too focused on her sister, spending most days and nights with her. She had hardly spoken to anyone else, especially not to the man who now was her husband.

Not that he had wanted to spend time with her. The few times they'd happened to meet he had only greeted her coldly before turning his back to her, showing exactly how despicable he found her.

His family behaved politely toward her, she had to give them that, but not one of them showed her any of the affection they openly showered upon Penelope. Her sister was already a part of this colorful family, as she had been coming here all her life. Penelope would always have a home here at Chester Park, even if she didn't marry Rake. She belonged here. Charmaine didn't.

Unfortunately Charmaine had no right or means to go anywhere. She was caught in this old castle, surrounded by obnoxious Darlings. Life here was proving to be a bit of a strain for her serenity, but she was determined to see it through because, in the midst of all the bad things happening, something good had emerged—she finally had time to spend with her sister.

"I have tried to talk to Sinclair, but it's like talking to a brick wall. He's not opening up at all," the duchess said as she sat down beside Charmaine, casting a suspicious look at the perfectly folded needlework. "The other day he sneered at me when I asked how he was feeling, and that is not the Sinclair we all know and love. So here I am, asking you what has made him so full of hatred. No, don't you deny it, my dear. Sinclair was a very levelheaded man before he had to marry you, and now he's practically seething with anger."

The duchess was genuinely worried about her

grandson, and such devotion was admirable. Charmaine's parents had never left her alone for a minute, always there telling her what to wear, what to do, and what to say. But not once had they uttered a word of love.

The Darlings, on the other hand, were constantly showing affection without either embarrassment or vulnerability. Maybe they bickered a little too much for her sanity, always discussing everything so thoroughly. At first the chatter had made her head ache, but after having all her meals with them for the last couple of months, she was becoming accustomed to it. To her surprise she even found it hard to stay serene sometimes when they were teasing each other, as many of them could be quite outrageous.

Meeting the duchess' worried gaze, Charmaine dug her nails into her palms in an attempt to not show any emotions. "I wish I could help you with the answers you seek, but as I have not seen nor spoken to Sin much since the day we were...married...I don't think I can be of much help."

"Something happened between the two of you, something which made Sinclair so furious with you he hardly can stand looking at you, and I want to know what."

"It is not my fault."

"What is not your fault?"

"That Sin can't stand looking at me. I have to admit I find it most disheartening. I'm used to men adoring me, telling me how much they admire me. But ever since I came here, not one of you have told me how beautiful I am, even though I am certain you all must think about it constantly."

This time it was the duchess who stared blankly at Charmaine, hiding her thoughts behind a mask. Not that it was hard to figure out what the older lady thought. Charmaine almost blushed at the mere thought of how selfish and self-centered she must seem, just as Sin had said.

"I can't help but wonder what—" The duchess interrupted herself and cocked her head to the side, looking Charmaine up and down as if silently measuring her.

"Yes?"

"What possibly could have happened that made a good girl pretend to be a bad girl?"

This time Charmaine couldn't stop the telling blush that crept warmly over her cheeks, and the duchess smiled knowingly, obviously quite pleased with her ability to pinpoint the problem.

"You don't have to say anything." The duchess brushed aside Charmaine's effort to come up with some explanation of either her blushing or her behavior. "As long as I know you are not what you pretend to be, it's fine. My beloved grandson hasn't married the dimwit he thinks he has. Thank goodness for small blessings."

"Your Grace, you have misunderstood—"

"Stop it." The duchess snorted. "You are only going to snare yourself with more lies if you try to talk your way out of this mess. You will have to tell me the truth about it later, mind you, but for now I don't want the why, I only want to hear about the what. What can we do to make Sinclair stop blowing steam out his ears?"

"I-I don't know."

"Of course you do. You are the one who made him

this angry from the beginning. What did you say to him to make him this furious?"

"Nothing, I…"

The duchess grabbed the needlework and threw it into the fire with one swift, angry movement. "Stop it! Why are you still saying you don't know, when we both know you do?"

"Your Grace, I was merely—"

"Your Grace me here, Your Grace me there." The duchess leaned back against the sofa, crossing her arms over her chest. She looked more like a surly child than an urbane matron of society. "If you are going to be a part of our family, you have to start treating us as such. You insist on keeping your distance, keeping everyone at least an arm's length away, but I think life here would be so much better for you if you just opened up a bit, instead of pretending to be something you aren't."

The duchess leaned forward and patted Charmaine affectionately on the cheek, silently offering what the girl desperately and secretly had yearned for since her arrival at Chester Park, the touch of a human hand.

Sin had not been an option there, since she had destroyed her every chance with him when tripping him into marriage. Not the best beginning.

"Tell me," the duchess begged. "I can sense the turmoil in your heart. Who knows, maybe letting some of it out will make you feel better in the end."

"I tripped him." Charmaine blanched as soon as the words left her mouth, regretting it immediately, but it was too late.

"Excuse me?"

"Sin. I tripped him so he would fall down on top of me."

To her surprise, Charmaine felt almost relieved when admitting what she had done. As if one of all the burdens on her shoulders had fallen to the ground, leaving her still weighed down but a little lighter.

"You forced him to marry you?" The duchess asked quietly, without her usual drama, and Charmaine rushed to explain her actions.

"I was desperate and acted before I thought it through thoroughly. I regretted it the moment the deed was done, but then it was too late, as Lord and Lady Newbury had already seen him covering me and wouldn't listen to anything he had to say to his defense."

"Being forced to marry someone against your own will surely is a perfect reason for feeling resentment."

The duchess was too cooperative, and Charmaine felt her eyes narrowing as she gazed suspiciously at the older woman. "You knew I tripped him. He's already told you as much."

"Yes, he did."

"So why have me confess what you already know?"

"I wanted you to open up a bit and maybe learn there is nothing wrong with letting someone know what's in your heart now and then," the duchess said with her version of an impish grin, and Charmaine felt a shiver run down her spine.

"Please do not force me into explaining myself to you," Charmaine whispered, catching the older woman's game.

"Why not?"

"Please…"

With a sigh that could have lifted the roof of

Chester Park, the duchess forfeited. "All right. It will probably kill me, but I promise I will not ask you too many questions. But don't you look so relieved yet, my dear. In return for not tormenting you, I want you to do something for me. I want you to talk to Sinclair."

"No."

"You have to."

"No. I refuse."

"You have to."

She felt like pouting. From the outside Anna Darling seemed soft and kindhearted, but now Charmaine knew that couldn't be farther from the truth. The Duchess of Berkeley was the toughest, most nosy woman she'd ever met, and it didn't end there—the woman didn't know when enough was enough.

"I can't. And besides, even if I did talk to him, he wouldn't listen to me. He hasn't uttered one word to me for two months, not since our wedding day."

"Still, you have to talk to him. This cannot continue. You two are married. You can't go through life avoiding each other."

Charmaine sighed, dejected. "Why not? It's not as if there is any love between the two of us."

The Duchess looked a bit strange for a moment before nodding in agreement. "Yes, you do have a point there. This is clearly not a marriage sprung out of love. But who knows? Maybe it will be one day. You can't deny the possibility the two of you will get over this and find a way into each other's hearts."

Fall in love with Sin?

Charmaine frowned. Was it possible for her to start loving her husband? She honestly didn't know. Up until their wedding they hadn't interacted much, only dancing now and then.

She'd always felt relieved when she noticed Sin's name on her dance card, as he didn't flirt with her. He barely said a word to her, and for a young woman who constantly had admirers whispering pretty words in her ear it was pure heaven to dance silently for a while and enjoy the music.

There was one thing she had noticed about him, though, now as she thought about it—his large, warm hands. They made her feel safe.

"My dear, what are you thinking about? You look almost terrified."

"I-I…" Charmaine didn't know what to say. She was too shocked at her own realization. She, who had spent the first nineteen years of her life constantly feeling insecure and afraid, had felt safe with Sin.

No one but her sister Penelope had ever made her feel that much at ease, not even Lord Dane in his best moments. The mere thought of *him* made her heart pound harder, and mentally she shoved him further back into her consciousness, just as she had done every day for the last year and half. This was not the time to dwell in the past. Lord Dane was no longer a part of her life, and now he definitely would never be.

"Is it the thought of falling in love with Sinclair that terrifies you so?"

Charmaine awoke from her thoughts, staring in confusion at the duchess. What was she talking about now? Terrified to fall in love with Sin? It took her a moment before she remembered what they had been talking about from the beginning, and she reached out a hand toward the duchess.

"No. Not at all. I was remembering Sin from the

past and my memories wandered—" She interrupted herself before she spilled too much, but the duchess already smiled compassionately.

"You started to think about the one man you did love."

Not trusting her voice, Charmaine nodded, grateful for not having to elaborate more.

"There's nothing wrong with remembering good times. But be careful you don't let old memories remove your chances of future happiness. No matter how it happened, you are now married to Sinclair, and if you want to be happy, it has to be with him, I'm afraid."

"I know." As much as it pained her to admit it, the duchess had a point. Charmaine had to talk to Sin. Not because she wished for marital bliss, but because she was in desperate need of emotional peace. Maybe Sin would still refuse to hear her out, but then she would at least have tried.

"May I ask what happened with Lord Dane?" the duchess continued, not ready to leave the delicate subject just yet. "It was obvious the two of you were deeply in love with each other, everyone waiting most eagerly for your engagement to be announced. But then, from out of nowhere, he marries someone else, and you continue with your life as if nothing out of the ordinary had happened."

"Not all fairytales have happy endings."

"But yours was supposed to."

"Was it?"

The duchess shook her head. "You know this doesn't mean you can't have a happy ending with someone else, someone like Sin."

Charmaine sniffed softly, unable to put her serene face back on as the need to tell the truth overwhelmed her. "I don't believe in true love any longer. If Lord Dane had loved me, truly loved me, he would have fought for me. But he didn't. Instead he left me without a word, and the next thing I heard was that he had married someone else, only one measly month after proposing to me."

The duchess stared with disbelief at Charmaine. "He *proposed* to you? I thought he hadn't, as we never heard a word about it. But what happened? I can't think you would have told him no, not if you were as much in love with him as I think you were."

Charmaine swallowed hard, not used to opening up this much to anyone other than Penelope. But then again, telling the duchess about Lord Dane was an easy price to pay if it meant she could keep the more important secrets behind lock and key.

"Charmaine, please indulge me. What happened when Lord Dane proposed to you?"

"He never proposed to me directly. As tradition demands, he went to my father first. I-I don't know wh-what exactly was said between them, but it ended with Lord Dane leaving London. Leaving me. Father ordered me to never talk about it again."

The duchess, too angry to sit still, paced to and fro in front of Charmaine. "Of course it was that father of yours. I can't believe I didn't think of it before. Considering how badly he treated Penny, it shouldn't have been so hard to figure out he went after you too in some way. I'm sorry."

"It's not your fault," Charmaine whispered, a bit surprised at how the duchess's anger made her feel a bit better. It was nice to have someone standing up for her, when she usually had to fight her own war.

"Am I wrong if I assume he is the reason you remained unmarried? You must have received hundreds of proposals over the years, all of them politely rejected. Why would a father keep a daughter unmarried? Especially yours, having such a gem as you."

Charmaine breathed deeply through her nose, not wanting the duchess to notice how much the subject upset her. "He had someone else in mind for me."

"He had? Who?" The duchess gazed encouragingly at her, impatiently waiting for an answer.

"I don't know the man personally. My father thinks quite highly of him, though."

"How strange." The duchess frowned, pondering Charmaine's answer. Suddenly she clasped a hand over her mouth, her eyes frightened. "Oh, dear God, don't tell me it's Lord Bolton?"

"No, it's not Lord Bolton."

"Thank the good Lord." The duchess let out a relieved breath. "That would have been horrendous."

"Horrendous, indeed," Charmaine echoed, another shiver running down her spine.

"Poor, sweet little Penny," the duchess sighed absentmindedly, but Charmaine had no problem following her train of thought.

Lord Nester had never hidden the fact he didn't care much for his younger daughter as he kept busy doting on Charmaine. His indifference toward Penelope had never been more obvious than the day an old acquaintance of his, Lord Bolton, demanded Charmaine for wife. Too impressed by the extremely rich man,

Lord Nester wanted nothing but to oblige him, but to give Charmaine away was not an option. In an effort to avoid Lord Bolton's wrath, he offered Penelope as compensation, not as a wife but to use in any way the sadistic Lord Bolton wished.

Luckily, Penelope had managed to escape from Lord Bolton's luxurious home and had found refuge with the Darling family. Lord Nester forbade his wife and Charmaine to ever contact Penelope again, to treat her as *persona non grata*. It had been a horrible time, both for Charmaine and the ailing Lady Nester, losing a loved one and unable to do anything about it.

That changed six months later, when her father managed to recapture Penelope and race toward London to pay his liability to Lord Bolton. For once throwing all caution away, Charmaine had run through the dark night to Chester Park, informing the Darlings about Lord Nester's plan.

Rake and his relatives rushed toward London, and she had known Penelope would be saved, and then, exhausted, she had fainted dead away. The kindhearted Lady Newbury had ordered her son to take their guest to a bedroom where she could rest, and as Sin had helped her into the room she had repaid his kindness by tripping him.

One week later they were married.

"When I think about what could have happened to our precious little girl… My heart dies a little every time." The duchess closed her eyes as if in deep pain.

"It won't happen again," Charmaine vowed solemnly, guilt over what her sister had had to endure clutching her heart. "I promise you I will do whatever it takes to make sure he never hurts her again, even if it means giving him what he desires most."

"You are such a good, devoted sister," the duchess praised through grateful tears, completely misunderstanding the meaning of the vow.

Charmaine, who had been speaking more to herself than to the duchess, accepted the compliment with a gracious nod. A quiet knock on the door ended the conversation as a footman informed them the duchess was wanted in the duke's study.

"I'd better go," the duchess sniffed, drying her tears with an exquisite handkerchief. "My husband obviously is in desperate need for me to save him. I overheard Diana mention that she needed to talk to him about her charities, and I guess he didn't hide well enough."

After a roll of her eyes as she spoke, the duchess floated out of the salon, leaving Charmaine alone with her thoughts. With a dejected sigh, she slumped back into the sofa.

Why did they all persist with asking her *why*?

Why this, why that…

She didn't know what to say. Soon she would run out of excuses, and what was left then? The truth? No, honesty wasn't an option. She knew they would never believe her, especially as she hardly could believe it herself.

Shivering as if an icy wind passed through the cozy little salon, she thought of Sin's large, warm hands. If she told him the truth, would he be as disgusted with her as she was?

She sighed deeply, knowing she couldn't.

How could she admit to him the sickening reason she had not married sooner, despite receiving hundreds of proposals? The very same reason she so desperately had used him as a way out, when he unbeknownst had offered it to her?

The mere thought of looking into Sin's dark eyes and telling him how her father kept refusing her suitors because he eagerly waited for her sick mother to die—it made her feel like fainting again.

Lord Nester wanted many things in life, but there was just one thing he passionately had declared himself unable to live without, and that one thing was Charmaine.

Chapter Four

Slowly, the carriage rocked down the dusty road, and Penelope growled with frustration as she tumbled to the small floor for the umpteenth time.

"It's bloody impossible. This infernal rocking should be making me drowsy, but all it does is making me nauseous. If we don't arrive at Pendragon soon, I promise you I'll throw up all over your beautiful gown."

"I'm sorry." Charmaine offered her sister a helping hand and Penelope scoffed, amused, as she accepted it.

"You're sorry? How can the condition of the Herefordshire roads be your fault?"

Charmaine laughed over her sister's teasing, so relieved over their travelling north and further away from their father that she could have danced in joyful celebration.

"I'm just sorry you're feeling sick. As for the roads, there is not much I can do about them, unfortunately. At our last stop, I overheard Lady Newbury tell Sin it was not much more than a few hours left, which would please you, I hope."

Penelope nodded absentmindedly, her thoughts already moving to the next subject of her heart. "Talking about that husband of yours, when are you and Sin going to reconcile? You can't continue with this strange marriage of yours—it's driving both the two of you and the rest of us crazy. There must be something you can do to make it better, isn't there?"

Charmaine blushed under her sister's probing gaze. Of course there was something she could do, but even though she more or less had promised the duchess to talk to Sin, she wasn't going to. It had been hard these last days, not being able to hide from him as they all were bunched together, travelling to Francesca's new home to visit the triplets she had given birth to a couple of weeks ago.

When Charmaine had heard about the trip they were planning, she asked the duchess if she could stay behind, without mentioning her need of space from Sin. Unfortunately he overheard her, and immediately she was ordered to pack her things. It was quite clear he enjoyed putting obstacles in her way.

What Sin hadn't thought about, when he stubbornly refused to let her stay behind, was how confining a carriage could be when one was travelling for days. After spending two days alone with Charmaine and stubbornly ignoring her presence, he had changed place with Penelope for the last day, instead joining his parents in their carriage.

He still hadn't said a word to her directly since their wedding day, not even answered the few questions she had dared to ask him in a desperate attempt to start some sort of conversation.

But to no avail.

His seething anger didn't seem to ease with time, and again she found herself alone and miserable. Thank goodness her sister Penelope was travelling north with them.

The duchess, as the sneaking matchmaker she was,

although her two victims already were married, had made sure Sin and Charmaine would travel alone in one carriage. She had probably nourished a wish that the confinement would force them to interact. But the duchess had failed miserably with her attempt, as Sin kept to his side of the carriage stoically, turning his broad back toward Charmaine as much as he could.

Even though she wouldn't admit it, she was relieved he mulishly had brought her with them. With the entire Darling family visiting Pendragon, she would have been too exposed to her father, something she hadn't considered when she first asked to be left behind.

In a way, they both had got what they wanted. Charmaine smiled wryly at the thought. She desperately wanted Penelope as far from Lord Nester and Lord Bolton as possible, and Sin just wanted to spite her. Against her will she had to admit being impressed at his ability to hold a grudge. Not once did he stray from his decision to ignore her, leaving her to spend the days reading and sleeping.

But now and then, when he thought she didn't notice, she could feel him watch her from the side, just as she couldn't stop looking at his hands when he gazed out through the window. His large, warm hands, which made her feel protected against everything evil, like her father.

"I'm afraid it is too late for me to repair the damage between the two of us," Charmaine admitted now to her sister sadly. "He's so angry, stubbornly refusing to talk to me, which doesn't make it easier for me to reach out to him."

Penelope frowned slightly. "Don't you find it

strange that we both have problems with our loved ones? Me with Rake, who's in London fighting himself black and blue because he's so bloody angry with me, and you with Sin, who is hiding in the other carriage with his parents."

"I don't love Sin."

"Of course you don't."

"It's the truth. I don't love him. I hardly know him."

"I agree with you."

"No, you don't."

Penelope arched an amused eyebrow so much like Rake's that Charmaine almost smiled. Almost. "Yes, I do. You don't love Sin, which I can well understand, as you have never had any close relationship to him before. But…"

"There is always a *but* when it comes to you," Charmaine teased, and Penelope put on a grave face.

"Life *is* filled with 'but's."

Penelope was such a silly minx sometimes, and Charmaine had missed her much during the time they were separated. Not that they ever had been able to be as close as she would have wished, but still…

Somewhere between their father and his sick infatuation and their mother's quiet, helpless effort to save Charmaine from him, their sisterly relationship had stayed solid. Penelope was probably the only person in the whole world who really did love her unselfishly, without strings.

"*But*…do you think you *can* love him?"

Charmaine woke up from her straying thoughts. "Who?"

"Sin." Penelope rolled her eyes, unamused by her

sister's lack of attention.

"I...don't...know. I've never thought about him like that before, and as for now... He's not so very lovable when he glares and snarls at me as soon as we meet."

Penelope laughed out loud, yet gave her sister her very best upset face. "Glares and snarls? Are you calling your husband a dog?"

"Why, yes." Charmaine laughed. "I think I am. He reminds me of Old Ben's retriever, the one who kept barking wildly, giving me his meanest eye, whenever I came too close."

"You loved that dog."

Charmaine blushed. The insinuation couldn't be clearer, and Penelope grinned more wickedly than Rake ever could have.

"I did," she admitted with an embarrassed grin. "At first I was terrified of him, because he sounded so angry and ready to take a bite of me if I ever got close enough. But when I got to know him, he turned out to be the friendliest and cuddliest dog you could imagine. I cried for days when he died."

"So maybe you should give Sin a chance? He might be treating you like something the cat dragged in, but when you get to really know him he will be the dearest man—trustworthy, reliable, and caring."

"You make him sound quite dull."

"Maybe dull is what you need?"

"You don't think I, like all other young ladies, wish for a knight in shining armor—a real Prince Charming—who'll take me by storm and whisk me away to live happily ever after?"

Penelope cocked her head to the side, looking at

her sister with a calm, steady gaze. "No, I don't think you do. You have already tried that once, with Lord Dane, and look where that ended. He rushed off to become someone else's knight, leaving you alone and miserable. No, I think you need someone you can rely on. Someone who will take you seriously and who needs you. Desperately so."

"Now you make *me* sound dull."

"I think somewhere, deep beneath that shiny exterior of yours, there hides a little scared girl who doesn't want to be the center of everything but would rather be a part of something."

It was such a correct insight of her deepest wishes it left Charmaine stunned. She had never asked to be the Incomparable Queen of the *ton*, put on a pedestal, always looking down on others, never belonging.

If the choice had been hers, she would have preferred to be unseen by the masses but cherished by a few. Like Sin's sister Francesca, who was no great beauty but highly loved by her closest family and her dearest friends.

Penelope too had a better life than Charmaine did, even though she didn't think so. Penelope had always been left on the outside of their small family circle, but in the end it was that separateness which had saved Penelope.

"What makes you think I don't thrive when surrounded by admirers?"

"Because you are the least self-centered person I know, and you have never, ever used your beauty to grant you something. Ever."

"Maybe I just succeeded with fooling you too?"

Penelope chuckled softly. "You can't fool me,

sister dear, because I love you too much to let your lovely face stand in the way of thinking straight. You are not what you pretend to be, and you are bloody good at hiding it."

The duchess had said the same thing the other day, and Charmaine couldn't help wondering why she didn't fool them. What had changed? Why did they think so much more of her than she wanted them to?

"Most people pretend to be more than they are."

"Yes, they do. But the strange thing with you is that you pretend to be less. It's like you don't want anyone to like you for who you really are, instead wanting them to dislike you for being something you aren't." Penelope patted her tenderly on the knee, taking the edge off her words. "If they all knew the Charmaine I know and love, they would love you too. But now most people think of you as a harpy who looks too good for her own good."

Charmaine arched her eyebrows, surprised over her sister's choice of words. "Harpy?"

Penelope shrugged, just as dainty and uncaring as Charmaine when she wanted to underline how spoiled and selfish she was. "Yes. That's what you want them to think, isn't it?"

"It might be."

"Aha!" Penelope waved her index finger excitingly. "You just admitted that you do want everyone to think less of you."

"No, I did not."

"Yes, you did."

"Not at all."

"Did too."

Charmaine sighed. They were too old for this kind

of argument. She was nineteen and Penelope eighteen, two grown-up women who should argue with more finesse than "did too."

As the carriage slowed she looked out the window, bending her head back to be able to see the whole front of the magnificent castle that was home to the Duke of Herefordshire.

"Oh, my, what a lovely home they have," she breathed, and Penelope leaned forward, gasping excitedly. It was like a castle out of a fairytale, with uncountable towers and pinnacles. As the carriage stopped at the front stairs, Francesca and her husband came out, closely followed by what looked like most of the staff.

Penelope opened the door with a shriek, throwing herself out from the carriage into the waiting embrace of her best friend. Charmaine moved back into the shadow, her heart aching as she watched the happy reunion in the courtyard.

What would it be like to be a real part of the big, loving family crying and laughing happily in front of her? For Penelope it was easy, being such a lovely person. For Charmaine it was harder. No matter what the duchess and Penelope thought, she wasn't able to remove the hideous version of herself she had created. It was stuck, and now she had to live with its side effects.

"Get out."

She winced with surprise. She hadn't noticed Sin coming up to her, being too occupied staring at the happy reunion in front of her. She looked down, meeting his icy stare.

"I beg your pardon?"

He growled impatiently and, before she had a chance to react, grabbed her hand, dragging her harshly closer to the door. Unprepared for his rude yanking, she fell forward with a yelp, landing in a quite unladylike fashion in his arms.

The feel of his body against hers made her knees go weak, and if he hadn't been holding her she would have fallen quite ungracefully down to the stony ground of the courtyard. Dazed, she looked up into his face, and for a moment he lost all anger. Something burned in his eyes, and, mesmerized, she stared at his full lips, silently demanding him to kiss her.

He looked as if in pain as he lowered his head, obliging her, but just as his lips almost touched hers, a sharp voice interrupted the moment.

"Sinclair Darling, for goodness' sake!"

Lady Newbury marched up to them and grabbed her son's arm, forcing him to release Charmaine and step away from her.

"That, my dear, is something you save for the bedroom instead of doing publicly in the courtyard of Francesca's new home, and especially not in front of all their servants," she hissed, and to Charmaine's surprise Sin's ears turned red.

"It won't happen again," he bit out before turning and heading straight to his sister, ignoring Charmaine, who stood still where he had left her.

Lady Newbury mumbled something, which may have been an apology for her son's outrageous behavior, before following him back to her daughter.

"What was that?" Penelope whispered excitedly as she joined Charmaine. "It looked like he wanted to eat you up. Am I wrong if I assume you two were *this* close to sharing your very first kiss?"

Charmaine's cheeks grew hot, and Penelope clapped her hands together. "Really? Ah, this is so marvelous. Maybe some time away from home was what the two of you needed. A chance to get to know each other on neutral ground."

"Penny, you put too much into it."

"So you weren't standing there, in front of everyone, staring up into Sin's hot eyes with shivering lips? I recognize the look, you see. Rake stares at me just as hotly all the time. Sin definitely wants you."

Charmaine couldn't stop herself. "He does?"

Penelope smiled excitedly. "Oh, yes, he does. Lady Newbury almost fainted when she noticed how he ogled you."

It was amazing how giddy her sister's words made her feel. Why was she this happy over Sin wanting her? Yes, he was her husband, but that didn't change the fact he still was Sin—the man she'd known her whole life and had never looked twice at.

To be completely honest, she had not looked at him a first time, either. Sinclair Darling had never been someone who made her heart flutter before. So why did he now? Why did he make her feel like she was falling in love with him?

She frowned, feeling a bit in despair.

Was she falling in love with her husband?

That thought scared her more than anything. She couldn't fall in love with him. She was nothing like what he needed, and he was far too good for her.

"Watching you...interact...with your wife tells me you won't be too upset about us running out of guest rooms. I need the two of you to share one so we can fit all of you into the castle."

Francesca's teasing voice to her brother broke through Charmaine's erratic thoughts, and she froze. Was she supposed to share a room with Sin? Share a bed with Sin?

"Oh, no," she whispered breathlessly.

"There must be one more room..." Sin too seemed a bit distressed by his sister's information, clearly not eager to share a room with his wife.

"Unfortunately not," Francesca said, seeming a little bit too pleased with herself over that revelation. It was almost as if she wanted them forced to share a bedroom, which surprised Charmaine.

Francesca had never hidden the fact that she couldn't stand her best friend's sister, and they had avoided each other as much as possible over the years. Charmaine had always been a bit jealous over Penelope's and Francesca's closeness, as it was something she'd never had herself—a best friend.

Sin stared, outraged, at his sister. "Really? Not one room left in that grand castle of yours?"

"No."

"How about a sofa?"

"No."

"A comfortable chair?"

"No."

Sin's frown deepened as he glared. "A bloody carpet, then?"

"Does she snore?"

Francesca's question caught him off guard, and Sin looked just as confused as Charmaine felt. "What?"

"Your wife." Francesca nodded lightly toward Charmaine. "Does she snore?"

"Eh…" That was one question Charmaine knew he couldn't answer, as they had never yet shared a bedroom.

"Maybe she speaks in her sleep," Devlin suggested kindly, and his wife nodded in agreement.

"That must be it. Why else would he be so upset about having to share a room with the woman he married?"

"Indeed, why else?"

Sin glared at his sister and brother-in-law, and if looks could kill... They left him no choice. He had to share a room with Charmaine. To refuse wasn't an option, not if he didn't want to embarrass himself, Charmaine, and his whole family in front of the servants and fuel gossip throughout the neighborhood.

"I want to see the babies," Lady Newbury squealed, effectively changing everyone's focus. Within minutes the courtyard was empty, leaving only Sin and Charmaine standing there, side by side, staring at the front door through which the family had disappeared.

"I can sleep on the floor," Charmaine offered softly, not wanting to destroy the fragility of the moment.

"Oh, yeah?" He snorted. "I don't think so. I sure as hell won't give you one more thing to complain about when it comes to me."

She looked at him from the side, following the lines of his proud face. "I have never complained about you."

"No? Well, there must always be a first time."

She put her hand on his arm, trying to reach through to him now as he finally was talking to her, but he shrugged it off, turning his back to her again.

"You can't hate me forever," she cried out to his retiring back. He stopped midstride without turning around, his large shoulders heaving with his deep sigh.

"I don't hate you."

She tried to get rid of the lump in her throat by swallowing, but her voice still sounded small, miserable, and pathetic. "But you despise me."

He glanced at her over his shoulder with unreadable eyes. "No, I don't."

"You said you did."

He sighed again. "I was angry."

"You're still angry."

"No, I'm not."

She took a step toward him but stopped as he stiffened. An overwhelming feeling of hopelessness filled her as she looked at his proud, strong back.

At that little moment when she had tripped him, she hadn't considered him or his feelings about being forced into marriage. All she had thought of was Penelope and her own last chance for redemption. It hadn't occurred to her that with her choice of action she effectively destroyed all the plans he might have had for his life.

Somehow, deep inside of her, she knew she could be happy and content with him, if she only let him through her walls. But could she throw every caution aside for her own happiness?

As long as her father was out there searching for a way to get to her, she couldn't rest, especially as Penelope still wasn't married. In the eyes of the law, Lord Nester was her sister's legal guardian, and if he demanded the Darlings send her to him, they would have no choice but to comply.

And then Charmaine would have to go to him.

A long time ago she had promised herself to never let Penelope know the truth about him, that Lord Nester wasn't their real father. He was only the heir who had inherited the title and its poverty when their real father died. Charmaine had been a mere baby and Penelope still growing in their mother's womb.

Elspeth de Vere, Lady Nester, had been just as beautiful as Charmaine when younger, before pain took over her body, turning her into an old woman ahead of time. As soon as the new Lord Nester laid eyes on the young, grieving widow, he had to have her. Without mercy he persuaded her to do what was best for her children—marry him.

When Charmaine was a child, he had constantly told her how beautiful she was, and stupidly she had been proud over his praise. When she grew older, she realized it wasn't the outside that counted but what was in your heart, but then it was too late already. She had already destroyed all her chances to find a friend among the girls in the county, always acting as though she was more than they were.

She didn't know when Lord Nester's fatherly pride had turned into a man's desperate need, but she was sixteen the first time he tried to enter her bedroom. Lady Nester had been in shock when she found her drunken husband outside her daughter's bedroom, yelling about how much he loved her and wanted her.

From that day Charmaine was never alone.

Either her mother or her mother's sour-faced maid was constantly with her, as her stepfather showed no remorse when he sobered up and realized the truth was out. Instead he seemed relieved over not having to pretend, and he tried harder to get to Charmaine, amused by his wife's desperate attempts to save her daughter.

"Why don't you just die, so I can marry Charmaine instead," he had told his wife over and over again, but Lady Nester never answered. She looked at Charmaine with her grieving eyes, silently promising she would never give up, never surrender to her husband's sick needs.

When Charmaine debuted into society, no one could have been prouder than Lord Nester, and he thrived as he watched how admired she was. One man after another went to him, asking for her hand in marriage, and every single one Lord Nester refused on her behalf.

She was his and his alone. No one else was to have her. At first Charmaine hadn't cared much about his efficient way of getting rid of her suitors; she hadn't considered any of them anyway.

But then she met Lord Dane...

As if sensing the turmoil inside her, Sin turned and, for the first time since their wedding day, looked straight at her without an insult.

"I'm not angry," he repeated hoarsely. "Only disappointed."

"Disappointed?" She stared at him in confusion. "Why are you disappointed with me?"

"Because you are not what I thought you were."

His strange admission made her frown. "What was I supposed to be, then? As beautiful on the inside as I am on the outside?"

He had at least the decency to blush.

"Something like that."

She wanted to laugh hysterically. When had her life become this twisted? As ever, it was her bloody looks creating the problem. First it was Lord Nester, possessively estranging her from everyone else to keep her. And now it was her husband who *didn't* want her, as she didn't live up to his high expectations.

"I'm sorry," she choked, tears filling her eyes.

He made a painful grimace. "Don't be. It's not your fault."

"Then why do you keep telling me it is?"

"Why? Because you were the one who made this marriage happen, not I. You were the one telling me you didn't even care if it was me you married. Of course I think it's your fault. If I'd had any choice I would never have married a woman claiming she doesn't care if I am the one who is her husband."

His jaw twitched with every harsh word he spoke, and his whole face became as hard as stone and just as cold. All his earlier embarrassment was long gone, and she knew she had to get away from him before she started to cry.

Because every word he said was true.

Not only had she behaved irrationally and selfishly toward him—she had behaved exactly as her stepfather did against her.

She bowed her head as she walked past him, wanting nothing more than to find somewhere to hide and lick her wounds. Without a word he reached out, grabbing her waist. He dragged her closer to him, pressing her soft body against his, and an unfamiliar feeling of excitement rose inside of her, scaring her more than anything else.

She wanted him.

Looking up into his dark eyes, she shivered with anticipation as she opened her mouth, searching for the right words to demand her release. Slowly he leaned forward until his lips were only a breath away from hers.

"Please," she whispered, and he lifted his free hand, planting it tenderly against her face, gently rubbing his thumb against her soft cheek.

"Tell me you want me."

She shivered as his thumb moved down over her mouth. "I want you."

He leaned down, brushing his lips against hers, and she whimpered for more, unable to hold back the feelings he created in her.

"No. Tell me you want *me*."

She couldn't resist his gentle demand. Dazed, she put her arms around his neck, pulling his ear closer to her lips. "I want *you,* Sinclair Darling."

With a growl coming from somewhere deep inside of him, he hardened the grip of her face and pressed his lips against hers, claiming her mouth.

His tongue made sweet love to hers, making it impossible for her to think of anything but kissing him back. Her knees went weak, and upon noticing how affected she was by his kiss, he growled again, behaving more like a savage claiming his woman than a civilized man of his time.

"Sinclair Darling, what *are* you doing?"

The high-pitched voice cut through their dazed minds, effectively ending the kiss. As Charmaine looked toward the front door, she saw Lady Newbury standing at the top of the stairs, staring at them in shock.

"He's just fondling his wife."

Lord Newbury came out through the door behind his wife and made a little beckoning gesture with his head toward Sin. "Come. Fanny is getting quite hysterical because you haven't seen her precious babies yet. You can kiss your wife later, preferably in your room. With the door closed, mind you."

"George!"

"Yes, dear?"

"Didn't you notice he was kissing her?"

"Yes, I did."

"In the courtyard!"

"Yes."

Lady Newbury frowned at him, tapping her silk-clad foot impatiently. "And?"

Her husband walked up to Sin, patting his shoulder. "Good boy, well done."

Lady Newbury rolled her eyes. "Fools. I'm surrounded by fools."

Lord Newbury chose to ignore his pouting wife, who disappeared into the castle again, expecting them to follow. Instead he sent his son a look that said, "Come before her nerves unleash hell upon us all," and Sin let go of Charmaine.

"I'll be right behind you," he told his father, who nodded before following his wife, leaving Charmaine alone with her husband.

A husband who had just kissed her.

She felt her cheeks growing warmer as he turned to look at her with his serious, dark eyes. He was such a nice-looking man. Why had she never noticed that before? He wasn't overwhelmingly good-looking, as she was, or as Devlin Ross, Francesca's husband. Sin was taller and leaner, more ruggedly handsome than magnificently beautiful.

He had a lovely smile, which one appreciated much more when it wasn't so often bestowed upon you. He was a man who preferred to spend his time dealing with the Berkeley estate rather than throwing his time away on every assembly to which he was invited.

When Francesca had been in London for her first season, he had been much more in attendance than earlier, of course, because his mother had required him to stay near his sister and protect her from all the fortune hunters.

The backside of being an heiress, Charmaine presumed. She had never had that problem herself, as her family was rather infamous for their poverty.

"I'm sorry," Sin said, looking as cold and repudiated as before his parents interrupted them.

Before the kiss.

His odd behavior made her feel uneasy, but she was too used to hiding her true emotions, so instead of letting him sense her insecurity, she smiled brightly.

"It's not your fault your parents decided to reappear at just that moment."

"I meant the kiss."

Oh.

"Nothing to be sorry about."

His eyes narrowed with suspicion, and a vein twitched at his temple. He had a really hard time coping with her indifference, she realized, and was already rebuilding the wall between them, the one the kiss for a moment had removed.

"Too used to sharing kisses with men, I presume?"

His nastiness created a lump as large as England in her throat, but she determined not to allow it to prevail, and swallowed it. This wasn't the time or the place for her to fall into pieces, in front of him.

For one small moment she had felt at home. For the tiniest of minutes she had felt blessed to be this man's woman. She had actually felt safe, something only he seemed to be able to make her feel.

"Of course not," she answered softly, in an attempt to not irritate him more. But it seemed he had decided that anything she said was wrong, as he looked patronizingly at her.

"All those suitors, and not one who has dared to kiss those lush lips of yours?"

"Unfortunately not. My father has been quite good at keeping a distance between me and my beaus."

Or me and anyone.

"I don't believe you, especially considering how you used to blush whenever Lord Dane was in sight."

Of course he had to bring Lord Dane up. She wished she had the ability to cut off all old emotions and leave them behind.

It wasn't as if she hadn't tried. Oh, how she had tried. When she first heard about Lord Dane's Yorkshire wedding, she had been devastated and had cried for days. She hadn't stopped until her father quite harshly told her to look uncaring at least when out amongst people, or he would punish her—or Penelope—badly.

"Lord Dane is a married man."

Sinclair snorted angrily at her. "And what says you'll let that obstacle stop you? You are now a married woman, which opens doors you never had before."

"I would never…"

"Never is such a strong word," he interrupted rudely. "Don't you think I've seen how all those so-called happily married women flirt with other men? As soon as they've given their husbands an heir, they behave worse than the most confirmed bachelor, roaming the *ton* for a man to satisfy their needs."

"I'm not like those women."

"Sure you aren't."

The insult in his voice was almost too much for her. Tears started to fill her eyes, and she looked down at her hands in an effort to hide her fragility from him.

She had to be strong.

Or he had to think she was, so he would leave her be. As soon as Penelope was married to Rake—or anyone else of her choosing—Charmaine would be able finally to rest.

She didn't know what she would do then, or how she ever could restart her own life again, but she would no longer have to watch out for her sister. She didn't care about herself. If her stepfather got to her, so be it.

She had long ago realized how unimportant she was, and in her darkest hours she had almost looked forward to finally giving in to Lord Nester and letting him have her. Then, maybe, for a short while, she would feel loved and cherished.

But as long as there was the smallest chance her stepfather could destroy Penelope's life in his quest for Charmaine, she had to stay alert. And that meant not letting her new husband make her sway from her mission.

"If you'll excuse me," he said with a small, insulting bow, "I think I will go where I'm wanted.

Why don't you find the room we are supposed to share, and make yourself comfortable on the floor, because that, my dear, is a bed you'll never have to share with me."

She returned his bow with a graceful curtsy and watched him stalk away from her. A footman beckoned her to follow him, a look of pity hinted on his face.

As she walked through the grand foyer of Pendragon, she knew she couldn't sway from her destiny, couldn't give Sin what he seemed so desperate for—the truth.

Penelope deserved happiness. Charmaine didn't.

As she passed the open door to the salon where the Darling family had gathered to admire and welcome to the world the three beautiful small babies, she saw Sin in the middle of the group, and her heart stopped beating. He sat beside Francesca, one of the lovely baby girls resting peacefully in his strong arms.

The love on his face and the pride in his smile was endearing, and for a small moment she imagined it was their baby he held so carefully. That it was their baby who had so mesmerized him.

She didn't know how she got to the bedroom, following the footman in a daze. When she noticed she was alone, she sat down on the bed, hiding her face in her cold palms, trying to breathe through the painful sobs tearing through her body.

The emptiness inside her echoed her tears until her whole body screamed with distress over the path she was forced to walk in life. Exhausted, she fell back into the waiting bed, letting sleep save her from reality, taking her into a world of peace and harmony.

A world of love.

Chapter Five

"I think she will crack the windows."

Charmaine looked up at Sebastian Darling, Sin's younger brother, who had come to join her at the back of the music room.

"She's not so bad," Charmaine said, trying not to flinch as Miss Annabelle Overton most impressively stretched her vocal range even higher.

He looked at her with an amused arched eyebrow, reminding her much of his uncle Rake's arrogance.

"Really? You actually think the girl can sing?"

"No, but she...sounds...quite...clear. That's always something."

He grinned mischievously, his green eyes dancing with mirth. "I think I'll have to agree with you there. The girl does indeed sound clear. Very much so."

He winced as Annabelle reached the final part of her song and screamed out the last high note as well as her poor, strained voice could muster before looking expectantly at the shocked audience, who needed a minute to catch on to what she was waiting for. Politely, they clapped their hands, trying to look as though they had enjoyed the performance.

"If she sings one more song I will cut my ears off," Sebastian groaned, and Charmaine couldn't hold back an amused laugh. He was such an impish young man, Sebastian Darling, quite the opposite of his older brother—and in her current state of mind exactly what she needed. Someone who didn't care about why.

"I think your sister desperately tries to repress the same urge." Charmaine nodded toward Francesca, who was almost pushing the young woman from the temporary stage. Sebastian grinned as the offended Annabelle sat down beside her proud mother, who showered her with praise.

"A mother's white lie," Sebastian whispered, and Charmaine giggled again.

"I wouldn't call it a white lie. That would be insulting the real white lies. Poor Mrs. Overton's tongue is probably black."

Sebastian laughed loudly, drawing attention from those surrounding them. And that included Sin, who glared at them with his dark eyes, and she couldn't help thinking he again thought the worst of her.

"Why don't you stop lying your own tongue black and tell him what he wants to hear?" Sebastian asked, following her gaze toward his brother. "Don't you deny it, little sister-in-law. You are the sole reason for your own unhappiness, and if you'll only talk to him, and I mean *really* talk to him, you can mend this marriage, turn it into something good. Something like Fanny's."

Charmaine wanted to sigh deeply with despair. What was it with this family? Why did they keep sticking their noses where they didn't belong?

First the duchess had been haranguing her about her relationship to Sin and now Sebastian, from out of nowhere, was telling her what to do.

She knew it was because they loved Sin and wanted only what was best for him. They couldn't do more than try to persuade her to work out the bumps in their marriage, but as no one knew the full story, they were unaware they nagged her in vain.

"It's just one small problem," she said, trying to put the focus on Sin instead of herself. "Your dear brother refuses to hear me out, and therefore there is not much more for me to do than wait until he feels ready to listen."

"You could seduce him."

What?

She couldn't hide her shock at his outrageousness, and his grin deepened. "You are such a beautiful woman, Charmaine Darling, something which you should use to your advantage. When I think about it, I don't think you ever have. You just stand there, looking absolutely gorgeous, with your long blonde hair and vivid blue eyes. But you never use it."

She blushed, hearing him call her by her new name, as she to her surprise found she liked being a Darling. It felt right to belong to this strange family, being a part of the chaos they called life.

But to be asked to seduce Sin…

As Sebastian cocked his head to the side, looking at her with his mischievous green eyes, a part of the wall she had built around her heart disappeared. It was strange to feel such immediate connection to someone she didn't really know, and she knew he could become her friend.

Not because he had to or because he wanted her, but because on some level they connected. The easiness between them was without strings, and she had never experienced that with someone before, and especially not with a man.

Before she could change her mind, she decided to

be honest with him. "I wouldn't know how to."

He didn't blink at all over her admission. Instead, he dragged her further back in the room, until they could have a private conversation without anyone overhearing.

"Get naked. That would work."

She didn't think her cheeks could get any warmer, but she ignored her embarrassment. "What if he denies me anyway? That would be too humiliating."

"He won't."

"How do you know? How can you be certain the man who constantly turns his back to me, pretending I'm not there, won't laugh at me before continuing ignoring me?"

"Because he doesn't ignore you."

"Yes, he does!"

Sebastian shook his head, his eyes dancing with amusement. "No, he doesn't. Even now, as we speak, he's watching you when you don't notice. The man can hardly take his eyes off you, and I guess ignoring you is his only way to save his poor heart from suffering too much."

Charmaine shook her head sadly. "He doesn't care about me."

"He doesn't? Then why do you think he's this angry with you? Because you made this marriage happen? Hardly. If you had just warmed up to him, he would have forgiven you that little mishap a long time ago."

He looked expectantly at her, waiting for her to come clean with him—and she wanted to, but couldn't. Not until Penelope was safe.

"It is too late. He can't even stand the thought of

having to share the same bedroom with me. Didn't you hear him when we arrived? He was desperate to sleep anywhere else as long as it wasn't in the same room with me."

The pain she had felt at his not wanting to be near her was clear in her small voice, and for once the mirth in Sebastian's eyes died as he looked at her with a compassionate little smile.

"Ask yourself one thing, then: *why* do you think he doesn't want to share a bedroom with you?"

"Because he can't stand the sight of me."

Sebastian shook his head and grabbed her chin, forcing her to look into his eyes. "No, because he knows he can't resist touching you if he has to share a bed with you. He wants you badly, Charmaine, and if you for once stop acting like an ice queen and instead show him the real you, the warm woman I can sense behind all the pretending, he won't be able to withstand you."

Tears ran down her cheeks, and he wiped them away tenderly. "Please believe me. A little warmth can do wonders. This ice-queen act of yours is starting to get really old, and I think you might find yourself in the midst of something much better if you let go of it. Something which might last a lifetime."

She found herself wishing that were true. A life filled with happiness sounded like heaven to her, and the more she pondered it the more she realized she liked the thought of sharing it with Sin.

The problem was Penelope.

She was still very much in jeopardy, although not aware of it, and Charmaine had long ago made a vow to put her sister's life first. Penelope would never know what her sister had sacrificed for her well-being, but Charmaine didn't care. As long as Penelope was happy, it was enough for her.

"What's holding you back?" Sebastian frowned at her, and she sighed deeply.

"Too much to tell, I'm afraid. All I can say is that for now I can't reach out to Sin. For his own good it is better he stays away from me."

"You sound like you are dangerous."

She couldn't help but laugh when she noticed the suspicious look he gave her. "I'm not. But sometimes we all carry things in our hearts we cannot ignore. I have such a thing, and I have to see it through before I will be ready for happiness."

Reluctantly Sebastian capitulated to her stubbornness. "For me it's hard to understand what can make a young, well-bred lady like yourself give up her own life, but as I can see it's important to you I'll leave it be. But, please, if there is anything you need help with—come to me. I will help you and ask no questions. All right?"

She nodded, tears in her eyes, humbled by his simple generosity.

"Well," he continued, with his impish smile back in place, "let's join the others before rumors start running around about me not being able to keep my hands off my lovely sister-in-law."

She put her hand in the crook of his arm and accompanied him back to the others, who were awkwardly praising the gloating Annabelle Overton.

Penelope joined them in the outskirts of the crowd.

"What an awful woman."

"Miss Overton?"

"She too, I admit, but I was talking about the mother. She's been telling everyone how important she is and how much everyone looks up to her. Fanny has been rolling her eyes so much I fear they soon will continue rolling, whether she wants it or not."

"That would be a sight to see." Sebastian grinned and Penny whacked him lightly on the shoulder.

"You imp. Go away and let me talk to my sister alone."

Sebastian bowed deeply. "As you wish, my lady. Who am I to go against such a gentle demand?"

He strolled away, leaving the two sisters alone.

"I need to talk to you," Penelope whispered intensely, nodding toward the door leading out to the hallway, and Charmaine followed her curiously.

"Alone at last," Penelope sighed as they entered the famous round foyer of Pendragon.

Charmaine, who could sense her sister's repressed anxiety, didn't waste any time. "What is it, Penny? You seem distraught."

"He's not here."

"Who isn't here?"

"Rake."

Ah.

Charmaine put an arm around her sister, offering her handkerchief to the now crying Penelope.

"He will come, you know."

"I know. Sooner or later he will appear, because he too wants to see the triplets. But how will I ever be able to reach him? I've been such a monster, pushing him further and further away from me when I didn't tell him the truth about what happened to me at Lord Bolton's house, and now he's just too angry to face me."

"Do you think he loves you?"

"I know he does."

"So why hesitate? When he comes, you just have to make sure he understands your point of view."

Penelope snorted angrily. "Like you have, you mean?"

Charmaine drew back slightly. "This was about you, not me."

"But you insist on holding everyone at arm's length, refusing to let anyone know what's in your heart. And yet here you are, telling me to do the opposite. Why don't you?"

"Because Rake loves you, that's the difference. You have something to build upon. I haven't."

The air went out of Penelope, and she smiled apologetically.

"I'm so sorry. You are right. Your situation and mine are quite different. You are married to a man you don't love and who doesn't love you, while I have a man I love and who loves me. I just seem unable to make him want to marry me."

Charmaine frowned. Why did it bother her how easily Penelope assumed she and Sin didn't care for each other? It was the truth, she knew that, but still... She didn't like it at all.

"I think I'll leave this little soirée for now." Penelope sighed. "I'll go and see how Fanny's doing with feeding the little ones. I need to distance myself from everyone for a little while."

"You are such a bad liar," Charmaine snorted, knowing her sister too well. "You are just trying to elude Mrs. Overton."

Blushing, Penelope grinned. "Yes, I must admit I

am. She's such a horrible woman. She keeps patting my hand, telling me not to worry about being less pretty than her daughter. I can't help that it vexes me a bit."

"As it should. But if I understand it correctly, that woman vexes everyone she meets, so you shouldn't take her words too seriously. You are very beautiful, and she's just jealous."

"Not as beautiful as you are."

"Maybe not on the outside, but you are the better person on the inside, believe me."

Penelope hugged her closely. "I love you, Charmaine. You know that, don't you?"

Charmaine nodded. "And I love you."

"I know. You can't help it. Nobody can. I'm just too loveable."

Charmaine laughed, and as her sister disappeared up the staircase, she couldn't help but smile. Poor Penelope. She hadn't had an easy life so far, and Charmaine wished there were something more she could do for her, but other than keeping Lord Nester and Lord Bolton as far away as possible, there was not much.

Too tired to return to the music room and keep up the appearance of indifference, she found her way to the bedroom she and Sin had been given, closing the door behind her. The silence of the room was manna for her pounding head, and she decided not to call for a maid. Instead, she started to unbutton her dress by herself, slowly working her way through the small buttons.

The dress had just fallen into a silky pile at her feet when the door crashed open and Sin barged in, stopping midstride as he realized she was undressing.

"Y-you left," he stuttered, and she felt an urgent

need to put the dress back on, but something made her think of what Sebastian had said: *Seduce him. He wants you.*

"I did," she whispered, but he wasn't listening. He was staring at her with an odd expression, slowly closing the door behind him without taking his eyes off her.

"Why?"

"I'm tired."

He took a step toward her, and she could see him convulsively clenching his hands as if trying to restrain himself from reaching out to her. From touching her.

Maybe Sebastian had been right. Maybe Sin did want her. A little flicker of hope started to dance inside her, and she wished she knew what to do.

How did you seduce a man?

Get naked, Sebastian had said, and before she could stop herself she took a step back and sat down gracefully on the bed. Sin's eyes never left her as she bent down and removed first her shoes and then the silky stockings.

She heard his ragged breathing when she removed the thicker chemise, leaving only her thin one. The silken layers didn't hide much of her body.

"What are you doing?" he whispered hoarsely, and she knew this wasn't the moment for lies. If she ever wanted to be able to reconcile with him, she needed to be as truthful as possible.

"Seducing you."

He staggered forward and grabbed her waist, hauling her closer to him. She let her arms slid up around his neck just as she had earlier that day, lifting her face to his in a silent invitation for him to kiss her.

His hands trembled as they moved over her back, touching her soft body under the silky chemise, but he didn't lean down and kiss her. Instead he closed his eyes as if he tried to find strength to withstand her.

"Kiss me," she whispered, unable to stop herself from wanting to feel the wonderful sensation his last kiss had aroused inside her.

"Why?"

She looked into his burning dark eyes—and, to her horror, she couldn't see him yearning for her; all she could see was contempt.

"Because I want you," she whispered as he took her hands from his shoulders and moved away from her.

"You do, do you?"

He looked her up and down in the most insulting way possible, and only her pride made her able to face him. Something had gone wrong, terribly wrong, and she didn't know what. He had wanted her; she had felt it in his trembling hands and in his hot breath washing over her.

But somewhere she had done wrong and lost him.

"What made you believe I want you?"

Tears filled her eyes, and she forced herself to stand still and not hide from him, even though his insulting gaze made her quiver. He did everything he could think of to make her feel small and humiliated, but she would never let him know how well it was working.

"You're quite the seductress," he drawled, circling the bed before lying down on top of it with his arms under his head, looking absolutely untouched by her almost naked presence. "One can't help but wonder where a virgin like you has learnt how to make a man want you. Or is that the thing—you are not a virgin anymore?"

She winced at the open insult and, with a whimper, dived to the floor and grabbed the thicker chemise to hide her body from him again.

"Oh, no, don't you put that thing back on. You were doing so well, Charmaine. Why don't you continue, and show me what other men have taught you. Show me how you have seduced them."

As she put the chemise on again, defying his order, she hid her face, not wanting him to see the streaming tears.

"I have never…"

"Liar."

She stiffened as he snarled at her, clearly not believing a word she was saying.

"I don't lie," she whispered. "I have never seduced anyone before."

"You just can't tell the truth, can you? This explains why you were so desperate to marry me, why you tripped me. You knew no one else would ever want to marry a used piece like yourself, and when I presented the perfect way out to you…"

His voice trailed off, and instead of continuing he patted the bed beside him. "Why don't you come here and show your husband what you have learnt."

"No."

"No? Why not? What's wrong with seducing your own husband? Don't you think there should be something in this for me? What else do you have to offer me but your body?"

Nothing.

She had absolutely nothing to give him but herself, and he was making it more than clear he didn't want her. Sebastian had been wrong. Sin couldn't want her any less than he did.

The humiliation of having tried to seduce him was nothing to the humiliation of being denied. She had known it could happen, but Sebastian had been so sure...

How could Sin believe this of her?

What possessed him to even consider her offering herself to other men before tricking him into marrying her?

"Please leave," she whispered, but he only laughed at her. A strained laughter, as if forced, but still a laugh.

"Why? So you can go downstairs and continue flirting with my brother and making a spectacle of yourself in front of everyone?"

Jealousy. That was what had ticked him off.

He had watched her and Sebastian when they stood at the back of the music room, and he had conveniently misunderstood everything.

The relief she felt made her stagger. Jealousy she could understand. Jealousy she could live with. Her stepfather had constantly lectured her about her indecent behavior toward other men.

Most men seemed to be overly possessive when it came to their wives. Why would Sin be different just because he didn't love her?

"I wasn't flirting with Sebastian."

"Well, let me tell you something, it certainly did look as if you were. You kept touching him."

She looked up at him, recognizing his lie.

"No, I didn't. I was merely standing beside him,

talking to him."

"So what were you two talking about so intently? How to best hide your lack of virginity?"

She grabbed her robe from the small chair beneath the window and put it on, not knowing what to say to him. Should she tell him the truth? That they had been talking about him? No, she couldn't. Not when he was this upset.

"We talked about the guests, Mrs. Overton and her daughter."

"Ah, the lovely young woman with the beautiful voice."

"Really? You liked her singing?"

"I thought she had the loveliest voice. Don't you agree?"

She shook her head without thinking, too caught in her thoughts about the awful Miss Annabelle Overton and her screechy voice. "No."

As if he had been waiting for this, he jumped from the bed and strode to her, stopping only a breath away. "Are you jealous of her beauty and talent?"

"What?" Charmaine frowned, still caught in her thoughts regarding Miss Overton's torture of their ears, not really listening to him. "I'm sorry, what did you say?"

Sin used her confusion, leaning closer to her until she only needed to go up on tiptoes to put her lips against his. But this time she didn't want to. He had destroyed the little confidence she had managed to gather, and now she didn't dare try to kiss him again.

"Are you jealous of Miss Overton?" he repeated hoarsely and leaned even closer to her, forcing her to decide to either move backwards to get away from him or stand still and wait for his lips to touch hers.

When she moved away from him, a wry smile played over his full lips and he straightened his clothes, moving toward the door. "I think I'll leave you be. The lovely Miss Overton told me she wouldn't mind taking a little stroll down the terrace, and what kind of gentleman am I if I don't oblige her wish?"

His open attempt to make her jealous made her uneasy. She didn't want this tension between them, not when nothing of it was true. She couldn't have him walk away from her believing she was a loose woman, believing she wasn't what she was supposed to be.

But wasn't that the problem from the beginning? That he couldn't face the fact that underneath her shiny exterior was only a young, lonely girl who wanted nothing more than to belong to someone?

Could this be a blessing in disguise? Maybe his disdainful thoughts about her were just what she needed for him to leave her alone, to give her space enough to be able to look out for her sister.

She shook her head mentally. No, it wasn't.

How could she live knowing he believed her capable of doing something as vile as giving herself to others and then shamelessly luring him into marrying her? Everyone kept telling her he was the most levelheaded of men, but she had seen nothing of that. Instead he seemed driven by his emotions, just as he had when triumphantly declaring his intention to flirt with another woman.

She closed her eyes, envisioning him with Annabelle Overton in his arms, and the terror she felt made it clear to her—she couldn't let him leave her without at least trying one last time to reach him.

"Sin!"

He stopped with his hand on the door handle, looking at her expectantly over his shoulder as if he had only waited for her to stop him.

"Yes?"

She took a step toward him, wanting desperately to make him hate her less, but she didn't know what to say. She hadn't a clue where to start, and in the end she just shook her head.

"No, nothing. I'm sorry."

He stood still for the longest of moments, frowning at her as if her lack of backbone disappointed him. In the end, he left the room without uttering another syllable, leaving her to go and flirt with Annabelle Overton on the terrace.

She staggered back until she reached the bed, dozens of erratic thoughts twirling inside her head as she sat down. How would she ever be able to live through this visit? Not only was she supposed to share this small room, and its small bed, with her estranged husband, but she would also have to watch him carry on with other women, all because he believed her guilty of infidelity and wanted to hurt her back.

An eye for an eye.

She hid her face in the pillow he had just left. She couldn't stand this much longer. This emotional stress was eating her up.

She needed to be alert, to have a clear mind, in case her stepfather tried something. But all the commotion with Sin was taking too much of her energy and attention. She simply couldn't keep her head straight when it came to him.

For someone who wasn't in love with her husband,

she definitely acted as if she were. So maybe he meant more to her than she had known? Maybe he was the man her heart had wanted all along, but she had been too caught up in the circus known as the Season to recognize the feeling?

She didn't know, and now she was too tired to figure it out. There was only one thing she was certain of, and that was that he was hers for life. He couldn't leave her and marry someone else like Lord Dane had done.

Sinclair Darling was her husband whether he liked it or not, and nothing he said or did could change that.

Chapter Six

"There it is, Gretna Green."

Penelope yelled, unladylike, hanging out through the window of the carriage, and Sin sighed deeply in gratitude. "Finally! I thought we would never get here."

"Oh come on, Sin, this trip hasn't been so bad, now, has it?"

Charmaine bit back a smile as he stared openmouthed at Penelope, clearly unable to grasp how she could say something so ridiculous.

"Not so bad?" If he hadn't been inside a moving vehicle Sin would probably have started to pace in despair. "We have endured one broken wheel, three snowstorms, and too many cold inns for me to count. And you have the nerve to say this trip wasn't bad?"

Penelope sat back on her seat, giving him a look that said just how ridiculous she found him. "I didn't force you to come with us, did I? Charmaine and I could have travelled alone, as I had planned from the beginning. But no, you just couldn't let Charmaine leave you, could you?"

"As I said, I don't trust her to act as your chaperone. If anything happened, she would have seen to her own protection first, not caring about yours at all. And I do care too much about you to leave you in the wind like that."

Not a word of caring about her, Charmaine noticed

sadly. The man couldn't have made his indifference toward her more obvious. It was Penelope's safety he thought of, not his wife's. As far as she knew, he probably would have rejoiced if something happened to her. Then he would be able to marry the horrible Annabelle Overton instead, and raise a whole bunch of tone-deaf children.

"You are despicable," Penelope scoffed. "How can you say such a thing about your wife? You are supposed to honor and cherish her, not stab her in the back verbally."

"*I'm* despicable?" Sin leaned forward, waving his index finger toward his sister-in-law. "If you knew what your precious sister has done…"

"I do know!" Penelope grabbed his finger.

"You know?" Sin slumped back into the seat, and Penelope released his finger.

"I do. She tricked you into marrying her and now you are upset over it, lashing out continuously at her. But you have to get over it, Sin, or at least try to be civil."

"You know how she fooled me, and yet you still defend her?"

"Her actions? No, I don't. But her person? Yes. She is my sister and I know her. She would never have done something like that with no reason."

Sin snorted angrily. "Try to make her tell you why, if you like. You won't succeed, I promise you. She's like a clam; she does not open up in the least."

Both turned to look expectantly at Charmaine, who wanted nothing more than to sink into the comfortable cushion behind her and disappear. This trip had been hell for her, confined inside the carriage with Sin, unable to avoid his dark, probing eyes.

Thank God Penelope had been chatting constantly since they left Pendragon and Herefordshire behind. Otherwise she would never have been able to endure having him so near for such a long time. Every time she looked his way she met his eyes, as he pinned her with his unreadable gaze. As if the carriage wasn't feeling too compact already…

"You can talk to us." Penelope put a supportive hand on Charmaine's knee. "We are here for you and want to share what troubles you. Something is slowly eating you up, and I…*we* need to know what it is so we can help you. Please, Charmaine…"

The honest compassion in Penelope's eyes made the lump in Charmaine's throat grow again. Could she share with them? Could she tell them the whole truth and not be judged by them?

No.

The answer was short and simple. No, she couldn't. Penelope's life had already been turned upside down because of their stepfather's sick infatuation with Charmaine, and now, when her younger sister was so close to getting out of his reach, she couldn't tell the truth.

And Sin…

Somehow she knew she could tell him anything and any normal day he would have backed her up against Lord Nester, making sure she would be forever free of him. But not now, not while his thoughts and actions were ruled by his current unstable anger. How would he ever be able to sort through his hatred toward her long enough to be able to help her?

No, she was alone in this, and soon it would be

over. Soon she would be able to live her life again, and she could only hope she hadn't destroyed things too much between her and Sin.

Maybe he still could care for her a little in the future and perhaps love her a bit. Maybe...

"There's nothing wrong with me. I'm perfectly fine," she finally chirped as icily as she could, and Sin snorted in response.

"A clam!" he snarled to Penelope. "A bloody clam. She will never oblige you, or me for that matter, with the truth. She would rather die than enlighten us with what really goes on beneath that glorious blonde hair."

As the carriage stopped, Penelope gave her sister one last probing glance, which told Charmaine this discussion wasn't over. It would continue another time and in another place, and without Sin's hateful presence.

"Do you think Rake's here?" she asked to change the subject, and Penelope lightened up.

"You think he arrived before us?"

"Of course he hasn't." Sin rolled his eyes. "Even if he arrived at Pendragon the same day we left he wouldn't have followed us immediately."

"Why not?"

"Because Francesca won't blurt it out as soon as he arrives. No, she will wait until he is comfortable and unprepared, and then she will spring it upon him. And I know he won't go running here immediately for you, not without thinking it all through properly. You have made it quite clear to him that if he comes here it is for forever, and he's got quite the decision to make."

Charmaine couldn't keep her tongue. "What decision? He loves her with all his heart, so what is it he needs to think about?"

Sin looked deep into her eyes as he answered, "He needs to decide if she's worth it."

"Of course she's worth it!"

Before Sin had a chance to snap back, Penelope's sad little voice interrupted. "He's right, Charmaine. Rake wouldn't come here without being sure this is what he wants. It might only take him a few hours or it could take a couple of days, I don't know. What I do know is that he won't come after me if he's not sure I am what he really, really wants. All I can pray for is that I haven't destroyed our future together with my behavior."

Sin's tender smile as he watched Penelope sent daggers into Charmaine's heart. If he would look upon her like he looked at her sister she knew she wouldn't ask for more. That was all she wanted—a smile filled with love and trust.

"Don't you fret about this now," he said softly to her sister. "We can stay for a couple of weeks, if needed, so please don't be stressed over this. Let's find somewhere to stay for a while, and then let's keep our hopes up. I know he will come, Penny. I just don't know how long it will take for him to make that decision."

"Thank you," Penelope cried out, throwing herself into his waiting arms. Charmaine had to look out through the window, pretending an interest in the dark building at which they had stopped, to avoid letting them see how envious she was of their closeness.

"Just one little thing," Sin said as he loosened his hold of Penelope. "Do you think he will understand the message? You did, after all, just inform him you were going to Gretna Green."

"He will. He once told me that if I ever eloped here, he wanted me to let him know so he could stop me beforehand. He knows what he said to me."

"Then let us get out of this infernal carriage and into the inn. Maybe they'll have some hot tea to warm us up," Sin said as he jumped out the opened door and then helped Penelope down. When Charmaine moved closer to the doorway, he looked at her darkly before turning his back to her.

The driver helped her down, and she followed her travel companions through the muddy snow into the warm inn. The sturdy innkeeper took one look at their shivering and immediately ushered them to a table next to the roaring fire, where he had a servant bring them hot tea and soup.

"Ah, that was exactly what I needed." Penelope yawned. "Now a soft bed would be the perfect ending to this long day."

"Of course," Sin said and beckoned the innkeeper to join them. In a moment they had been handed a key to a small suite, theirs to use for as long as they needed. It was a nice suite, with a salon between a smaller bedroom on one side and a larger one on the other.

"You two can have the large bedroom," Sin said as the servants brought up their luggage. "I'll do fine in the smaller one."

Charmaine bent her head, not knowing if she should feel grateful or humiliated over his stubborn refusal to share a bed with her. They had spent a couple of weeks at Pendragon, and she had slept alone in the small bedroom they had been given. She didn't know where he spent his nights, but she had no trouble imagining where.

"Of course not," Penelope scoffed. "You two must be so tired of me constantly being around, and so I will take the smaller bedroom and let you have the larger one for yourselves."

"Really, there is no need for you to insist." Sin's voice was icy. "You would be doing us a favor if you shared the bedroom with your sister."

Charmaine pressed her nails into her palms in an effort to stop herself from starting to sob hysterically. Could he want her any less? His constant refusal to be near her hurt more than she had thought possible. She wanted nothing more than to be as far away from her two companions as possible.

"That's enough, Sin," Penelope said harshly. "I'm not going to separate the two of you, so stop insulting my sister, please. You can put that bag in the smaller bedroom and the rest in the larger."

The last was directed to the driver, who couldn't hide a small smile as he did as asked. As soon as her things were inside the small room, Penelope went through the door and slammed it shut behind her, leaving Sin and Charmaine alone in the salon. Awkwardly they stared through the doorway at the large bed they were supposed to share.

"Don't think this changes anything."

She straightened her back and forced her ice-queen face on before turning to face him. "Why don't you talk to the innkeeper and see if he has another room available."

"No use. He made it quite clear this is the high season for Gretna Green, as the winter always makes too many couples eager to get married. Can't understand what makes them eager. I find marriage quite the drag."

"Maybe another inn?"

"And leave you alone? No way."

She felt herself warm up to him. Was he only looking out for her? "It would be the best solution, if there was a possibility."

He moved toward her, and she took a few steps back, until she bumped into the door leading out to the hallway. "Don't think I will let you live by yourself, free to share your bed with anyone you chose."

"W-what?" She stared up into his angry face without understanding what he was talking about. Free to share her bed? With whom?

"I will not let you have lovers sneak into your bed, leaving me with the possibility of you giving me a bastard I will be forced to call my own."

When she understood what he meant, the air went out of her, and she grabbed the door handle behind her back, thankful for it being there, as she would have fallen to the floor otherwise.

There seemed to be no end to his low opinion of her. She thought she had made it clear to him that she hadn't had any lovers, and that she still remained the virgin she was supposed to be. But it appeared she hadn't. He still thought of her as a whore, luring him into marriage because no one else was stupid enough to become her husband.

She forced her tears back as far as she could. She wouldn't give him the satisfaction of seeing her cry in front of him, of letting him know how much he hurt her with his cold words and his contempt.

"It's late, so why don't you go and get ready for

the night. And don't you put on some thin chemise to try to seduce me, because I'm too tired for you tonight. Tomorrow I might feel differently, though, and I'll let you know."

"As you wish." Somehow she managed to sound almost normal and uncaring, and without looking at him she walked slowly into the bedroom, silently closing the door behind her.

How could he think such low thoughts of her? She had never even been kissed before that day in the Pendragon courtyard, thanks to the jealous guarding by her stepfather. She was more pristine than a nun, and yet he thought the complete opposite of her.

She looked at the bed, trying to imagine sharing it with him, and she quivered with expectation mixed with fright. The thought of having his large body lying beside hers made her feel small and exposed.

Lord Nester had taken every opportunity to whisper to her exactly what he wanted to do to her, and the thought of Sin doing those things scared her. She didn't know what exactly happened between a normal man and woman in bed; all she knew was what that insane man had mumbled in her ear.

But Sin wasn't Lord Nester.

Sin wasn't evil. He was just a good man who'd had the carpet ripped away from under his feet and now was desperately trying to learn how to walk without it. She knew she wasn't helping him along with her refusal to tell him what troubled her, but that shouldn't render her all the insults and humiliation from him.

She rang for a maid and had her help her unpack and undress. Then she dismissed the girl and climbed into the bed to breathlessly await Sin. She could hear him moving around in the salon, and every time his steps brought him closer to the bedroom she held her breath.

But he never came.

In the end, she was too exhausted to stay awake, and she fell asleep still alone in the bedroom, still waiting for him to join her.

That night she dreamt about her stepfather. Twisted dreams of him hunting her through the deformed rooms of Harveyfield, reaching for her with his bony hands. His ghastly laughter echoed as she desperately stumbled from room to room, not finding salvation anywhere, and in the end he caught her in her childhood bedroom.

Along the walls, all the suitors from her past stood looking at her as if they thought she deserved what happened to her. When Lord Nester pushed her down on the bed, she screamed and screamed to get someone to save her, but all the men remained at the walls, looking at her with gleaming eyes…

"Charmaine, please wake up."

The soft voice cut through the horrendous nightmare like a guiding star, and she let it lead her away from her stepfather, away from Harveyfield and all the suitors. When she opened her eyes, Sin's worried face hovered above her. A shiver of fright ran through her body as she noticed how close his body was.

"Good evening," he breathed when he saw she was awake, and she could feel his anxiety.

"Good evening."

"You were dreaming."

She almost snorted but managed to stop herself from doing something to destroy the moment, because for once he was looking at her without contempt.

Without disappointment.

"Yes."

"You screamed. I thought someone was…" His voice trailed off, but she could see him wince over what he had thought happened to her.

"Thank you for waking me up."

"Don't mention it." He leaned back again, offering her some space, which made her feel much better. She didn't like being caught in small spaces and especially not by a man, even though it was Sin, who had nothing to do with her dream or her life before their marriage.

"Do you often dream like that?"

She pulled the bedspread closer, until it covered her whole body from his eyes. "No."

He chuckled softly as he lay down beside her, careful to not touch her in any way. "You look like a little girl, with your braids, and the bedspread all the way to your chin."

When she didn't answer he rolled over to his back, stretching out beside her without taking his serious, unreadable gaze from her. "You screamed about your father."

She couldn't stop a shiver. "I did?"

"If hadn't known better, I would have thought you were afraid of him."

She forced herself to giggle. "How strange."

"My sentiment exactly."

"What girl would ever be afraid of her father?"

He didn't react to her pathetic attempt to joke. Instead, he gazed at her, a gaze that made her feel more insecure than ever. What more had she said in her dream?

"Penelope is."

"Y-yes…"

He turned to his side again, and she sank back further into the pillow, trying to get as far away from him as she could without him noticing it. But he did. She could tell by the frown growing on his forehead.

"I'm sorry," he said softly, and she frowned back at him.

"For what?"

"For accusing you of having lovers."

His apology surprised her, and she wanted desperately to ask him why he had changed his mind. But she dared not, as she was too afraid it would only make him ask her more about her dream and about her stepfather, and she wasn't fit for that now.

"I was too caught up in my own anger to consider how overprotective your parents always have been toward you. Now, when I think about it, I can't remember ever seeing them leave you alone, and definitely not with a man."

His levelheaded insight brought new tears to her eyes. This was the Sin she had known before. The steady, calm man who didn't lash out verbally, trying to hurt her as much as he could.

"Are you *crying*?"

"No," she sniffed.

"Yes, you are."

He shifted position, slipping his hands in under the bedspread to grab her waist and haul her closer to him. Gently he forced her to rest her cheek against his broad chest as he put his arms around her, hugging her closer to him.

At first she lay stiff as a board, not able to feel at

ease in his embrace. But as the minutes passed and he did nothing but softly caress her back, she started to relax. His warm body against hers was soothing, and, drowsy, she slowly fell asleep again.

She dreamt of babies.

Chapter Seven

Something changed between them that first night in Gretna Green. Saving her from her nightmare seemed to soothe Sin's anger, making it possible for him to be around her without yelling like a madman.

He still held her at arm's length mentally and behaved more like an old uncle than a loving husband, but she didn't mind. To her it was the perfect solution.

Finally she could breathe.

After the first week in Gretna Green, she started to act less like an ice queen and more as her true self, carefully letting him see pieces of what no one else had before—the real Charmaine. He never mentioned it, but she could sense him appreciating her more every day.

He liked her. He truly liked her.

Not the Incomparable Queen. *Her*.

They joined the social life in Gretna Green, and she loved to arrive on Sin's arm as Lady Chilton. He escaped to the game room as soon as he could, but she didn't mind. She knew he was there and would come to her if she needed him.

She introduced her sister to as many unmarried men as she could find, in case Rake didn't show up. They had even found a new friend in a kind local girl, Miss Lydia Woodley, who generously introduced them to everyone she knew, bringing them with her to every party and assembly she was invited to.

It was a strange feeling, being able to act as a chaperone when only a short while ago she hadn't been able to go anywhere without one herself. But she thrived in her new freedom, making sure both Penelope and Lydia did too.

Sin rarely joined them during their outings, as he spent most of his time writing letters to the supervisor at Chester Park, unable to let go of his responsibilities toward the estate.

Not until their third week in Gretna Green did a problem present itself to them, causing uproar in their temporary matrimonial heaven.

"Don't you ever grow tired of it?"

Looking up from her needlework, Charmaine smiled inquiringly at her sister. "Of what?"

Slumped in an unladylike fashion in her chair, Penelope waved her hand toward the surroundings. "This."

"The inn, you mean?"

"No. Or, yes…" Penelope sat up, frustrated. "This life we lead here. Nothing ever happens. Day in and day out we do the same things, talk to the same people, and discuss the same subjects. It's like we have entered a wheel of eternity we can't escape, and it is driving me crazy."

Charmaine laughed sympathetically. "I have to agree with you that life in a small town like this doesn't challenge your brain much, but to me it's peaceful and what I needed. What *we* needed."

Penelope plucked a sandwich from the plate and started to dissect it. "Lord, I'm so bored. Soon I will do anything just to get a reaction from the locals. I've never seen such a bunch of slow-minded people in my life. Thank God for Lydia!"

"Indeed," Charmaine agreed. "Lydia is the best thing here. I have to admit I thought less of her at first, but she has proven to be a truly good friend and an entertaining companion."

"You hated her guts."

"I did not!"

Penelope snorted loudly enough to catch the haughty attention of the people sitting near them, and the two sisters tried to keep from giggling too loudly.

"We must seem so strange to them," Charmaine said, when their neighbors at the next table started to whisper while casting eyes toward their table, apparently talking about them.

"I know exactly what they say," Penelope said with a mischievous glint in her eyes. "Look at that amazingly beautiful woman who sits there with her not-as-pretty sister. Isn't she married to that boring man who keeps avoiding them as much as he can?"

"Sin's not avoiding us." Charmaine sighed impatiently. "And you are quite as beautiful as I am."

"Uh-hum." Penelope nodded knowingly. "So how are things between you and Sin? You seem to get along quite nicely nowadays, compared to before Gretna Green."

"We do, don't we?" Charmaine couldn't hold back a satisfied smile. "I can hardly believe how good life has become now, when we have gotten past our earlier differences. It's like a marriage made in heaven."

"I have to agree, since you both look very pleased with yourselves."

"You make us sound too good to be true." Charmaine frowned, and Penelope shrugged indifferently.

"You behave more like two siblings than a married couple passionately in love. You are the image of happiness to everyone looking at you, and yet there is something missing. There's something that's simply not there."

Penelope slumped back in her chair again, obviously pondering what was wrong with her sister's marriage, and Charmaine groaned inwardly. This wasn't a subject she wanted to discuss with her sister. Especially not her unmarried sister.

"What do you feel when he kisses you?"

"I beg your pardon…"

"Oh, don't you beg-your-pardon me. I know you, remember? You always say that when you don't want to answer a question."

Charmaine sighed deeply. "Penelope…"

"So do you?"

"Do we what?"

"Kiss."

"Of course we kiss." Charmaine rolled her eyes to show her sister just how ludicrous she found her.

"Pecks on the forehead don't count."

Oh. "I can be happy without kissing."

"Can you?"

Charmaine could see her sister didn't believe her, and she couldn't blame her. She hardly believed herself. Ever since that first night in Gretna Green, when he had held her so gently, comforting her, Sin hadn't touched her.

Not once, although they now shared the bed, sleeping side by side. He just lay down with his back toward her, breathing a polite and very bland, "Good night," before promptly falling asleep, leaving her feeling miserable and unwanted.

She wanted more. She wanted hot kisses and trembling hands desperate to touch her. She wanted to feel his need of her, and her alone. As it was now, she couldn't help but think he wouldn't even notice if someone else were in her place.

"I hope so," she admitted to her sister. "I do hope so, because I don't know how to make him want to kiss me."

"But you share the same bed…"

Charmaine just shook her head in despair. "As if that helps. He just turns his back to me, ignoring me. I have come to the conclusion he doesn't want me in that way, and I guess I'll have to learn to live with it."

"What about the kiss in the courtyard at Pendragon? We all saw it, and I'll tell you, he wanted you desperately."

"I know." Charmaine sighed longingly. "But unfortunately that was merely his anger speaking. Now, when we are at ease with each other, he has lost all his tempers and is quite levelheaded again."

"Boring, you mean." Penelope snorted, and Charmaine couldn't do much more than agree.

Sin *was* boring.

She almost wanted him to be angry with her again so he would get more interesting. His favorite subjects of conversation, or more usually of his longwinded monologues, seemed to be lectures about agriculture, such as the best way to grow various plants. She couldn't remember a word he'd said; she was always too busy with keeping herself from yawning.

Penelope continued with her dissection of the

sandwich, and Charmaine bit back a smile. Her sister was an innocent child sometimes, letting her emotions rule her mind. Charmaine, on the other hand, had always been forced to put a lid on her emotions and had learnt to think before acting.

She felt a bit envious of her sister's ability to react honestly to everything that happened to her. She knew she almost never did. Under their stepfather's roof she had repressed her feelings over and over again, to avoid catching his unwanted attention, and in so doing she had learnt to hide her true self.

As a married woman she did the same thing, pushing her real needs and wants aside to be what Sin needed her to be—serene and seemingly happy.

"I can't believe it." Penelope interrupted her thoughts, staring at the door with a strange mix of angst and expectation, and when Charmaine turned to follow her sister's gaze, she froze.

There, just inside the door and still covered with snow, stood Lord Dane, looking as perfectly handsome as ever. Watching him drag his fingers through his long blond hair, emotions she thought long gone started to rise from their hiding place, and she lost her ability to breathe for a short moment.

As if he felt her watching him, he stiffened before slowly letting his gaze roam the large room until he met her eyes. A fire started to burn in his blue depths, a fire she remembered too well.

Lord Dane still wanted her.

And to her despair she felt her treacherous heart skip a beat. Oh, how she had loved him! He had been a fresh wind in her life, with his warm smile and irresistible laughter. He had brought joy into her dull life, and for a short time she had felt alive.

But then her stepfather had destroyed it all by telling Lord Dane she didn't want to marry him, brutally sending him away. It hadn't surprised her much that he had married someone else immediately. He was the most free-spirited and spontaneous person she knew.

"Don't you do anything stupid now," Penelope breathed beside her, and Charmaine tore her eyes from her old beau.

"Whatever do you mean? What is it you think I might do? Elope with him? We are both married to other people now, and I certainly will not fool around with him and destroy what Sin and I have succeeded in building."

"But the way you look at him…"

Charmaine blushed. "I can't help it if I still have feelings for him. He used to mean a lot to me, Penny. I'm sorry, but I can't turn my emotions off so easily."

"What do you think Sin will say?"

Charmaine made a little grimace. "I don't think he will be too pleased. He made some rather crude remarks about Lord Dane earlier. But then again, why would he care? Lord Dane is just an old friend, and why should not I be able to have old friends?"

"I think there is a difference between old friends and an old suitor, in the eyes of a husband."

"Sin won't care."

Penelope didn't reply, but the pointed look she gave her sister told Charmaine she didn't agree with her at all.

"He won't!"

"Of course he will. He's your husband."

"Just because he is my husband doesn't mean he will mind me spending some time with Lord Dane, catching up on old times."

"I still think you should send for Sin."

Charmaine sighed, defeated, and was just about to beckon a serving wench to come to their table when a smooth, vibrant voice filled her ears.

"Hello, Charming."

She tangled her fingers tightly together in an effort to hide her inward shiver. Her smile, looking up at him, was small and utterly polite.

"Lord Dane."

Without being asked, he sat down beside her. He nodded politely to Penelope before grabbing Charmaine's tangled hands in his, squeezing them tightly.

"Seeing you like this makes me realize how much I've missed you. What has it been, a year?"

She nodded, not able to speak as she gazed into his blue eyes. Usually they sparkled with mirth, but not this time. The laughter was gone, and instead he looked at her sadly, and tears filled her eyes.

She had missed him too.

He had filled her heart with joy and her life with laughter and for a short time made her believe in a happy future. But then her stepfather's intervention had brought her back to earth and to her private hell again.

For one season her life had been perfect.

For one season she had been happy.

"You look as beautiful as ever," he mumbled as he lifted her hands to put chaste kisses on her knuckles. "I could sit here all night admiring your magnificent loveliness. It's a wonder you can leave your bedroom.

If I were you I would stay put and spend both day and night staring at my own reflection."

"You are such a tease, Lord Dane." Charmaine laughed. "You flatter me with your fancy words. And yet here I stand, untouched by every last one of them."

His eyes twinkled in a very familiar way as he wiggled his eyebrows at her. "What? Are my ears hearing what I think they hear? Are you, Lady Charmaine de Vere, the Incomparable Queen of the *ton*, telling me you don't give a bloody damn about my lavish compliments?"

"I don't mind the compliments. It's the false flattery I'm having trouble swallowing."

"False flattery? My lady, you hurt my tender feelings." Lord Dane's amused grin was contagious, and Charmaine couldn't stop herself from smiling back.

"Tender feelings? My, oh, my. Much can indeed happen in a mere year."

"Much can, indeed." The laughter disappeared from his eyes again, and it was obvious he thought of what had happened since the two of them met the last time.

"How *are* you?" Charmaine asked sincerely, and he shrugged lightly.

"I'm fine. Really I am. I've been hiding in the countryside for a year and missed the last season, unfortunately. Did you attend?"

"Yes."

He gave her a disappointed look. "I wanted to go, but things happened... I had to stay in Yorkshire for a while. I got married, you know."

"I know."

She forced herself to look serene and not show him

how much it still hurt that he had married someone else, and he looked even more disappointed, as if he had wanted a different reaction than the one she gave him.

"She died two weeks ago."

"I'm so sorry." She blushed, and he leaned closer to her with an eager look on his face.

"Don't be. I'm not. I was forced by my mother to marry the woman, even though she was sickly and already almost lying on her deathbed. But now I'm free. Free to live life again. Free to marry whomever I want."

Something about what he said irritated her a bit. Maybe it was his cold attitude about the woman he'd married, or the uncaring way he talked about her death. She couldn't put her finger on exactly what, but all in all, something about him bothered her.

"What brings you to Gretna Green, Lord Dane?" Penelope asked politely, effectively ending the tension between Charmaine and her former beau. "Are you here to get married again?"

Lord Dane grinned toward Penelope, showering her with the brightness of his smile. "No, as a matter of fact I'm not. Not yet, at least."

He sent Charmaine a quick look, and she understood he would have nothing against resuming what they once had shared. "I've friends, though, who are just married, and they have asked me to join them in celebrating the occasion."

"How fortunate for us."

He didn't look at Penelope when answering, instead he smiled hotly toward Charmaine, who blushed in response. "I couldn't agree more."

"Take your hands off my wife."

Sin's cold voice cut through the warm bubble Lord

Dane had created, and Charmaine blanched as she looked up at her husband.

He looked ready to kill. Gone was the levelheaded man of the last couple of weeks; in his stead the hateful avenger had returned with full force. Quickly Charmaine removed her hands from Lord Dane's grip, but her former suitor didn't notice—he was staring at Sin with confusion written all over his handsome face.

"Y-your wife?"

"My wife."

"But…" Lord Dane seemed incapable of grasping what Sin had said and turned to stare at Charmaine. "You are married?"

She nodded. "Yes."

"To him?"

"Yes."

"But you can't be. Not now."

"I'm sorry," Charmaine whispered, and his eyes filled with pain.

"I thought you were going to wait for me."

She looked at him with disbelief, unable to grasp such self-confidence. "Wait for you? Why should I have waited for you? I didn't know…"

"You could have asked," he interrupted. "But you never answered any of my letters, in which I tried to explain to you over and over again what had happened and why."

Charmaine frowned. "Letters? What letters?"

"The letters I sent you every day for the first month, until I realized you didn't intend to answer me."

She looked at Penelope, who shook her head sadly, and she could have cried in despair. She had never received one single letter, and it was not hard to guess where those letters had ended up.

Lord Nester.

"Charmaine, it's time for us to prepare for dinner," Sin snapped, and she nodded slowly, not knowing what to say or think anymore.

What her stepfather had done to her was beyond wrong. He had without remorse selfishly declined Lord Dane's proposal and sent the man away, to make sure Charmaine would stay single and unmarried until he was able to marry her himself. Then he had confiscated the letters Lord Dane sent her, letting her feel abandoned and unwanted.

"You never got the letters?"

"No, I didn't."

"I'm sorry to hear that. I had quite big hopes for my future. For our future... And now you are..."

Lord Dane looked up at Sin, his blue eyes turning as dark as her husband's gray ones.

"You are one lucky man, Chilton. You have succeeded with what most of our gender only dreamt of, securing the hand of the Incomparable Queen."

"Lucky indeed." Sin's voice icily echoed Lord Dane's envious words.

"If you don't mind my asking, how did you do it? How did you get past that father of hers? I never once managed to get her alone without one of her parents there as a chaperone."

Why did it vex her that Lord Dane kept mentioning her beauty and her social status as the most sought-after young woman? Not once did he mention love, or having had any emotion for her at all. Was it the shock of finding she was lost to him forever, or had his love been no more than shallow?

Sin touched Charmaine's arm lightly, telling her without words he wanted her to come with him. Obliging him, she grasped the arm he offered her.

"I've had no problems at all with her parents. Now, if you will excuse us, we have more important things awaiting us."

Sin dismissed the gaping gentleman with a curt nod before beckoning Penelope to walk ahead of them as he propelled Charmaine out of the room. Numbly she went, leaving Lord Dane alone at the table to stare after them, seemingly devastated.

"I can't believe this," Penelope breathed as they reached their private salon. "He sent letters? But you never got any, did you?"

Charmaine let go of Sin's arm as he stalked across the room and poured himself a large glass of port. "No. I didn't."

"How could he?"

Charmaine didn't answer her sister, although she knew the answer.

Because he wants to marry me himself.

But she couldn't say that out loud. She couldn't let Penelope and Sin become aware of what an awful person she was, a person who had made her stepfather want her.

Chapter Eight

Sin poured himself another glass, which he finished in one gulp, and Charmaine noticed the telling vein at his temple pulsating. Her husband was furious with her, and she knew she was partly to blame.

Penelope had been right. She should have sent for him before Lord Dane joined them, just because of their history together. But she had been too caught in the moment. Meeting Lord Dane, the one man who had managed to touch her heart, had turned her whole world upside down.

He still wanted her, but now it was too late. Now she belonged to the angry man who stood by the fireplace, looking more like a menacing, dark demon than a loving, contented husband. Sin practically oozed anger as he stared into the fire, and she saw his jaw twitch over and over again.

"Charmaine, why don't you join me in our bedroom? I would like to talk to you in private. If you'll excuse us, Penny."

It was an order and not a question. After sending the compassionate Penelope an apologizing look, Charmaine followed him into their bedroom. As soon as she'd closed the door behind her, he started to unknot his cravat, throwing it on the bed as he stalked across the room.

She walked over to the chair at desk, twitching her

skirt between her fingers while waiting for him to acknowledge her. Not until he had removed his jacket and unbuttoned his shirt did he look at her, but not with anger as she had presumed. Instead he looked tired and worn as he dragged his fingers through his brown hair.

"Life never stops surprising you, does it?"

She shook her head. "No."

"You shouldn't have talked to him without me."

"I'm sorry."

"Of course you are." He snorted angrily, and she frowned at him, not appreciating his tone of voice. So she should have had her husband by her side when she met her old beau, but still… It wasn't as if they had planned the meeting, or had it somewhere private. They had been in the inn, for goodness' sake, in the midst of a chatting crowd, accompanied by her sister. What more could he ask of her, except for him being there?

"What do you mean? I *am* sorry for what happened."

"You are always sorry for something. It seems to be your most employed word. Whatever you do or say, you always end up telling me you're sorry afterwards. Honestly, it annoys me exceedingly to hear you say it time after time. You never explain yourself. You never acknowledge me or my opinion. The only thing you do is tell me you're sorry. I'm so sick of it!"

She gaped at him, not understanding where this outburst came from. This was the first she'd heard of the problem, and yet it seemed to have bothered him for quite some time.

You are always sorry for something.

As she looked at his frustrated face, she knew she was losing him again. Not that she'd had him in the first place, but she had at least been on the verge of turning their marriage into something good.

But it had only taken the appearance of Lord Dane to send them back to where they'd started, he furious and she devastated.

"I'm sorry," she whispered before she could stop herself, and he shook his head with disgust.

"I'm sure you are. It must have felt like a punch in the stomach to you, finding out the love of your life is now available and all yours if you want him. Especially considering you were the one who made sure we *had* to marry just a few months ago. If you had bided your time…"

He sat down on the bed as though utterly fatigued and tired, and her heart went out to him. It hadn't been the easiest of times for him, these last couple of months. His normal life had been turned upside down, and all because she had forced him into something he hadn't asked for.

Something he didn't want.

She had succeeded in forcing into marriage the only man who didn't want her. Maybe it would have been easier for her to spend the rest of her life with someone who was awed by her and wanted her, but in that short second when she had to make up her mind whether to trip Sin or not, she had found him a good choice. And somewhere deep inside her she knew she wanted to spend the rest of her life with him.

The strangest thing was that downstairs sat Lord Dane, the man she had thought was just what Sin had called him, the love of her life. And yet here she sat in the bedroom, looking at Sin, knowing in her heart she didn't want life different. She didn't want anyone but him.

Not even Lord Dane.

Sin made her feel safe. He made her feel whole. And as she stood there looking at him, she knew she didn't want anyone else. But as long as she kept her secrets from him, he would never come to care about her. He had more than once made it perfectly clear to her that he needed the truth from her.

He needed her to confide in him.

As long as she didn't, he couldn't open up to her and trust her. The foundation for a solid marriage was mutual respect and trust, and she offered him neither. Maybe when Penelope was secure and out of reach of the evil that threatened her she could tell him everything and pray he would understand without blaming her too much for her stepfather's wrongdoings.

"I don't know how to continue," he whispered hoarsely. "It's not as if I didn't know your heart belonged to him. But until now it wasn't really a problem, because he was out of your life."

"Lord Dane is still out of my life," she said softly, searching for the right words. "I can't change that I am married to you now, and I don't want to, either."

"How utterly encouraging of you," he sneered, misunderstanding her completely. "I must say it really warms my heart to hear you admit you are married to me, because you can't change it now. It almost beats hearing you admit you didn't care whom you married."

She blushed, embarrassed over what she had said on their wedding day. That hadn't been her best moment, when she had unthinkingly admitted to him he hadn't been her choice, that it was only opportunity that had made him the one. It hadn't been completely true then, and now she knew it was a downright lie.

Sin *was* her choice. Subconsciously or not.

"But it *did* matter it was you," she tried. "With you I can relax and let my guard down. It's something I've never…"

"You feel relaxed with me?" He put his head in his hands, looking more and more defeated with every word he spoke. "My God, Charmaine, how can you even admit such a thing to me? Relaxed? I know you don't love me, but I had hoped…" He took a deep breath. "After the kiss we…"

His voice trailed off and instead he chuckled quietly, a harsh, strangled noise, echoing the turmoil in his heart.

"How pathetic am I, who thought these last few weeks were actually making a difference in our marriage. I even nourished a silly wish about us building something everlasting between us. But once again I have succeeded in fooling myself. What we have together is not important to you, which becomes clearer the more I get to know you. You are the most self-centered person there is, and you always make sure it is about you. You feel relaxed? My God, woman…"

"But Sin…"

He held up a hand toward her. "Don't. It's no use. I have no wish to hear any more bad excuses from you."

"But Sin, you have to…"

"Have to what? Let you rant on and on about how you feel and how sorry you are about everything? I don't think so. I have much more important things to do than humoring you."

He accused *her* of being self-centered? Had she not been so upset over not being able to reach him, to make him stay silent long enough for her to actually be able to finish a sentence, she would have laughed straight out. Probably hysterically.

Anger rose inside her, as she watched him sitting there on the bed, sulking over her being such an egotistical person.

"Don't you have anything to say?" he asked, looking more like a pouting child than an adult, and her nostrils flared as she took a deep breath to calm herself.

She was so tired of this.

Why was she always the one to blame? It didn't matter who or what it was regarding, it always seemed to be her fault. Frankly, she was sick and tired of always having to apologize to everyone about everything.

"Be quiet," she hissed between her teeth, and he looked up, frowning.

"What did you say?"

"You heard me," she hissed again, walking closer until she was just in front of his knees, so he had to bend his head backwards to be able to look into her eyes. "I asked you to be quiet."

"Asked?" He snorted. "I would rather say you ordered me to be quiet. Not politely at all, I would say."

She poked a finger hard on his chest and had the pleasure of seeing him wince. "You are supposed to be the quiet one, aren't you? I find that very hard to believe, because ever since we got married you have been, when not ignoring me, nagging on and on and on constantly, and I'm so bloody tired of all your wrongful assumptions that I could strangle you with my bare hands!"

He stared at her, openmouthed, and she grabbed

the opportunity now when she finally had his attention.

"I might be a bit self-centered, but so, my for-the-moment-not-so-dear husband, are you. Ever since we got married I've tried to bend to you so we could find a way to make this work, but it's not possible for me to make amends with you because you have already decided who I am, and you won't give me the benefit of any doubt."

"How can you…"

"Shush!" she yelled, shoving him hard enough that he fell backwards onto the bed. "Please just be quiet for once. This time it is *you* who has to listen to *me*, whether you like it or not."

She put her thumb in front of his nose.

"One: I *am* trying to work on this marriage too. I've been shutting my mouth so hard that my jaws ache, stopping myself saying something which will offend you, but it doesn't matter, does it? No, because you have already decided you are *very* upset with me and therefore you won't listen to me at all."

He frowned at her and opened his mouth to say something, and unmerciful she held up her index finger, pointing it at him.

"Two: Yes, I am beautiful, something of which I am very much aware. But I don't care about it, and never have. Actually, to be completely honest with you, most of my life I've wished I were homely, because my looks have never brought me anything but sorrow. It's not my fault men consider themselves in love with me just because they think my looks astonishing. I haven't forced them to stand there gawking at me, filled with their shallow feelings of love."

She saw him blush slightly as she waved her

middle finger in front of his face, near to poking his eyes out.

"Three: I'm married to you. *You*, Sinclair Darling. Not Lord Dane or any other man. *You*."

She took a step away from him, too tired to keep feeding the fire inside her. "If you can't find it in you to meet me halfway, this marriage will never work. I can't be doing all the bending, forever trying to be what you think I should be. I have done that my whole life, and for once I would like to be just me. Nothing but me."

He sat up, looking at her with narrowing eyes.

"But you still want him, don't you?"

She frowned, confused. "Who?"

"Lord Dane."

She took another step back, not believing her ears. "Of all the things I've said to you *that* was the only thing you heard? Me mentioning Lord Dane?"

"You can't get him out of your head, can you?" He sat up, scowling at her. "It doesn't matter what I say or do, it always comes back to Lord Dane."

"Oh, for goodness' sake."

She threw her hands out in despair, feeling angrier than she ever had before. Or than she ever had let herself feel before. She had been angry a lot during the first twenty years of her life but had always had to push the feeling away, always put the lid firmly back on.

But this was Sin.

And for what it was worth, she hadn't lied when she told him she could relax with him. It might not mean anything to him, but it did to her. And to be able to show your true feelings, to be able to be upset, was pure freedom, in her mind.

Her breast heaved as she watched him stand up

without once letting his glaring eyes leave her person. He usually looked very proper and perfect, with not a wrinkle daring to touch his person.

But not now.

For once he didn't look like a perfect Roman statue. Instead he looked like he had lived in the same clothes for days. His hair was tousled and his shirt unbuttoned halfway down his chest.

He was normally gravely composed and not the one to be noticed among his more colorful relatives. But with her he reeked of emotions he couldn't, or wouldn't, control. And to her surprise she found she liked this emotional Sin, because he didn't hide his true self from her as he did with everyone else. He let her see his emotions, and she liked that.

"Why don't you just admit what's in your heart?" he asked coldly. "We both know the man downstairs is the one you want, not me. It must be so distressful for you to find yourself caught in a marriage by your own hand. It must make you so frustrated that you can't blame anyone else but yourself for throwing yourself away on me."

He took a step closer to her, nailing her with his dark eyes, but she didn't mind. Because all she could do was stare at his lips. The lips that had woken emotions inside her she hadn't known she was able to feel.

That one kiss they had shared…

It had been pure heaven to her, so sensational it still made her lips tingle when she thought about it. Like now.

"Are you listening to me at all?"

His frustrated outburst broke through her thoughts, and she looked at him with narrowing eyes.

"No."

Her honesty took him by surprise.

"No?"

"Can't say I am."

"My God, Charmaine," he blurted out. "How are we ever going to make this marriage work if you don't listen to me?"

"You don't listen to me either."

He glared at her angrily. "Yes, I do."

"No, you don't," she snorted, and he took another step closer to her, and her head went back so she could look into his eyes.

Or at his very kissable full lips.

"What is going on inside that beautiful head of yours? You tell me you are trying very hard to not offend me, and yet you do, all the time. You refuse to tell me the truth about what made you force this marriage. You refuse to oblige me with your true emotions regarding Lord Dane. When we are among others you are a completely different person than you are when it's just you and me. I-I just don't know what to do with you."

His honest admission went straight to her heart, and she wished she could be as honest with him. But not yet. Not before Penelope was safe. Then she could tell him, if not the whole truth, at least enough parts of it to satisfy his need of knowledge and insight.

"Can you wait for me?" she whispered softly, and he looked at her suspiciously.

"Wait for you? Whatever do you mean? Why should I wait for you?"

She put a hand against his chest, feeling his heart beat faster under her palm. "Do you want me?"

He took a step backwards, as if he wanted to escape from her. "W-what?"

"Do you want me?"

"Want you?" He shook his head, taking exception to her question. "Why would I want something I've already got? You already are my wife."

"But do you *want* me?"

Her intense behavior seemed to make him a bit distraught, and he took another step back, bumping into the bed. "I'm sorry, but I don't know what you're getting at. You are my wife, and…"

"Do you want to kiss me?" she interrupted, and had the satisfaction of watching him blush.

"Eh…I…uh…"

"It's a simple question. Do you or don't you want to kiss me?"

He drew his fingers through his hair. "O-of course I-I want to kiss you."

"Why?"

"Why what?"

"Why do you want to kiss me?"

He chuckled nervously. "Because you are a beautiful woman and every man wants to kiss you."

"But you are not every man."

"No, I'm your husband."

She nodded. "So, do you?"

He frowned. "Do I what?"

"Want to kiss me?"

His blush intensified. "Yes."

"You do?"

He nodded nervously. "I do. Sorry."

"For what?"

"For wanting to kiss you."

She couldn't stop a smile. "I don't mind. As a matter of fact I like the thought of you wanting to kiss me. It makes it a bit easier, you know."

His dark eyes narrowed. "What is easier?"

"Asking you to kiss me."

He visibly froze, and she grasped the moment she was given and put her arms around his waist, pressing her body against his.

"Sinclair Darling, would you please kiss me?"

She didn't have to ask him twice. With a growl he grasped the back of her head with his hands and did what she had wanted for quite some time.

All the feelings he had awakened inside her that day at Pendragon, when he kissed her for the first time, came back with a rush, and she lost her ability to breathe. She latched onto his shoulders, kissing him back with all the flaring emotions he created in her, and she felt him tremble in her arms.

Again and again he played with her lips and her tongue, and not until she felt close to fainting did he lift his head and end the kiss.

She moaned, disappointed, and a little light started to shine inside his dark eyes. A light fired by the knowledge that she wanted him.

"I want you," he whispered into her mouth as he again demanded her lips against his. Her hands slid up around his neck again, this time to hold his head. Without words she forced him to deepen the kiss until they both moaned with the need of each other.

A knock on the door broke through their dazed minds, and they hardly had time to let go of each other before the door burst open and Penelope came in.

"There's a man at the door, asking for you," she

told Sin, quite unaware of the emotional situation she'd interrupted. "He says you promised to join their table in the gambling room."

"Damn," Sin said between his teeth. "I had forgotten all about that. Thank you."

"You're welcome."

He looked at Charmaine with unreadable eyes, and she smiled nervously.

"I have to go. I promised an old friend to join them, and I can't back down on that now. If it's all right with you?"

"Of course," she said curtly, trying to hide the turmoil he had created inside her behind her old ice-queen façade, and he sneered with disgust.

"Of course it's all right with you. You must thank your lucky star your sister unbeknownst saved you from having to endure me touching you."

"Sin…"

He shook his head. "No. Don't. No more lies."

She took a step closer to him again. "I didn't lie to you."

"Of course you didn't."

His voice dripped with sarcasm, and before she had a chance to come up with a reply he turned and left the room. In the doorway he stopped, looking directly at her with his dark eyes. "Don't wait up for me."

And with those last words he disappeared down the hallway in search of his friends, leaving Charmaine abandoned in the middle of the room, ready to scream out her frustration.

What had happened?

For a little while it had felt as if they had connected through the kiss, and maybe found a working foundation upon which to build their marriage.

But no.

It took only one unexpected interruption for him to rush away as quickly as he could, leaving her with a strong desire to throttle him.

What was wrong with him? Why did he so stubbornly bounce back to believing everything she said was a downright lie? It was as if the kiss hadn't meant anything to him. At least not as it had to her.

"Did I do something wrong?"

Charmaine turned to look at her sister, who gazed at her earnestly, and at first she wanted to scream out "Yes!" at the top of her lungs. But she couldn't put the blame on Penelope, who was completely innocent in all of this.

This was their problem, hers and Sin's.

"I hope I didn't destroy anything?"

Charmaine shook her head. "No, my dear, you didn't. Why don't we get ready for bed? I feel quite fatigued, and you heard Sin—he's not coming back for a while."

Penelope nodded sadly. "I'm so sorry, Charmaine."

Against her will, Charmaine laughed before hugging her sister tight. "It's all right. I'm quite used to you not thinking, as you mostly have your sweet head among the clouds. Please don't fret. Our problems will be solved soon, just not now."

Penelope smiled ruefully. "All right. If you say so. Come here, and I'll help you with your dress."

As her sister unbuttoned all the small buttons down her back, Charmaine stared silently at her image in the dark window, against her will remembering the glorious sensations of this second kiss.

She belonged in his arms, she knew it without a doubt. The only problem was how she would ever be able to see the threat of Lord Nester through to its defeat and still be able to hold on to this fragile thread of engagement in her marriage.

She sighed deeply as Penelope dragged the gown over her head, frustrated over her own lack of ability to find an easy solution.

She knew she wanted Sin.

Not Lord Dane or any other of the beaus that had passed through her life. She wanted to belong to her husband, and to him alone. But did he want to belong to her? His reaction to her during their two kisses told her as much, but not once had he said or hinted anything which could clarify this for her.

She was falling head over heels in love with a husband who thought she was in love with someone else. As she kissed her sister goodnight and closed the door tightly behind her retiring back, she knew she had to do something. But what? What could she do to make him understand that her heart belonged to him and not Lord Dane?

Chapter Nine

The annual January Ball in Gretna Green was everything they had been told it was, and more. The Assembly Rooms were filled to the brim with fashionably clad ladies and gentlemen, and if she hadn't known better, Charmaine would have thought she was in London at one of the grander balls.

Standing beside Penelope and their new friend Miss Lydia Woodley, sipping on lemonade more vile than that offered at Almack's, she found comfort in returning to the life she had known best, socializing.

When in London, she had always felt bored and wanted something else, but after being without it for quite some time she felt revived, almost giddy, as she entered the ballroom on Sin's arm. With a tight smile he excused himself, disappearing into the gambling room, but she didn't let his surly behavior take away her pleasure at being back where she thrived.

"She's like a jar of honey to a bear," Penelope explained to Lydia as a swarm of gentlemen eagerly approached them, and Charmaine didn't know whether she should be offended or amused.

"I beg your pardon?"

Penelope didn't care about her sister's outburst. Instead she affectionately patted Lydia's hand. "It's even better now that she's married, because she's off the prospective wife list, and instead you will stand next in line to be courted."

Lydia's eyes grew round with disbelief. "Or you. You are much prettier than I am. If Lord Elmsley has to choose between the two of us, he will most definitely choose you. I know I would."

"Then we will make sure he chooses you," Penelope said sententiously, and Charmaine rolled her eyes over her sister's antics.

So she was attractive to men like a jar of honey to a bear? Well, that surely didn't include her husband. Ever since their second kiss last week, Sin had returned to evading her as much as possible, and she felt quite abandoned.

What was it with that husband of hers?

All she wanted, besides freeing Penelope from their stepfather's vile plans, was to be with Sin. She wanted things to work out so they could be friends, a perfect beginning to the rest of their life together.

"Lady Chilton."

A smooth voice broke through her erratic thoughts, and she met the glistening eyes of the local scoundrel, Lord Elmsley. Lydia whimpered behind her, and Charmaine bit back a smile, too aware of the poor girl's unwonted affection for this man.

"Lord Elmsley," she said, offering him her brightest smile, perfectly happy to see him blush like a young man instead of an experienced libertine. "How nice to meet you again. Let me introduce to you my sister, Lady Penelope de Vere, and her friend, Miss Lydia Woodley."

Lord Elmsley nodded coldly to Lydia, by whom he seemed quite unimpressed, before bending his head over Penelope's small hand, kissing it in a lecherous fashion.

Then, gazing adoringly once more at Charmaine, he breathed, "Lady Chilton," and sent her what must be supposed his most alluring smile. "Would you mind if I borrowed your sister for the upcoming dance? It would be an honor for me."

"Oh, the honor would be hers, I guarantee you," Charmaine replied, hoping she didn't sound as bored with him as she felt. She was too used to good-looking, flirting men to be impressed by this local libertine. "But unfortunately my sister will have to decline. She has already promised my husband this dance."

She ignored Penelope's astonishment and prayed her sister would stay silent and not destroy the little moment of white lies. If she could get him to dance one dance with the starry-eyed Lydia, she would have done her good deed for today.

"I'm sad to hear this." Lord Elmsley turned all his attention to her instead, just as she had hoped. "Then maybe you would do me the honor?"

She almost felt sorry for him as she declined as elegantly as she could. "I'm afraid I've already promised the upcoming dance to our host. But Lydia here is, amazingly enough, still available."

Lord Elmsley's smile faltered as he looked at the blushing maiden, clearly having no problem understanding why she wasn't spoken for. But as a gentleman he couldn't deny the offer Charmaine had manipulated, and with a forced smile he held out his hand toward Lydia, who let him lead her out onto the dance floor, stars in her eyes.

"We have to find Sin," Charmaine said as the couple disappeared. "He will have to remove himself from the gambling tables to dance just this dance with you."

"I can sit this one out."

She looked at her sister, knowing that would have been the easiest way out. But a part of her wanted to see Sin, if only for a minute, and she used her sister most selfishly.

"No, you will not."

Using her most pointed tone of voice she, the one she knew Penelope wouldn't disagree with, she easily won the small discussion. Resolutely she dragged Penelope through the crowd, searching for her elusive husband, who now, unbeknownst to him, was her sister's dance partner.

As Sin joined them from the gambling tables, he sighed when he got her curt explanation. "I guess I have no say in this?"

"None," Charmaine said as coldly as she could muster. "Penny needs you to dance with her."

"For Penny I'll do anything," Sin replied, just as icily, before leading her sister into the dance.

She stood there alone, watching the two of them talk while dancing, and a sharp jealousy crumbled her heart as she watched their light conversation and easy smiles.

What was she trying to accomplish? Woo a man who didn't want her? She was the bloody Incomparable Queen, for goodness' sake, and could have any man she wanted by just looking at him.

But not Sin. Not her own husband.

When the host came rushing to excuse himself from dancing with her because of some accident with the lemonade, she graciously sent him away and instead walked over to the refreshment table, trying hard to cover her feelings of abandonment. It wasn't easy for her to not be wanted. All her life she had met men who wanted her, and she didn't really know how to pursue a man *she* wanted.

It seemed nothing she said to him worked, mostly because he didn't listen. Kissing him had seemed to work wonders until his head started to work its madness again, alienating him from her more every time.

She sighed profoundly, and in a wink three eager gentlemen joined her, as if they'd just waited for an excuse.

"Lady Chilton," Gentleman Number One said jovially. "Why is such a beautiful woman standing here all alone?"

She hid her confusion behind a radiant smile, as she couldn't remember the chap's name. "My dance partner had to attend to more important things."

The three gentlemen looked just the appropriate degree of appalled. "How very ungraceful to abandon someone as lovely as your ladyship," Gentleman Number Two pronounced, sending her a smile meant to subdue her, while Gentleman Number Three took her hand and lifted it to his lips. He brushed a lingering kiss against her knuckles, and she almost sighed over his ludicrous attempt to look as lecherous as Lord Elmsley had nearly accomplished.

"Can I get you a glass of lemonade?" Gentleman Number Two interrupted the flirtations of Gentleman Number Three, clearly irritated by the latter's indecent behavior.

She shook her head slightly. "No, thank you. I'm perfectly fine as I am."

"Can I get you your coat?" Gentleman Number Three threw himself into the conversation, trying to outdo Gentleman Number Two's chivalrousness.

She shook her head again, but this time Gentleman Number One joined the game before she had a chance to verbally decline.

"Maybe your ladyship would need a dance partner, now that you've been so rudely abandoned?

All three men looked at her like eager puppies that would do anything for a piece of candy, and she held back a smile. Why was she standing around moping because one man didn't want her? Watching these three fall all over each other in an attempt to be the one closest to her, she realized how much she had missed this, too—being wanted.

Being incomparable.

As if they could sense her favorably inclined hesitation, the three gentlemen stepped closer, showering her with their admiration.

"Lady Chilton, you are as beautiful as the sunrise in May."

"Lady Chilton, next to you, Venus and Aphrodite have no chance. Even Helen of Troy was nothing compared to you."

"Lady Chilton, I would die a happy man if you only would grant me a little of your precious time."

"Leave my wife alone, or I promise I'll fulfill that last wish with great pleasure."

As one, the three gentlemen jumped backwards, with Sin appearing from nowhere to stand by Charmaine's side, glaring at them with murder in his dark eyes.

"Excuse me..." Gentleman Number One dared to

say, but a deep, threatening growl from Sin had the men scattering in all directions.

"How dare you?" Charmaine said icily to her husband, outraged over his impoliteness toward her admirers. "They wanted nothing more than to converse and maybe dance a little. You know, what normal persons do, socialize!"

"Hell, no," Sin sneered, lowering his voice so only she could hear. "If you think socializing was all they wanted, you are too naïve for your own good. No, my dear wife, all they want to do is to rip your expensive gown from your delicious body and bury themselves deep inside of you."

She felt her cheeks burn hot as he spoke, as if they were on fire.

"Y-you…" She knew not what to say in response to such brutal honesty, and he laughed coldly at her.

"Come on, Charmaine, your sweet ears must have heard worse from all those men who have been hovering around you."

She shook her head, numb, and he snorted with disbelief.

"I don't believe you. At least one of all those men you have been flirting with must have whispered more than odes to your beauty. Someone must have told you exactly how much he would like to fondle those swelling breasts of yours?"

She shook her head again, her cheeks burning even more fiercely at his outspokenness.

"No." Her voice was only a meek shadow of a whisper, and he snorted again, although with a bit less heat than before.

"I don't believe you. I've been standing there for

years, watching you at different parties. You have always been surrounded by men fighting for a place by your side. I find it hard to believe none of them has ever told you what he wants to do to you."

So he had watched her?

She liked that thought—Sin standing aside, his dark eyes never leaving her person. It made her feel more powerful, knowing he had been interested enough to seek her out in a crowd. Straightening her back, she pushed her embarrassment away.

"Exactly," she hissed through her teeth. "As you just said, I was never alone. I was always surrounded by too many men, who searched for anything that could give them an inkling I had a special interest in them."

"Aha!" Sin scowled at her. "You admit it, then? You admit I was right and you're not as innocent as you'd like us to believe?"

"Sin…"

"Who was it?" The vein in his temple pulsated angrily, and she took a step back with surprise.

He was still jealous!

Her indifferent husband, who didn't care about her at all and who had been against her and their marriage all along, was jealous. Suddenly everything changed, including his present brazen accusations of her, and she clenched her jaws to avoid gloating too openly.

So he didn't care about her?

Maybe he didn't love her as much as she wanted him to—as much as she yearned for him to do—but he still cared enough for her to stand in the midst of a curious crowd and demand that she tell him whom she had let remove her innocence.

"It was Dane, wasn't it? Don't deny it, the way you

used to look at him is answer enough. So how was it, throwing away your decency on a man who left you to marry another woman? It must have been devastating for you to find out how little your virginity meant to him. How little your honor meant to him."

"You told me you believed me, the other day. You told me you knew I'm as innocent as I claim."

"Why don't you just admit the truth?" he said, ignoring her pleasing voice, too caught up in his jealousy to recognize how badly he was behaving. "Sooner or later I will find out the answer, so why deny me the pleasure of knowing who?"

She blushed again, as the image of them together in bed filled her mind's eye—not side by side, as far away from each other as possible, as it had been up until now. No, instead he was close to her, his skin against hers. His hot mouth kissing hers, craving her so much he made her weak with the need of him.

She shivered with anticipation as she took a step closer to him, looking up into his dark eyes, the knowledge of his jealousy brazening her. He stiffened when she put her hand lightly against his chest.

"So why don't you?"

Her husky whisper had him frowning suspiciously. "Why don't I what?"

"Find out."

"Find out what? What are you talking ab—"

He broke off as he caught her game, and she felt his heart start to pound faster under her hand.

"Find out if I'm a virgin or not."

"My God, Charmaine. You don't know what you're asking of me."

For the first time ever she thanked her lucky star

she was used to keeping her facial expression under control, and she maintained the seductiveness of her smile. She felt more embarrassed than ever before, but she had to see this through.

This was Sin—her husband.

The man she wanted to fall in love with and spend the rest of her life in obscure happiness with.

"I'm asking you to rip off my dress."

He stopped breathing for a second as his eyes turned even darker.

"Charmaine…"

"I'm asking you to fondle my breasts."

"For goodness' sake…"

She lifted her face to his ear, and whispered into it, "I'm asking you to bury yourself…"

He clamped his hand over her mouth. "Stop it."

She shook her head, unable to speak behind his hand, and he laughed hoarsely. "You don't know what you're asking me to do."

Still with his hand over her mouth, she nodded.

He closed his eyes briefly before looking at her again, and she knew she had won. Somehow she had reached through his prejudice regarding her person.

"Come."

He let go of her mouth and instead grabbed her hand, hauling her behind him as he stalked out of the ballroom, not stopping for anything or anyone until they were inside their bedroom, the door firmly locked.

His fingers shivered as he tried to unbutton her dress, and feeling strangely frivolous she grabbed the delicate fabric and tugged it hard, so all the small buttons flew all over the room.

"Didn't I ask you to rip it?" she breathed and did

the same to his shirt, sending more buttons flying.

"Oh, my God, Charmaine," Sin breathed, with so much need in his voice she couldn't wait longer for him to move. Bravely she grabbed his hands and put them on her breasts, almost fainting from the sensation of it.

"Didn't I ask you to fondle them?"

Her outspoken question broke through the last of his resistance, and with a moan he did what she had yearned for all along: he kissed her.

Again and again his mouth ravished hers and his hands moved over her, and she forgot everything but him and the passion he woke inside her. The pain, when he finally entered her, brought her for a moment back to her senses, and she looked up at him.

"You asked for it." He grinned as he met her eyes, and she laughed, too happy at finally being close to him to take offense at his outrageousness. She had, after all, started it with her own blunt behavior.

"What took you so long?" she purred, and with another growl he bent and kissed her hotly as he started to move inside her. She hadn't known she was capable of such overwhelming desire and subsequent satisfaction.

"Did I hurt you?"

Lightly he caressed the soft skin of her cheek, and she shook her head, still dizzy from the explosions of sensation he had taken her through. "No, not much."

"You are so beautiful."

She heard the honesty in his raw voice and for once didn't let the words pass. Instead she took it for what it was, an apology and an outstretched olive branch.

"I know," she teased, and he laughed lightly, seeming almost relieved.

"I know you know."

"That's good to know."

They shared a sated smile as he rolled off her, dragging her with him so she ended up as if glued to his side, her head on his arm. It was such an intimate position it brought tears to her eyes.

"Are you crying?"

She shook her head. "No, not much."

"No? Or not much?"

She giggled through her tears. "Not much, then, I guess."

"Why?"

She let her hand caress his stomach, feeling his muscles flex under the gentle pressure of her hand. "I thought this would never happen."

He hugged her closer to him, and she felt his hot breath in her hair as he planted a tender kiss on the top of her head.

"Well, all you had to do was ask."

Something warm started to build inside her at the tenderness in his voice. She let her hand travel downwards, as far as she dared, bending her head backwards as she tried to look as inviting as she could.

"Please?"

He put his hand over her wandering one just as she was about to reach his most manly part, and his eyes narrowed. "Are you asking me what I think you are?"

She had no chance to reply as his hot mouth clamped down on hers, fulfilling her request. Eagerly she followed his lead, following him into a state of perfect bliss.

Chapter Ten

"If you don't stop blushing soon, everyone will know what we have been doing all night."

She threw a bun at him, and he ducked to the side, sending her an intimate smile that made her heart flutter in response.

What a night it had been!

Over and over again they had made sweet love, and when the morning sun found its way in through their window, they'd still been in each other's arms, unable to fall asleep. She didn't mind the drowsiness or the soreness between her legs that made it almost impossible for her to sit without pain. She was a new woman today.

She was Sin's woman.

As if the knowledge of her being all his and his alone had released the last splinter of doubt in his mind, he had been more than loveable toward her ever since they'd got up from their bed.

He didn't seem able to stop touching her.

She had lost count of all the times he had hauled her into his arms, kissing her until she was only a shivering pile of human flesh. It was almost as if he couldn't stop kissing her now that he was allowed.

She didn't mind.

"You missed," he enlightened her unnecessarily, and she couldn't hold back a giggle.

"Did I, now?"

"Uh-hum."

"Sorry."

He raised his eyebrows. "What have I said about being sorry?"

"That I shouldn't be."

"So stop it."

She grabbed another bun and took a bite of it, staring at his mouth over the edge of it.

"Stop it," he hissed hoarsely, and she arched her own eyebrows, mimicking his earlier move.

"Stop what?"

"Looking at me like that."

"Like how?"

"Like you wish I was that bun."

Oh.

She liked that thought and ripped a large chunk of it with her teeth.

"Ouch," he growled, his eyes glistening with laughter. "That hurt."

"I hope so."

"What have I done to deserve this?"

"You still haven't apologized to me for thinking what I hope you found out I hadn't done."

"Still dwelling on that?" He sighed, and she nodded.

"Yes. And still waiting for the apology."

"I'm sorry."

"All right."

He chuckled over her quick acceptance. "You don't even know what I'm sorry about."

"I don't care," she admitted, sending him her brightest smile. "As long as you've told me that you *are* sorry, I can fill in the rest of it myself. Much more satisfying, I assure you."

"A woman of my liking."

"I salute that."

She raised her cup of tea toward him, and he saluted her with his. "To my wife."

"When I heard you two got married I didn't believe a word of it, and yet here you sit making love to each other with your eyes."

"Uncle Rake!"

Sin smiled broadly toward the elegant man who had approached their table unnoticed. Behind him stood Penelope, looking extremely happy, and Charmaine felt like the worst person alive.

"Penelope! My goodness, I forgot all about you yesterday. How are you? Oh, I'm the worst chaperone who ever set foot on this earth."

Her sister laughed and threw her arms around Rake's waist. "Oh, I don't mind, as Rake arrived shortly after Sin dragged you away from the ballroom. We got married!"

Charmaine squealed with delight, throwing herself at her sister and Rake, the latter moaning as the force of her body hit them.

"Oh, my, Penny, how fantastic! I'm so happy for you!"

Rake sent Sin an amused grin over the heads of the laughing and crying sisters in his arms. "I must say, it makes it a bit easier to get married when the love of your life runs away to Gretna Green."

"Penny is a smart girl and knew she would have to act quickly when you finally gave in," Sin mocked, and his uncle raised an eyebrow.

"*I* gave in? Who do you think has been keeping at least an arm's length between us the last couple of years? Not I, I assure you."

He let go of the teary-eyed sisters and sat down in the chair Charmaine had vacated. With a wave of his hand he sent a starry-eyed serving wench for two more cups.

"You look tired," Sin said, noticing the dark smudges under his uncle's eyes, and Rake nodded, for once without a mocking grin.

"I am. It's been...hard...for a while. But now I can rest. She's my wife—finally—and now I know she will be where *I* want her to be and nowhere else."

Penelope walked over to her husband and sat down beside him, grabbing his hand in hers as if afraid he would disappear if she let go of him for more than a minute. The look Rake gave her was so filled with love that more tears filled Charmaine's eyes out of sheer happiness.

And maybe just a little bit of envy.

She met Sin's warm eyes, and he beckoned her to come to him. She sat down beside him with her hands in her lap, as close to him as she dared without being scandalous.

Rake and Penelope might not care about what the surrounding people thought, but for Charmaine it had always been most important to behave according to all the rules of etiquette, down to the letter. All her life, until now, she had been desperate to behave correctly, because just one wrong move would have her stepfather at her immediately, lecturing her for her mistake and trying to touch her wherever he could as long as he had her alone.

Luckily her mother had always had a sixth sense when it came to Lord Nester's infatuation for Charmaine, always knowing when to arrive and save her daughter from his unwelcome advances.

She felt Sin's glance, but she held her pose, noticing how the others in the room looked their way, all because of the lovesick couple across the table. Rake didn't seem able to stop sending his wife smoldering looks, and Penelope looked as smug as a cat with a fresh-caught mouse.

"It's good to see you," Sin admitted warmly, and Rake gave a brief nod, without words telling the nephew two years his junior that he felt the same way.

"I was just about to give up on you," Penelope told her husband sweetly, and he raised his infamous eyebrow toward her.

"Really?"

"We have been here for almost a month now, and Sin has duties which await him. It's not his fault you took your time getting here."

Rake chuckled, and Charmaine noticed how all the ladies nearby looked ready to faint as they watched the handsome man. He had such charisma, this Lord Richard Darling, and he knew exactly how to use it. The only woman he had never been able to coax into whatever he wanted was Penelope, all because she was too much in love with him—and knew him too well—to fall for it.

As Rake caught Charmaine watching him, he winked to her with a smile filled with wicked amusement, and she shook her head lightly. He was such a scoundrel, but a very loveable one.

He, who flirted with all women, had never flirted

with her, something she always had been grateful for. It had been a relief to know he didn't have to conquer every woman around. Maybe he had avoided her because she was Penelope's sister.

"I must admit it was a surprise to hear you two had gotten married. As far as I knew, you two were never an item."

Sin moved his hand under the table and put it lightly on Charmaine's knee, as if he wanted to offer her some strength. She should have known Rake would be curious. He had not been in Chester Park when they were found in the guestroom, as he had been heading toward London at that moment, to save Penelope.

"Our marriage was forced by my parents, something I think you are well aware of."

"I am." Rake grinned. "But that you were obliged to marry doesn't mean there isn't a story behind it. You two were, after all, found in bed together, as I heard it."

"We are married. That's it."

"Ah," Rake breathed. "There *is* a story."

"There is?" Penelope glanced curiously at her sister. "Have you been hiding something from me, Charmaine? Here I've been telling you everything about my feelings for Rake, wrenching my heart inside out, and not once have you mentioned you might have feelings for Sin. Not once. Should I be upset?"

Charmaine felt Sin stiffen beside her, and she wanted desperately to stuff a bun into her sister's too-large mouth.

Bloody hell!

Why couldn't Penelope just be quiet? So she might not have spoken much of Sin, but then again, she had never spoken much about anyone during their small chats.

Not even Lord Dane.

Mostly because her sister had been chatting constantly about her love for Rake, and Charmaine had not had the heart to interrupt her. But also because Charmaine had been too afraid she might by mistake mention her problem with their stepfather.

"If I know you right, my love, you probably ranted on and on constantly about how wonderful I am and never gave your poor sister a chance to come clean about it," Rake teased his wife, and Charmaine could have kissed him as Penelope glared at him, removing her attention from her sister.

"Rant?" she hissed. "You think I rant?"

"Well, I must admit you do talk a lot. You can't help it, though. You are, after all, a dweller."

Penelope gasped, outraged, and Rake's eyes darkened until they were almost as black as Sin's, which made his wife blush instead.

"You look tired, my love. Why don't we go up to that bedroom of yours again, so you can get some sleep?"

Penelope quickly stood and grasped her husband's outstretched hand, and they disappeared up the stairs without even saying goodbye.

"I don't think she will get much sleep."

Charmaine giggled. "No, I don't think so either. Thank God he finally came. My belief that he would was starting to falter a bit, and I could see Penelope's was, too. She looks so happy…"

"They both do." Sin squeezed her hand under the table. "And you look happy for her. You love her very much, don't you?"

She looked at him with raised eyebrows. "Of course I do. She's my sister, and until now the most important person in my life."

"Until now?" Sin grinned, and she blushed just as much as Penelope had.

"Until now."

He sat silent for a while, just watching her tenderly with his dark eyes, and her heart responded to him. Every day her feelings for him grew stronger, and as they finally had managed to reconcile, she couldn't possibly be any happier than at this moment.

He was such a wonderful man, even though he had a tendency to bring up the past when he was angry with her. But she didn't mind. He was so refreshingly honest in his reactions to her, and being able to read him so easily made her feel even more secure with him. She'd had enough of secrets in her life and wanted nothing more than openness and honesty.

"You too look a bit drowsy, my dear wife. What do you say to going upstairs and taking a little nap?"

His eyes told her how little rest she would get, and her blush intensified as she nodded. With a grin, he stood and offered her his arm. She put her hand in the crook of it, amazed how wonderful it felt to belong to this man.

Slowly he led her through the inn toward the stair, not stopping for anyone they met, until a clipped voice was heard behind them.

"Look at the happy couple, all smiles and not a thought of all the broken hearts in their wake." Lord Dane's usually jovial face was stern, with lines she'd never noticed before clearly visible.

"Lord Dane." She curtsied politely, and he returned

her courtesy with a bow just as polite.

"Lady Chilton, I presume?"

"Yes, she's still my wife," Sin scoffed and pulled Charmaine closer to his side, where she could feel the warmth of him.

Lord Dane sighed deeply. "Just checking. When I woke up the day after I met you last, I thought it might have been merely a bad dream, but I guess that was the liquor speaking."

"I'm so sorry," Charmaine said compassionately, and she meant it with all her heart because she was truly sorry for him.

For them.

Once he had been everything she'd dreamt of, and her stepfather had made sure that dream would never come true. She had been devastated when she heard of his marriage just one short month after he had proposed to her, promising her everlasting love.

But then, she knew him. Lord Dane wasn't the dwelling kind, and she had assumed he had simply moved on with his own life. That he had been forced by his mother to marry another woman had never crossed her mind.

And then there were his letters. What if her stepfather hadn't snatched them away from her? What if she had read them and been enlightened about what was happening, what he really felt? Would things have ended differently then?

Knowing herself, she assumed she would have decided to wait for him. Even though she wanted nothing more than to get away from her stepfather, she wouldn't have thrown away her one chance of love.

But for how long?

The fact was that, even if she had received his letters, Lord Nester would still have given Penelope to Lord Bolton. Charmaine would still have been caught in her stepfather's web, unable to save her sister or herself.

Lord Dane might have waited for her for a while, but sooner or later his mother would have succeeded with her plans and had him married to the woman of her choice. The snare would still have tightened around Charmaine, and in the end she would still have had to force someone into marriage to save herself. She would still have been standing here, looking at Lord Dane as someone else's wife.

"You have such a kind heart, my dearest Charming." Lord Dane smiled sadly as he used the nickname he'd once given her, and she heard the grief in his voice.

"Will you be all right?"

He nodded solemnly. "I think so. At least I hope so. But I will miss you. I've been so set on spending the rest of my life with you, and now I don't know where to start over."

"I have missed you."

Her admission brought a smile back on his face.

"Thank you. I needed to hear that. I've missed you so much too. Being caught in an old drafty castle in northern Yorkshire is not much fun. The girl I married was kind, but there was no laughter there. No dancing. Just talk."

"She became a good friend to you?"

"Sort of, I guess. I did like to talk to her, but then again—there was not much else to do."

"Were there no servant girls to entertain you?" Sin

138

added coldly to the conversation, and Lord Dane shrugged indifferently.

"Some, but no big challenge there, I'm afraid."

It took a minute for her to grasp what Sin had meant, but after a night in his arms, learning more about what could happen between a man and a woman, she caught the implication in his words. She almost gasped as she caught how blasé Lord Dane's answer was.

Sin, who must have sensed her hidden outrage, grinned mischievously, and she had to bite her lip hard to keep from lashing out at him.

"I'm so sorry she died," she continued from where they had been before Sin's interruption, and Lord Dane gazed, confused, at her.

"Who died?"

"Your wife."

"She did? Ah, yes. Yes, she did."

It wasn't so hard to see the man was lying his teeth off, and this time Charmaine didn't hide her outrage.

"She's still alive?"

"Eh…"

"My God, Lord Dane! Are you telling me the wife you told me was dead—isn't?"

"Eh… No."

He fidgeted uncomfortably, and she looked up into Sin's laughing gray eyes, not knowing what to think. She could hardly believe what Lord Dane had done.

What if she hadn't been married to Sin? Missing Lord Dane as much as she had, she would probably have suggested they should sneak away and get married and face the consequences—and her stepfather— afterwards.

And she would have married an already married

man.

"What were you thinking? What would you have done if I hadn't been married to Sin? Married me anyway?"

"Probably."

"Probably?"

Her voice was a mere squeak as she repeated his answer. The nerve of the man!

He shrugged again, just as indifferently as before. "Well, sooner or later she would've died, and if I'd been able to keep the two of you apart I would have had the best of both worlds."

"The best of…"

Charmaine's voice trailed off as disgust at his attitude overwhelmed her, making her want to cry for the loss of her good memories of him. Now all she could think was how inconsiderate he really was.

Sin, who again astonished her with his insight, pushed her toward the stairs. "If you'll excuse us, Lord Dane, my wife and I have something to do."

"Ah, yes. Good, good."

Without mercy Sin pushed her toward the stairs, where he grabbed her hand and didn't let go until they reached the privacy of the small salon.

As husky laughter was heard from Penelope's room, he continued into theirs, dragging Charmaine with him. Not until he had closed the door behind him did he open his mouth. But not to talk. Instead he howled with laughter, not once caring about her pursed mouth as she watched him cry with joy until his whole body convulsed with mirth.

"Can you believe the man?" Charmaine spat when he started to calm down enough to listen to her, and she paced to and fro over the wooden floor. "Can you believe how callously he told me his wife was dead? To even consider marrying me although he already was married…"

Sin dried his eyes as he finally managed to compose himself. "He's just burning his candle at both ends. But I must admit I found this quite amusing. Lord, I almost wish you had married the chap, as long as I could have been there to watch when you found out that not only were you not legally married to the man but he already had a wife."

Charmaine threw off her coat as she moved around in the small room, close to exploding. How could she ever have thought herself madly in love with that man? She had thought the best of him, and in the end he turned out to be one of the worst examples of mankind.

That poor girl he married!

As she passed Sin for the umpteenth time, he grabbed the opportunity and pulled her into his arms.

"Don't let the man get to you. He's just a fool who is too used to having things his own way to even consider how impossibly he behaves."

He had her stand between his legs while, carefully, he started to unbutton the small buttons of her lovely dress.

"Don't think about Lord Dane and his outrageous and selfish behavior toward you. It's better if you use your lovely head to think about the reason we were heading this direction in the first place. As I recall, we were on our way up here for a purpose."

She frowned at him, not able to cast Lord Dane's treason aside at first, but when Sin started to place small kisses on her naked shoulder she couldn't withstand him for long, and soon she was moaning with pleasure.

Their lovemaking was just as consuming and satisfying as it had been earlier. Afterwards, as he placed a light, thankful kiss on her sweaty forehead, she couldn't think of any other place she would have preferred being than here in his arms.

Had it not been for the problem with her stepfather, she would have been perfectly happy and content. But as long as Penelope stayed unmarried she wouldn't be able to let her guard down. There was no one who could stop him. He was her legal guardian, and...

She sat straight up as the truth hit her, Penelope *was* married. She was now the very much beloved wife of Lord Richard Darling—and out of their father's evil clutch.

Penelope was married.

She was safe.

"What is it?" Sin mumbled drowsily as he noticed she wasn't lying beside him anymore.

"Penny's married."

"Eh, yes."

"She's *married!*"

"Yes, she is married. And we are upset over this because...?"

Too relieved to speak, she threw herself into his arms, hugging him closely. His chest rumbled as he chuckled, amused at her frantic cuddling.

"I must admit I don't mind you being a bit upset, if this is how you deal with it."

She snuggled her nose into the crook of his neck, inhaling the scent of him. His large hands softly caressed her back, removing more and more of the tension from her body with every tender touch.

The truth was almost too much for her to take in. After all these years of living with the stress of her father's desperate attempts to be near her, to touch her, she could finally relax and enjoy every minute of life as everyone else did.

Finally, she was free.

Chapter Eleven

"For goodness sake, Uncle Rake, stop staring at Penny and concentrate on the game."

"I'm not staring at Penny."

"Yes, you are. Constantly. It's getting quite old, you know."

"What is getting old? You?"

"Says he who is at least five years my senior."

"At least?"

"It's hard to tell, you know. It seems much more than a mere five years when one looks upon your wrinkled old face."

"Caroline, I think your youngest son is losing his eyesight!"

"Don't you try to get me to join your silly discussion."

"Silly?" Sebastian grinned mischievously, and his mother shook her head with a sigh.

"Why don't I ever learn? I tell you this—never enter a discussion between Darling men. It will only bring you frustration and sorrow," Lady Newbury enlightened Charmaine, who sat beside her mother-in-law on one of the plush sofas filling the salon where the Darling family gathered every afternoon for tea. It wasn't the quiet affair it had been at her childhood home, as the Darlings hadn't it in them to be quiet. Ever.

They were constantly discussing various things, and it didn't matter to them if it was a bump in the carpet or how much flour the cook used when she baked her delicious scones. They still made it into a war of words.

"Sorrow?" Rake chuckled, his eyes never leaving the game of cards he was playing with two of his brothers and his nephew Sebastian. "I get the frustration part. But sorrow?"

"Nursing a headache every evening that's been caused by this family's constant bantering makes one feel sorry for oneself." Lady Newbury's grave voice sounded almost hollow, and the duchess, who sat on a sofa facing them, nodded just as gravely in agreement.

"It most certainly does. I don't know where they get it from. Hannibal is, as you all know, not the most talkative person, and neither am I."

All the men in the room started to cough, and the duchess put on her best injured expression, together with her wettest puppy eyes.

"They are not very respectful toward their elders, either." Lady Newbury sighed, and her mother-in-law turned her head toward her so quickly she almost snapped her neck.

"And who are you calling elderly?"

"Oh, God." Lady Newbury sank back deeper into the sofa, looking mortified, and Charmaine bit back a smile as the duchess humpfed on the other side of the sofa table.

"Elderly…"

"So how did you find Gretna Green, Charmaine?" the duke asked kindly, and this time she didn't hold back her smile.

"Very nice. It was such a beautiful place, and we met lots of new people, some of whom became really good friends."

"Do you mean that girl Lydia, who keeps sending three letters a day?" He frowned at her with his bushy, white eyebrows. "She's got speed in her fingers, I have to say."

"And way too much time to spend writing."

"Rake!" Penelope glared at her husband. "Lydia Woodley is a sweet, caring girl who became a dear, dear friend to us."

"I'm only saying she needs to find a man to fill up all those empty hours of hers."

"It's not so easy to find a man, especially when they tend to run in the opposite direction," Penelope admitted with a wry smile, and her husband raised an amused eyebrow as the other men howled with laughter.

"Really, my love? Aren't you being a bit harsh against your friend now?" he drawled, his voice dripping with sarcasm.

"Am I?" Penelope asked sweetly, something which Charmaine thought should have told Rake he was walking on thin ice. But Rake was too busy sharing gloating gazes with his manly relatives to think twice about how deceptive Penelope could be in all her innocence.

"I think you are. I met the dear Lydia, you know, and I don't think she's such a hag as you make her sound. She is a bit..." He made a grimace as he searched for the right word. "She is just a little bland, I would say."

"Homely, you mean," Sebastian offered, and Rake

nodded gratefully.

"Thank you, Ian. To say the dear Lydia is blandly homely describes her perfectly. She is a nice girl, even though she tends to talk too much most of the time. And she stares a lot, especially at men. But otherwise…"

"Sounds like a catch," Sebastian drawled, and Rake grinned wickedly in response.

"Doesn't she?"

Penelope winked at her sister, her eyes twinkling with mirth, and Charmaine had to bend her head so she could hide the laughter which threatened to escape. Penelope was such a minx sometimes, and it surprised her Rake didn't catch how she was pulling him along. But she had to admit he was pushed into it by the other Darling men, who joyfully engaged themselves in cheering him along against his wife.

"She is a catch, I agree with you there," Penny said, holding her hand up in front of her as if inspecting her nails. "The problem for dear Lydia is how most men seem to not notice that. I'm glad she never had a London season. The poor girl would have had an awful time, abandoned in a corner by all the eligible men. Some people are just destined to become wallflowers."

"Penny, what a low comment to make about your own gender." Sin scowled at her. "Being homely doesn't equal being a social failure."

"Of course it will. She's no great beauty, and she has no money to speak of. She is the youngest child to a penniless country squire without social connections. She's made to be a wallflower."

"No one is made to be a wallflower."

Penelope raised her eyebrows at Sebastian, who had sounded just a bit too self-assured. "I tell you, Ian, looks and money are all that matter to men. And even if she had been somewhat pretty she still wouldn't have been wanted by the men of the *ton*."

"Oh, come on, Penny." Edward, the fourth of the duke's seven sons, snorted. "Among us we could make any girl just as Incomparable as our Charmaine here. It wouldn't be a problem for us at all."

Our Charmaine.

It was amazing how much one little word could affect a person. Charmaine's throat lump grew as her happiness caused problems with her breathing. Not that she minded. She belonged.

"Now you are exaggerating," Penny mocked Edward, and he shook his head in response.

"No, I'm not. With a little work, we could turn her into a diamond of the first water."

"Eh, no, we couldn't," Rake put in as he finally grasped what his sweet little wife was after, but too late. Edward had already walked straight into Penny's trap, and now he was caught.

"Of course we could. I say, bring the girl here, and we will make her the most popular girl in London."

"Deal."

Penelope gave Edward another sweet smile, and this time he caught Rake's warning glares, but too late.

"Oh, no."

"Oh, yes."

"Penny, you are not going to write to the girl and tell her to come here."

Edward tried to humble her by glaring darkly, but she just nodded daintily. "Oh, I promise I won't write and ask her to come."

Relieved, Edward exhaled. "Great."

"No need to," Penelope continued, putting the last nails in his coffin. "I have already sent her an invitation. She should be arriving here by the end of March, just in time for the Season. She will be so happy when she hears you all have decided to transform her into one of the *ton*'s most sought-after women."

"Rake!" Edward whined, but his younger brother just shrugged.

"You have only yourself to blame for this, Ward. You were the one who didn't stop when Penny showed us her true colors. And now it is you who will transform this blandly homely girl into a perfect beauty."

"No."

"Oh, yes."

"You have to help me."

"No, we don't." Rake grinned, pleased with himself. "We are not the ones who bought her bluff."

"Mother!"

The duchess ignored her son's desperation and instead smiled encouragingly toward Charmaine. "It's wonderful to hear the four of you had such a lovely time in Scotland, but as we have missed you all so much during the past month, I must say I'm glad you're back. Life is not perfect unless our family is complete."

"It's nice to be back," Charmaine admitted politely, and was granted a grateful look from the duchess.

"For a while, at least—it's February, after all, only two more months until the Season kicks off again. Are you ready to conquer the *ton* as Lady Chilton?"

"I don't think I ever will get used to that name," Charmaine admitted. "Every time someone calls me Lady Chilton I look over my shoulder to see whom they are addressing."

The duchess gave an amused snort. "Oh, I know exactly what you're talking about. When I was first married to Hannibal, I didn't answer when the servants called me Your Grace. I was Anna Howard, no more and no less. It took me quite some time to realize they meant me."

The duke laughed heartily, his wonderful, booming laughter that was as contagious as the Spanish Fever. "I thought you were never going to get used to being called Your Grace. Do you remember how upset the servants were? They refused to call you anything else, and you never answered them and kept ignoring them when they tried to catch your attention."

"I do. Poor Butler still hasn't forgiven me the slight."

"Not hard to understand why. You effectively removed all his dignity in front of the other servants when you didn't listen to him when he tried to talk to you."

With a dramatic snort, the duchess replied, "I still think he could have called me by my name instead, at least until I got used to the new married me. But no, the man is just too stubborn."

"Just like you."

The duchess gasped, outraged, glaring at her husband. "I'm not stubborn at all."

"Of course you're not. Just as you don't talk very much, either."

The other men in the room snickered, and the duchess pursed her lips at her husband, who blanched and moved back away from her.

As the duchess lectured her husband about rude comments, Sin went over to Charmaine where she sat and beckoned her with a nod of his head to come with him. Relieved to escape the wrath of the duchess, she followed him out of the room.

"How are you?" he asked as soon as they were outside the door, alone. "You seem tired."

"I am," she admitted. "I still haven't recovered from our trip back here, or the constant lack of sleep."

"I'm sorry." He gave her a wicked smile that told her he was anything but sorry.

She couldn't blame him. She too enjoyed their nights of making sweet love too much to care about sleep, or the lack of it.

"No, you're not." She giggled, putting her arms around his waist and her cheek against his chest.

As she felt him lift his arms up, embracing her, she couldn't help being thankful for having him as her husband. They had been married for over three months now, and every day it got better and better.

Sin was a husband made in heaven.

His thoughtfulness and kind heart had done wonders for her jumpy nerves, and finally she had begun to stop looking over her shoulder all the time, instead enjoying her newly won freedom.

The only thing that saddened her was how he constantly avoided telling her of his feelings for her. She knew, without doubt, that she loved him with all her heart, that he was everything she had ever wanted or could have wished for.

He made her feel safe and complete. He made her feel free and needed. It was what she had dreamt about in her most secret dreams, the ones she had cried herself through, and now she had it.

If he only would love her back.

It was the only negative part of their marriage, but she had no one but herself to blame, as she knew too well what his problem was. He would never open up his heart to her until she told him the truth. Even though he never mentioned it, she knew he was still more than desperate to know why she had tripped him, why she had forced them to marry.

Why.

Her problem was that she didn't know how to tell him the truth. How could she ever admit to him what an awful person she was? What if he loathed her for making her stepfather fall in love with her?

She knew it sounded worse than it was. Lord Nester was, after all, not her real father, although she had grown up under the impression that he was. But the mere thought of losing Sin because of it had her sick with angst, and it became harder and harder for her to open up to him.

"I've missed you today," Sin mumbled into her hair.

"I've missed you too," she admitted and felt him hug her a bit tighter, obviously liking her answer. "But isn't there just too much for you to do with managing the estate?"

"Yes, there is. As I am the heir to the dukedom, my grandfather wants me to know as much as I can about running everything. Father, even though he is next in line, has never been interested at all, and therefore Grandfather wants me to know what it takes to keep everything alive and in order."

"Why can't your father step in to ease your burden?"

He shrugged lightly. "It's not such a big burden to

me, and besides, I have the interest and my father doesn't. So I spend my time learning everything I can from Grandfather while he's still alive, and then I can continue with taking care of the estate when Father becomes the duke."

"Doesn't your father mind that you get all the knowledge and he gets none?"

Sin looked at her with a frown marring his forehead. It was clear he didn't like her assumption.

"No, he doesn't. Why should he? I'm taking care of what he doesn't want to be bothered with, and as I'm next in line after him to get the title, it is nothing but in his best interest to let me take over."

"It's quite uncommon, you know, someone being that generous."

"No, it's not," he said, disgruntled.

She gave him a tender smile and held her palm against his smooth cheek. "Yes, Sin, it is. Most men wouldn't let anyone else handle what they consider theirs, and that goes especially for a family estate and family wealth. Your family is different in so many ways, and this is just one of them."

He looked at her, his dark eyes unreadable. "And is this a good thing?"

"It is."

"Well, consider me different, then."

She laughed over his tender teasing, and he smiled back at her with affection. At moments like this she could almost believe he cherished her deeply, and maybe even loved her.

But she knew better than to indulge herself in impossible fantasies. For now it was enough for her to know they got along as well as they did.

Penelope would probably have thought her beyond stupid if she had known. Her younger sister had never let reality rule her world of dreams. But life had treated them differently so far, and where Penelope could escape into her perfect fantasy world, Charmaine had to be constantly on guard with her armor in place.

The Darling family was indeed different, and she knew she had already changed a lot since becoming one of them. Letting go of her ice queen façade had been a huge step in the right direction, and she had noticed in more ways than one how much the family appreciated her effort.

The greatest change, though, was her relationship with Sin. To let someone else become as close to her as he now was had been unthinkable before. But she couldn't stand his anger and resentment when she had acted as the selfish Incomparable Queen, so she had let that façade go, too. He had seemed relieved when he noticed she wasn't the spoiled harpy he had thought her in the beginning of their marriage, and it made her want to give even more effort to making their marriage a happy one.

If only she could make herself get rid of the last splinter parting them. The one with the ugly truth stuck to it. But she had gotten too used to his warm eyes and tender smiles to dare losing them.

"Not sharing the management of the Berkeley holdings with my relatives makes it easier for me to be prepared to carry the responsibility by myself in the future," Sin was continuing solemnly. "I will be the one who has to make sure my family fares well and that the people of our estate have good lives. It's a huge responsibility, and it is mine, whether I want it or not."

He seemed almost fatigued, and her heart went out to him. It couldn't be easy to be the one person in this free-spirited family who had a future that lay in a direction he couldn't change.

"So do you?" she asked quietly, and he looked at her inquiringly.

"Do I what?"

"Do you want it?"

He raised his eyebrows with surprise. "I don't know. To be honest, I've never considered what my life would have been like without the responsibilities of the Berkeley estate."

Watching him stare into the air, his thoughts seemingly miles away as he pondered his answer, she couldn't help being amazed that he had never considered leading the same normal, easygoing life his relatives did, a life without duties. Lord Newbury was, after all, the real heir and the one who should be taking care of everything, not his son.

"I don't mind being the heir," he finally let out in a slow, almost uncertain manner. "But I would like to have other options, too. Some other roads to choose from, leaving it to me to decide which not to take. In that way my life would have been my choice and not filled with things I'm supposed to do just because I was born to it."

"But you do have options," she prompted. "You decide how much time and effort you spend as the person responsible for all these people. If you chose to not care, you could easily live another life, having time for anything else your heart desires. But that's not you, is it?"

"No." He shook his head. "It's not."

"So in reality are you quite satisfied with the life you lead, and wouldn't have it arranged any differently?"

"I guess so, my intense little wife. Besides, I have had quite a large change in my life lately—you. My life will never be the same."

She blushed, feeling oddly satisfied with his conclusion, and he gave her another of those unreadable smiles that made her feel so cherished.

"Lady Chilton, you have a visitor awaiting you in the salon."

Charmaine looked at Ivanoff, the Chester Park butler, who had joined them in his unobtrusive way. "A visitor? Who is it?"

"I don't know, my lady. He didn't introduce himself, only stressed his urgency to see you, although I think I recognize him as one of the Harveyfield footmen."

A dark, awful feeling spread throughout her stomach and without thinking she moved backwards, wanting nothing but to escape the truth waiting for her in the salon. It had to be about her mother. Why else would someone from Harveyfield dare to visit Chester Park, probably against his master's profound wishes?

She felt Sin's hand on the small of her back and she closed her eyes, grateful for his presence.

"Do you want to go alone?"

"No."

He took a step closer, enveloping her cold, lifeless hand in his large, warm one. The comfort he offered with the simple gesture overwhelmed her, and tears filled her eyes.

"Charmaine?"

Penelope had stepped out of the salon, Rake behind her, and her small voice cut through Charmaine's emotional numbness. She forced an easy smile but must have failed miserably, as her sister started to weep.

"It might not be about Mother…"

"Of course it is," Penelope interrupted hoarsely. "What else could it be? No one would bother coming here if she wasn't dead."

"Penny…"

"Stop lying to me!" Penelope's heart-wrenching sobs increased alarmingly. She clearly didn't believe a word of what her sister said, and who was Charmaine to blame her? She herself didn't believe one word she had just spoken.

Rake put his arms around his wife's small shaking body, silently offering her his chest to cry against.

"My lady?"

Ivanoff waited for them further down the hall, and Charmaine nodded solemnly to him, knowing she and her sister had to face the waiting man, the sooner the better. Ten minutes later, as the man left Chester Park, Charmaine stared numbly out through the window while Penelope screamed out her grief in her husband's arms. For every devastated sob her sister let out, Charmaine felt the lump in her throat grow larger and larger, until she thought she was losing her ability to breathe.

"I'm so sorry," Sin whispered in her ear as he put his arms around her statuesque body, offering her comfort in her hour of need.

She closed her eyes and took a deep breath, not wanting to believe what she just had been told.

Her mother—the lovely, kind woman who had

spent most of her life tormented by pain—had lost her will to fight the sickness which had forced her to spend the last months bedridden. As quietly as she had lived, she had taken her last breath.

Elspeth de Vere, the Countess of Nester, was dead.

Chapter Twelve

Looking down on the only grave not covered with snow in the silent graveyard, Charmaine tried to grasp the horrible truth—somewhere under the packed dirt lay her mother's worn body.

Nothing more than a small piece of tarnished wood with the name Nester hastily carved onto it told who rested here. The little plank, thrown down by an uncaring hand, showed more than anything how little her stepfather had respected or cherished the woman who had been his wife for almost twenty years.

"He didn't...place her in the family tomb," Penelope whispered, her voice breaking. "He had them dig her grave in the darkest, most secluded part of the graveyard, the one the caretaker keeps forgetting to care for."

Charmaine couldn't answer her sister. Anger flooded her mind and soul, and she was too overwhelmed to get even one little word out.

That despicable man.

If the kindhearted servant had not taken it upon himself to inform Lady Nester's daughters about her demise, they would probably still be thinking she was alive. Lord Nester had not only chosen to not inform them, he had also, as quickly as possible, put his wife in the ground in such a secluded spot they would never have found it.

Thank God for the snow, which made it impossible for the caretakers—or their stepfather—to hide where they had buried her. It was the small rectangle of dirt under the hanging branches of an old tree that had shown them their mother's last home on earth.

Alone under an ancient willow.

Charmaine felt the lump grow larger again until it almost choked her. She fisted her hands hard inside the muff as her heart cried for her mother and the love lost forever with her.

"We have to put a gravestone here," Penelope whispered, and her husband put his arm around her waist so she could lean her cheek against his shoulder, wetting the soft fabric of his coat with her tears.

"Of course we will," Rake said softly as he pecked a brief kiss onto her forehead. "Just tell me what you want, and I will make sure it will be done."

"Thank you."

Rake gave his wife another peck before looking up at Charmaine, and the compassion in his eyes almost did her in, but she hardened herself and forced the tears away.

"We should go. It's getting cold."

With one last lingering look at the lonely grave, the threesome walked back toward the church, where their carriage waited.

"I wish this were Uncle Charles's church," Penelope said, her voice still shivering with anger. "Instead, we have to deal with that snickering, sniveling, idiotic clergyman who is too much under Father's thumb to listen to us."

Charmaine looked up at the cold, dark stone church and couldn't have agreed more. "It's too bad the Nester family always has belonged to this church instead of the Chester Park one, which is so much closer to Harveyfield."

"Indeed it is." Rake offered his hand to help her up into the carriage. "But as our family always has been the patrons of the Chester Park church, I guess the Nesters felt they wanted to join a different one."

She accepted his hand, climbing gracefully into the carriage to sit next to Penelope, who stared unseeingly out through the window. Charmaine settled herself, then looked in surprise at her brother-in-law as he closed the door from the outside.

"Aren't you going home with us?"

He shook his head. "No. I have some errands to run that can't wait. I'll have someone drive me home later."

He looked at his wife sitting lost in her thoughts. "I won't be too long, my love."

Penelope nodded without facing him, and again his eyes filled with compassion and love. For a moment he seemed to hesitate, unwilling to leave his wife alone, before calling out to the driver. With a jerk the carriage started to roll, back toward Chester Park. Charmaine leaned closer to the window and looked at her brother-in-law where he stood on the snowy road watching them leave, looking more determined than ever.

As he turned and walked back toward the vicarage, she knew exactly where he was going. Lord Richard Darling was about to take matters into his own two hands.

She almost felt sorry for the poor clergyman, who was about to have a visitor he had never asked for. But only almost. The man had made it quite clear to them that he was on their stepfather's side, refusing to tell them where he'd laid their mother to rest.

"I hope it will hurt."

Penelope obviously had come to the same conclusion about her husband's sudden hurry to do some errands. Silently they rocked through the familiar grounds, watching their old childhood home slowly come closer. It was such a lovely house, Harveyfield, and had belonged to the Nester family for hundreds of years.

Despite her stepfather and the limited freedom he had allowed her, she had spent nineteen peaceful years in that house. It pained her to think of not being able to enter through the low garden gate, walk up to the creaky old front door, and enter the worn but comfortable home. Never again would she be able to walk into her mother's warm embrace, feel her love make everything worthwhile.

As they came closer to the house, she got a clear view toward the stables in the back and noticed Lord Nester's carriage was gone. Before she had a chance to change her mind, she called out to the driver to stop.

"Why are we stopping here? I never want to see that man again for the rest of my life." Penelope's eyes were red and puffy as she pulled her coat tighter around her shivering body.

"Because I want my things. But more importantly—I want something to remember Mother by, something that was hers and hers alone. Something I one day can give to my daughter."

"What about Father? Do you really want to face him? Isn't it enough that Rake soon will, or at least his fist will?"

"He's not here. The carriage is gone."

Penelope stopped tugging her coat and stared silently at Charmaine with her dazed eyes. Not until the carriage halted at the front of Harveyfield did she move. But as soon as the driver opened the small door she flew up from her seat. "I'm going with you. I can't stand the thought of that man selling Mother's few possessions!"

Together they almost ran to the front door, and, ignoring the outraged gasps from the footman, they burst into the house.

"You are trespassing," the footman yelled as they pushed him aside, heading for the stairs and their old bedrooms. "His Lordship told me to have you two arrested if you ever dared to show yourselves in this house again, and if you don't get out of here immediately, I will."

But the poor footman never had a chance to fulfill his master's request, as the cook came up behind him and hit him quite hard on the head with a pan. He fell to the floor like a pile of clothes, and the cook couldn't hide a satisfied grin.

"Never liked him, you know." She beamed as she waved her hand toward the stairs. "You two hurry up and gather your things. I'll watch him and make sure he don't interfere again."

"Thank you," Penelope breathed, tears in her eyes.

"Go on," the cook prompted gruffly as she sat down on the bottom step of the stair, her pan ready to land on the footman's head again if he dared to wake up.

As Charmaine stepped into her old room, a wave of childhood memories washed over her. How she had loved this bright room with its large windows!

It wasn't as grand and luxurious as the bedrooms at Chester Park, but to her it had been enormous. She had felt like a princess, sleeping in the old four-poster bed which took up almost half the space of the room. A small desk sat beneath one of the windows, and a comfortable chair was placed next to it, a chair in which her mother had spent most of her time when in Charmaine's room.

A small door led into a dressing room that was just as large as her bedroom, filled to its brim with clothes and knick-knacks. She grabbed one of the bags she had used when travelling and filled it with her favorite clothes, shoes, and accessories.

When it was full, she grabbed another one, sentimentally packing her old doll and other toys she had played with as a child and which she now wanted to hand over to her own children. She removed the loose panel in the wardrobe behind which she had hidden her journals and all her personal correspondence.

She hesitated when she reached Lord Dane's letters, remembering how much they had meant to her once. Before she could change her mind, she put the letters into the bag, too sentimental to throw them away just yet.

"Are you finished?" Penelope said from the doorway, and Charmaine shook her head.

"No, not yet. I want to make sure I don't leave anything important behind for Father to find. Are you finished?"

"I am. I think I will continue in Mother's bedroom, though, if that's all right with you?"

Amazed at how relieved she felt about not having

to go through her beloved mother's things, Charmaine nodded in response, and with a small, tight smile Penelope left. Charmaine closed her eyes as the pain over her mother's death grew again inside her heart.

Why hadn't she taken her mother with her? Why hadn't she forced the Darlings to have Lady Nester brought to Chester Park before her father's return from London?

The answer was as simple as it was embarrassing—she had been too distraught over her own entrapment of Sin to think twice about the one she had left behind.

But her feelings about her own shortcomings didn't matter. She knew her mother would have asked her to do the same thing all over again. Lady Nester had spent the last years of her life desperately trying to keep Charmaine safe from her stepfather, and in her heart she knew her mother had died happy knowing her daughters were safe.

But still... Charmaine couldn't help but feel she had let her mother down by leaving her to face the wrath of their stepfather alone. Lady Nester had been too sick to ever get well again, but at least she would have been able to spend her last days with her daughters, and they would have been able to say goodbye to her.

Able to tell her how much they loved her.

With a sigh, she grabbed the two bags containing the first nineteen years of her life and carried them out into her bedroom. She put the bags on the bed and went to the desk, where she efficiently collected the things she wanted to take with her.

She put the pile of unread mail aside, knowing there wouldn't be anything worthwhile for her to read.

Since meeting Lord Dane and hearing about all the letters he had sent her, she knew her father would have held on to anything of any importance.

How would she ever be able to explain to Sin how it had been for her to live under the same roof with a man as obsessed as her father was? Even if she could make Sin believe her, she knew he would never understand. Even though he was brought up by free-thinking parents, Sin was quite traditional and very much square in his opinions.

Not even Penelope, who had grown up under the same roof, would understand. She had never seen that side of their stepfather. As much as he adored Charmaine, he had neglected the younger sister, like two sides of a coin.

Charmaine was too caught in her thoughts to notice the man who quietly joined her in the room. Not until she heard the telling sound of the door closing did she look up and met the hungry eyes of her stepfather.

"Scream and you will regret it." Lord Nester's smile was soft, but the threat was visible in his pale eyes.

Charmaine forced herself to breathe calmly, digging her nails deep into her palms to keep her head clear, as she had done so many times before. Becoming hysterical wouldn't help her now. She knew that by experience. If she remained calm, she might be able to stall him. Sooner or later Penelope would come back, and hopefully her presence would stop whatever plans the man had spun.

"I've missed you so much," Lord Nester whispered as he came toward her, putting his hand against her cheek. "I could hardly believe my luck when I came home and the footman told me you were here. Finally back where you belong."

She wanted to tear herself away from him, to scream and scratch his eyes out, but instead she held still, as she always had done before. Having been caught in this situation too many times before had taught her not to deny him. It would only make it worse. Better let him have his way and offer him as little back as she possibly could.

"Why did you leave me?"

When she didn't answer his whining question, he lost the sweetness and his true, ugly soul became visible: the person beneath the surface whom only she and her mother had fully met, and whom Penelope had sensed that day when he gave her away to Lord Bolton.

"I worshipped you. I adored you. I gave you everything. And how did you repay me?" He sneered as he removed his hand from her cheek and grabbed her arm instead, dragging her closer until his lips was alarmingly close to hers. "By letting that...that bastard soil you, destroy your lovely innocence and your virginity. It was mine to take, not his. How could you let him do this to me? To us?"

"He's my husband."

"By your choice."

His voice had risen to a high pitch, and she knew he was about to lose stability, lose his sanity, and so she played along just so she could get away from him, away from his delirious fantasies.

"It wasn't by my choice."

To her relief, he calmed down, moving slightly backwards, a sad smile softening his face. "I know. I heard how he made sure you had to marry him. I thought I'd taught you better than to fall for such a thing. You are too beautiful. Men want you."

"I know."

"*I* want you."

"I know."

A wave of nausea hit her as his lips came closer to hers again, eagerly wanting to do what they had longed to do these last couple of years: kiss her. She tried to look indifferent, tried to hold on to her serenity, but something must have shown, as he suddenly gasped and drew back with flaring nostrils.

"What is this?" he hissed, looking as though he was on the verge of crying. "W-why are you looking at me like that? Like you are..."

He took a deep, shaky breath as he took another step back from her, and she had to use all her mental strength to not take a deep breath of relief.

"You look like you detest me!"

"I don't detest you."

Her answer came fast and automatically, and any other day it would have satisfied him. But not this time. No, for the first time ever, he looked at her with doubt, and that scared her immensely.

What if he had changed? How would she then know how to handle him? How would she ever be able to read him correctly? If she couldn't foresee his every move, she could be in real danger, if she didn't know how he would react.

"I don't detest you."

The lie flew as easily as ever over her lips, but this time she didn't get the usual response of utter relief as she always had before when denying darker feelings for him. Instead, he walked over to the bed and grabbed one of the posts as if he were unable to stand upright without its help.

Charmaine didn't know what to do.

She looked at the closed door, calculating whether or not she had a chance of escaping the room without being caught before she opened it.

Probably. But what would happen if she did? Would he follow her? Would he hurt her?

More importantly, would he hurt Penelope?

The memory of how easily he had given her sister to Lord Bolton gave her the answer without a doubt: Yes, without remorse or second thoughts.

"Do you love me?"

His strange behavior and unusual intuition confused her, and she hesitated too long over what to reply. With a growl of pain he let go of the post and stalked back to her, pushing her hard on the chest.

Caught by surprise, she stumbled backwards, bumping into the wall behind her. Using her passiveness, he grabbed her wrists, pressing them against the wall over her head. Caught between him and the wall, Charmaine could hardly breathe, and she couldn't stop a whimper of pain as he harshly twisted her arms in a show of power.

"Tell me you love me."

His voice was clipped. He left no room for playing games. She had no choice but to try to soothe him and make him release her.

"I love you."

He snorted angrily. "You lying whore."

"Please..."

His cold laughter made her shiver with fear, and he pressed his heavy body closer to hers, until she could feel his arousal against her stomach.

"Can you feel how much I want you?"

He snickered as she turned her head away from him, too embarrassed and disgusted to answer.

"It pains me to know you have spread your legs for that husband of yours, that you have let him soil your perfect, pristine beauty. But I guess I'll learn to live with it once you're mine again. So maybe I lost your innocence to him, but he will lose the rest of you to me."

She frowned unwillingly, deeply disturbed by his strange conclusion. Even if Sin had wanted to get rid of her he wouldn't be able to. She was his deflowered bride and could already be carrying the future heir to the Berkeley dukedom.

"You are mistaken," she whispered, trying to reach through his madness. "Lord Chilton will never let me go."

His apparent satisfaction over catching her attention so easily was a bit upsetting, but not as much as the subject of his choice.

"Of course he won't. Sinclair Darling is not known for being daft, and only a daft man would give you up. Someone like Lord Dane."

"I-I don't un-understand," she stuttered, too dizzy to be able to think straight.

Lord Nester loosened his painful grip on her arms, and she let them down with a relieved sigh as the tearing pain ended. Instead he put his hands against her cheeks, as he had done so many times before, smiling triumphantly.

"A dead man has no say about what happens to his widow, and if she wants to move back to the security of her loving parent, I'm sure his family won't stop her."

Oh, God.

Fear like none she'd ever felt before ripped through her body as she looked into his insane eyes, reading the truth in them: Her stepfather was going to kill her husband.

"Please, don't."

Lord Nester sneered, disgusted. "What is this? Why are you so upset that he will die? You should be rejoicing that I am handing you this gift of freedom and the opportunity to finally become mine." He gave a sudden outraged gasp. "A-are you in *love* with him?"

Good God!

"No!" She took a deep breath. "No. There are no feelings between the two of us. The marriage was forced."

His eyes narrowed suspiciously. "Now I think you are lying to me, because I'm quite aware of how madly in love with you Sinclair Darling is. Year after year he has been standing around, staring at you with those puppy eyes. If I hadn't known for sure that you neither cared nor noticed his feelings, I would have had to ask him to cease the endless gawking. It was starting to get a bit irritating."

Her heart started to beat faster as she listened to her stepfather's ranting. Could it be true? Could Sin be in love with her? The joy which filled her heart almost made her smile, but then reality hit, and she shook her head mentally.

No, this was her stepfather speaking, her very insane stepfather, who thought it would be all right with everyone that he married his stepdaughter.

But then again...

He had always seemed to have a sixth sense about other men's feelings toward her. He had more than once told her to expect proposals from certain men, and he had always been right. The only thing he ever had been wrong about had been her feelings for him. But then again, he had always been blind when it came to her, which his sick infatuation for her was evidence of. "So do you?" Her stepfather interrupted her thoughts by harshly lifting her up from the floor and tossing her on the bed.

She blinked and sat up, confused. "Do I what?"

"Love him."

"I-I..."

He grabbed a vase and threw it into the fireplace with so much force it broke into hundreds of small pieces all over the floor. "You love him!"

She shook her head frantically, desperately trying to find the right words to use to persuade him into believing her indifference toward her husband.

But she was too late.

With a guttural cry, he slapped her hard across the mouth, and she felt queasy at the taste of blood as she fell back onto the bed.

"I would recommend you cherish your marriage as much as possible from now on," Lord Nester hissed, "because I am going to kill that husband of yours as soon as I have a chance."

He gripped her chin, forcing her to look at him. "And then it's just you and me."

Without forewarning, he bent and pressed his lips hard against hers. A wave of nausea trapped her as he tried to press his tongue through her pursed lips. Just as he succeeded in forcing her mouth open, she lost the inner struggle as well, and with a whimper she threw up all over him. He bolted back, cursing loudly as he tried to brush the vomit from his clothes and his face with his bare hands.

"When you are mine, I am going to make you pay for this," he snarled as he grabbed a blanket and used it to clean the worst of the mess. "I promise you, I will make you pay for every time you have denied me my right to your body and every time you have turned your delicious mouth away from mine."

When he had cleaned himself as much as possible, he threw the dirty blanket at her, letting her know just how little she now meant to him, before he opened the door and looked out into the hallway.

"Until next time." His smile toward her was pure evil, and she shivered in response to the barely hidden threat. With one last lingering look upon her, he disappeared out through the door, and not until she heard his footsteps fade away down the stairs did she dare to breathe again.

Oh, my God!

What was she going to do?

She knew Lord Nester never made empty threats. He was far too ignorant to even think of playing games. He was going to kill the unknowing Sin, to be able to get his hands on her. How could she warn Sin without telling him the truth about her stepfather? Again she felt caught between her desperate wish to come clean with Sin and her fear of losing him when he found out the truth.

She closed her eyes in despair, not knowing what to do. Not telling Sin about the threat wasn't an option: he should be able to defend himself, to be a bit more cautious, and especially to have a chance of not putting himself in a position where her father could fulfill his dreadful quest.

"I've gone through Mother's things and packed the ones that meant something to me. Do you want to see if I there's something I've missed?"

Penelope stood in the doorway, too caught up in their mission to notice her sister's disheveled appearance and the faint odor of vomit. Most of the time Penelope's bad habit of daydreaming and walking with her head among the clouds would vex Charmaine, but not this time. For once she was grateful for her sister's tendency to not notice details.

"Did you get the little box with her ancestors' heirlooms?"

A frown marred Penelope's forehead as she dug through her bag, but it disappeared as she held up a small leather box. "Aha! Yes, I did get it."

"Good," Charmaine acknowledged, ushering her sister toward the stairs. "We'd better get going. One never knows when Father will return."

As they sat in their carriage, slowly leaving Harveyfield behind them, Charmaine's gaze met the triumphant eyes of their stepfather where he stood in the large library bow window. He lifted his hand and made a cross in the air with his finger and she sank back into the cushioned seat, her heart filled with anxiety.

"Charmaine, what is it? You look like you've seen a ghost."

Penelope's inquiring voice was filled with compassion as she for once could sense her sister's distress, and Charmaine forced a light smile.

"It's nothing, really. Just a few old memories of our childhood days."

"Ah."

Apparently satisfied with the meager answer, Penelope lost interest in her sister and instead started to turn the pages in an old diary of hers, while Charmaine sighed silently with relief. She had no wish to start explaining herself to her sister. It was bad enough that she had to say as little as possible to Sin. Having to face Penelope's disgust, too, would be a bit too much for her. At least for now.

The mere thought of Sin made her heart beat faster. Could he be in love with her? Lord Nester seemed to think he was, and he was usually right about such things.

Her stepfather had always loved turning her suitors away and had more than once encouraged a beau just to have the satisfaction of denying him her hand. In her name, of course. No one knew she never was told about the interview until much later.

"What do you think Father will do when he hears about our visit?" Penelope looked a bit worried. "He has a tendency to act rashly, after all."

"Don't you worry." Charmaine patted her sister's hand affectionately. "Father has no use for you anymore, as you now are married to Rake, who most effectively made sure Lord Bolton never would look your way again."

"But what about you? You are Father's diamond. Do you really think he will let you go so easily? He has always seemed a bit too obsessed with you, and sometimes it felt as if Mother was the only thing that held him back from misbehaving."

Charmaine forced a giddy laugh to take the edge off the subject. "Yes, I do have to be aware of the man who is desperate for loving me to death."

"Putting it that way, it sounds quite ridiculous, I have to admit." Penelope laughed and lifted her old diary, again dismissing her sister, and Charmaine closed her eyes briefly.

Thank God for her sister's fickle mind.

Penelope had been a bit too close to the truth. Luckily, she had never understood just how twisted their stepfather's feelings were.

Which brought the killing of Sin back into her mind, and Charmaine shivered again at the mere thought of Lord Nester's intentions.

She had to do something to stop him from ever hurting Sin. She was too tired to think about it right now, but as soon as she had rested she would sit down and try to figure out what to do.

Lord Nester might think he held the upper hand, but somehow she was going to prove him wrong. Sin was her husband, and she was desperately in love with him. And if she dared to believe what her stepfather said, Sin might be loving her back, at least a little.

A good night's sleep, and then she would be ready for Lord Nester. He might think it was going to be an easy killing, but she would prove him wrong and save Sin. All she had to do was come up with a good, if untrue, explanation of why her stepfather was threatening him.

That couldn't be too hard now, could it?

Chapter Thirteen

"Don't you think it's time to stop hiding behind your ledgers and instead go and find out what's bothering your lovely wife?"

The sarcastic voice cut through the thick silence of the study, and Sin lost track of the numbers he had been adding. Irritated, he looked up and frowned at his younger brother, who strolled across the dark study to throw himself down into one of the visitors' chairs across the desk.

"Bloody hell, Ian, now you made me lose my count."

"And?"

Sin sighed heavily. "*And* I've been trying to find an error in the ledgers which has been eluding me for days, and now you've made me lose it all over again."

"Honestly, Sin, you should lock those boring, unimportant books away and throw the key as far as you can and start living life instead."

"This *is* my life, Ian. These, as you call them, boring and unimportant books are what make you able to live the comfortable life you have. If I didn't follow up on all things accountable, we soon would lose more money than we earned."

Sebastian grinned mischievously. "Lord, how dull it sounds."

"Everything in life can't be fun."

"Maybe not, but I still believe everyone needs to at least smile now and then. And you, my dear brother, never smile."

"I smile."

"No, you don't."

Sin closed the ledger with another sigh. He could tell Sebastian wasn't going to leave him alone without informing him about what was on his mind. Thank God he wasn't the longwinded kind.

Leaning back in his chair, Sin crossed his arms over his chest, trying to look just as annoyed and dejected as he felt. "I smile when I have something to smile about."

"You have Charmaine."

"And I smile when I'm with her."

Sebastian looked a bit too surprised. "You *are* with her sometimes? I would never have thought so, considering how you insist upon spending all your time in this dungeon."

So this was about Charmaine. Sin closed his eyes briefly. He had no desire to discuss his wife with anyone, including his only brother.

"My marriage is no concern of yours."

Unfortunately, Sebastian didn't care about his older brother's wishes. "Of course it is. We all have to sit there every day, watching her fade like a flower as her grave-looking husband pretends she's not there."

"I do not pretend she's not there."

"You don't? Are you just ignoring her out of old habit, then?"

"I don't ignore her, either. She's my wife and I speak with her when we're in our private chambers. You know, when the rest of you aren't there listening to every word we say."

"You make it sound as if we eavesdrop. How utterly rude."

Sin ignored his brother's wicked grin. "You are constantly eavesdropping, the whole bunch of you, and there really is no need for my wife and me to have our intimate discussions while with the rest of you."

"So you *do* talk to her, then?"

"Of course I do."

"So why does she sit there like a sad, beautiful puppy, never taking her eyes off your person, waiting for you to throw her a bone?"

Sin's heart flipped at the notion of Charmaine secretly yearning for his attention, but he pushed the feeling aside. When they arrived home from Gretna Green, he had realized Charmaine craved his presence much more than he had time for, and when he realized how much he preferred spending time with her instead of managing the estate, he had mentally grabbed himself by the ear.

Chester Park and the Berkeley estate would one day become his responsibility, and as he had told Charmaine, he couldn't let down the people depending on him. So, instead of spending his days with his wife as he wanted to, he locked himself into the study and filled his head with numbers and amounts. He had a large family for her to socialize with, including her very own sister, so he knew she couldn't possibly feel lonely just because he wasn't around.

"We are still acclimatizing to each other and our marriage. In time she will learn."

Sebastian arched a very Darling eyebrow. "*She* will learn?"

"We will both learn how to compromise to make our new life together work out for the best." Sin blushed as Sebastian grinned knowingly. Of course he had no inclination to change his own life, especially not for a wife and even more especially not for Charmaine. She was too used to getting all the attention from her parents, and it was his task to bring her down from her pedestal and teach her the important lesson of how unimportant she really was.

"I can't help feeling sorry for your poor wife. Here she has had her whole life turned upside down and ends up with a husband who has made it into a sport to ignore her as much as possible."

Sebastian was a bit too close to the truth there, and Sin felt his cheeks grow even hotter. "I don't ignore her as much as possible. But she must understand my work here is important and I don't have the time to dally with her and her every whim."

"She's ordering you about? I'm sorry, old chap. I didn't know that."

Sin's eyes narrowed as he looked at his brother and tried to see if the imp was serious or making fun of him as usual, but Sebastian's face was more than usually bland.

"Well, I wouldn't say she's ordering me about…"

"Oh, don't say she's the nagging type." Sebastian made a compassionate sound. "They are the worst, and I must say I would never have thought Charmaine was one. But then again, what do I know?"

"Clearly not much. Of course she doesn't nag. It's Charmaine we're talking about. She never does anything that would make her look bad."

"So she's just ignorant, then?"

Sin was starting to get a bit upset with his brother. Of course she wasn't ignorant. She was much more caring than he ever had envisioned her to be. As a matter of fact, she had turned out to be just as beautiful on the inside as on the outside, and every time he was with her he could feel himself falling in love with her all over again.

The thing was, he knew what she had been like before, all egotistical and uncaring. He certainly didn't want her to fall back into such behavior again. So he held her at arm's length, to make sure she could never turn him into her puppet as she had her parents.

At first, after their return to Chester Park, she had seemed confused and hurt, clearly not understanding why he treated her as if she were a piece of furniture during the daytime and among others. But after a couple of days she must have understood what he had tried to teach her, as the confusion disappeared and she instead looked serene and sated.

The perfect wife.

Strangely enough, he had found himself missing the spontaneous and emotional Charmaine he had met in Gretna Green, but he couldn't complain, as she now acted as sophisticated and urbane as she had always been before. The well-behaved lady with an even temper was, after all, the Charmaine he had fallen in love with. Wasn't it?

The duchess had told him she thought Charmaine behaved as if she were a glass of milk, all tasteless, neutral, and utterly boring, and he'd had to bite himself in the cheek to not agree. Only in bed, when they made love, did the girl from Scotland come forward, and only then did he leave all his restrictions aside, throwing himself headlong into the fire they created together.

She had been acting a bit snuggly in the aftermath, though, and as he found himself liking the feel of her in his arms all night a bit too much, he had forced himself to turn away from her warm, inviting body. Instead he gave her a fatherly peck on the forehead before leaving her bedroom for his own, where she wasn't a distraction.

"Can't you sleep here?" she had asked the first time he had got out of her bed since returning to Chester Park. She had looked shy, almost scared, and for a second he had hesitated, wanting nothing more than to slip back under the bedspread and pull her warm body close to his. But instead he had forced himself to shake his head before escaping from her alluring presence.

To him she was a siren, like those in Greek mythology who lured sailors to destruction with their luscious beauty and their tempting songs. He had to harden himself against her so she wouldn't drag him away from everything that mattered to him—everything that mattered to his family. She would have him live every day as it came, instead.

He looked at his brother, who had turned the easy life into perfection, and knew he couldn't do that. He hadn't it in him to let go of everything and simply live life. Not even for a day.

He had given Penelope a month, though, when he went with her and Charmaine to Gretna Green, but that was different. Penelope was a dear, dear friend, and it had been necessary for her chance at happiness. And in the end, the unusual neglect of his responsibilities had paid out: Penelope was now happily married to Uncle

Rake.

"Why this sudden interest in my marriage? You never seemed to care much about it before, so why now?"

Sebastian shrugged lightly. "It's such a waste to have someone as astounding as Charmaine in your home and then have to watch her turn into a miserable and disappointed wife."

"She just lost her mother. Of course she is feeling a bit low. Wait and see. She'll be back to her normal composed self in no time, and then you can go back to your drooling."

It was disdain in the look Sebastian sent him, and Sin frowned again. What was with his brother? He, the happy and contented scoundrel, seemed almost distressed over the fact that his sister-in-law was a bit under the weather. Quite a bit distressed, apparently, to actually come to Sin with his concerns.

He felt a cold shiver run down his spine as a thought flew into his mind and settled like a thorn in his palm. *Could Sebastian be in love with Charmaine?*

Sin wouldn't hold it against him. He knew exactly how easy it was to fall in love with her. He did it every day himself, over and over again. Charmaine was too alluring for her own good, and she didn't even have to flirt to make men follow her every whim.

She was just too loveable.

Bloody hell.

"I can see you are not interested in your wife and her feelings, so I'll leave you to your precious ledger. I hope the two of you will live happily ever after, as it's clear to anyone who has eyes in their head that you won't be with your wife." Sebastian's smile was just as icy as his clipped voice as he turned and headed for the door.

"She's *my* wife," Sin called out after him.

"I'm glad you're aware of that," Sebastian said over his shoulder, not bothering to turn and face his older brother, and Sin felt another cold shiver.

"You leave her alone, Ian."

"Like you do?"

And there Sebastian had the last word again as he disappeared through the doorway and the door crashed shut behind him.

"I'm *not* ignoring her," Sin pouted to the closed door as he slumped back into the chair again, not feeling as content as he had before his brother's interruption.

What if he was right? What if Sebastian had feelings for his sister-in-law? How could they ever see that through? He didn't want to lose his closeness to his only brother because of a woman, and especially not over his own wife.

It was a bloody nuisance to have a magnificent wife. He had been secretly preparing himself for the Season in London, which was closing in too fast. He guessed it would be Gretna Green all over again. Charmaine had been constantly surrounded by eager men who did anything to catch the attention of the beauty and maybe perhaps win the way to her heart, and her bed.

There had always been lots and lots of bets in the infamous *Book of Bets* at White's about her:

Who would win her heart.

Who would win her hand.

Who would sneak the first kiss away.

And now Sin was afraid there were more bets scribbled down, considering the notorious crowd of bored young men who had made a game of becoming a new wife's first lover. All newly married women had a list of bets, and claims, from different men, over who the lover would be and how far into the marriage he would succeed with his quest of getting into the woman's bed.

There were many women who were simply crossed off, in the end, as not one man had succeeded. But then there were the ones with whom someone had become the winner...

I wonder if Sebastian's name is scribbled down on Charmaine's page.

With another sigh he pushed the heavy ledger aside, unable to continue with the counting Sebastian had interrupted when he barged in. Instead, Sin stood and followed his brother's footsteps out of the study. Soon enough he found Sebastian in the family room, having tea with the rest of the family, including Charmaine.

She sat beside her sister on a small sofa, looking lovelier than ever, clad in a lovely pink dress in the same shade as her full lips, her thick blonde hair tumbling down her back. She acknowledged him calmly with an almost invisible nod, inviting him to sit down in a chair across the table from her with a small, elegant movement of her hand.

So composed. So serene. So cold.

He sat down in the chair, accepting the cup of tea she handed him gracefully, before he crossed one leg over the other and tried to seem more relaxed and at ease than he was.

"I'm sure he won't be able to sit for weeks," Rake drawled, oozing with manly satisfaction, and his wife clapped her hands joyfully.

"That's wonderful news! You are the best."

"I try." Rake's grin was more wicked than ever when he glanced hotly at his wife.

"This is the best day I've had in a long time." Penelope's sigh reeked with satisfaction. "Not only will that horrible man have troubles with his behind for a while, but we also managed to sneak into Harveyfield and gather our things without Father noticing."

"You did what?"

Catching the tea in his throat as he sat up too fast, Sin started to cough.

"There, there," Rake murmured, helpfully whacking his nephew on the back.

"St-hop ta-hat!"

"Excuse me?"

Sin glared at Rake, who looked as innocent as a newborn baby. Not an easy task when one was *the* libertine of all time. "Stop the whacking."

"Oh. Sorry. Just wanted to be helpful."

"You were not."

Rake shrugged indifferently and grabbed a sandwich, ignoring his sulking relative. Sin shot another sour look at him before turning to the two sisters and scowling darkly at them.

"You two were at Harveyfield?"

"Yes." Penelope looked a bit uncomfortable.

"What were you doing there?"

"Gathering our things."

"Your things?"

"Our memorabilia. A few childhood things, which

mean something to us and nothing to him."

"Are you two out of your minds?"

Penelope sat up straighter. "It was the perfect, most sensible thing to do. They are our things, little memories from our childhood, and they wouldn't have any value to him. Only to us."

Sin looked at Charmaine, but she kept her eyes on her sister, sending her compassionate glances, and he felt a cold hand grab his heart. What if Lord Nester had returned? The man was insane, something he had proven more than once, and just the thought of his wife getting caught in that man's hands made him shiver.

"Did you see your father?"

"No. He wasn't at home," Penelope answered lightly. "And that's why we emptied Mother's room of her small things, too."

"You did *what*?"

The room became as quiet as a tomb as the rest of the family halted their conversations and looked at them, wondering why Sin had yelled at the top of his lungs. He knew it wasn't common for him to show this much feeling in front of others, but to hear that they had been in that house...had been in *that* man's house...

"We had to save Mother's things."

Penelope's voice was stiff, and seeing the tears lurking in her eyes made him feel like a cad. They had just lost their mother. Of course they weren't thinking straight.

He looked at his wife, wondering if she were just as upset, but she seemed just as composed as ever. No tears hung in her eyelashes. Not one emotion was seen on her beautiful face as she looked back at him with her vivid blue eyes.

"They had to," Rake interrupted Sin's thoughts. "Considering how the man had tried to hide Lady Nester's grave, it's not too hard to guess what he would have done with her things."

"Burnt them, probably," Penelope offered in a heartbroken whisper. Immediately Rake went to his wife, scooting her into his arms before sitting down again with her on his lap. Charmaine calmly collected her skirt, saving it from becoming wrinkled, and Sin couldn't help wondering how she would have reacted if he had done the same thing to her.

Would she have liked him putting her on his lap so she could hide her face against his chest while he embraced her tenderly? His heart said yes, but his eyes told him no. She didn't seem touched at all by all the emotions being shown beside her in the sofa. Instead she continued to sew on her embroidery with perfect little stitches.

Always the lady.

For a second he thought about that first time he had left her alone in her bed, when she had looked hurt and lonely as he harshly abandoned her. That was the last time he had seen any sign of feeling on her lovely face, other than when they made love.

Even at the news of her mother's death she had stayed calm and unemotional, while Penelope had cried all over the room and particularly all over Rake.

"I still think it was a stupid thing to do," he continued, forcing his voice to be steady and low. "What if Lord Nester had returned? What would the two of you have done then? Penny, he could have grabbed you again and sent you one last time to Lord Bolton. Or didn't you consider that?"

Penelope paled visibly as she took in his words, and he held back a satisfied smile. This wasn't the time or the place to gloat. Instead he just harrumphed and pretended not to notice how well his lecture had taken.

"Aren't you being a bit too obnoxious now?" Sebastian asked as he joined their little circle. "Nothing happened, after all, and it's not as if they are going back there again."

Sin wanted to growl out his frustration over the interruption just as he had the situation under control, but as always he forced his feelings back and shrugged as indifferently as he could manage toward his brother. "If caring about the safety of your wife and your sister-in-law means being obnoxious, then I have to confess I am."

Sebastian grinned impishly as he sat down in an empty chair. "I'm just saying you could ease your stance a bit. Nothing happened. End of story."

"Indeed," the duchess agreed, as she too joined them. "Let's just leave what could have happened and instead direct our attention to what *did* happen. You found Lady Nester's grave?"

"Yes, Your Grace." Charmaine nodded. "They had buried her in the furthest part of the graveyard."

"Horrible." The duchess shook her head sadly. "Truly horrible. Thank God the four of you found the site before that evil Lord Nester managed to hide it beneath a bush or something."

"Oh, Sin wasn't with us," Rake said with a faint smile. "He had more important things to do."

The duchess turned to stare angrily at Sin. "More important than accompanying your wife to her newly deceased mother's grave? Sinclair Darling!"

189

"I've been away for a month," Sin answered, filled with the righteousness only a wrongly accused man can feel. "A month! Do you know how much work there was piled up, waiting for me? Stacks upon stacks upon stacks of paperwork? Don't berate me for taking care of neglected business instead of going with Charmaine to the graveyard. She had her sister with her, for goodness' sake."

"A sister is not a husband."

She had him there, he had to admit. Anna Darling, Duchess of Berkeley, was infamous for her illogical logic, and when she was upset about something—which was most of the time—there was no possibility of persuading her to change her mind.

"You have a point there," Sin agreed. "A sister isn't and can never be a husband."

"Are you patronizing me, boy?"

Sin wanted to roll his eyes heavenward, but managed to stop himself in time. Instead, he shook his head and mumbled something the duchess correctly interpreted as an excuse.

"You should have chosen your wife, in that situation," she lectured him, wagging her index finger at him. "The books haven't got any feelings, but a wife does. Your wife just lost her mother."

"It's all right," Charmaine interrupted gently. "I managed quite well without him."

She obviously didn't mean to be rude, she was probably just trying to stand by his side against his grandmother, but he couldn't help feeling a bit vexed over how easily she erased the importance of his presence. So she had managed quite well without him?

Somehow her words made him feel more

unimportant than ever, and he clamped his mouth shut so he wouldn't say something to be regretted later.

Managed quite well without him?

"Sinclair, for goodness' sake, please cease that harrumphing. It's making my head ache!"

"Yes, Grand-Mama."

"And the eye-rolling."

"Yes, Grand-Mama."

"And the pouting."

"Oh, no, Grand-Mama, Sin doesn't pout," Sebastian interrupted before Sin had a chance to answer, his green eyes alive with an unmistakable mischievous sparkle, and Sin braced himself for the sarcasm he knew would be poured over him. "Sin *never* pouts. He's just being his ordinary solemn self—too boring and too occupied with much more important things."

"Who are you calling boring, you bloody…"

"Enough!"

Sin looked up at his grandfather, who had quietly joined them and was now staring hard at them under his bushy eyebrows.

"You two have been at each other's throats every day for the last couple of days, and it's starting to get tiresome. Solve it or forget it. Just don't force the rest of us to listen to you squabble."

"It's not my fault that…"

Hannibal held up a hand, and Sin closed his mouth. This was not the time to continue. His grandfather usually had the patience of a saint and almost never lost his temper with his children or grandchildren. But when he did…

"I'm sorry," Sin and Sebastian mumbled,

unanimous, and Hannibal gave them an approving nod.

"That's my boys. Now scoot over and make some room for an old man to rest his tired legs."

"They found Lady Nester's grave," the duchess enlightened her husband when he had made himself comfortable. "That awful man hadn't placed her poor, tormented body with the rest of the family but instead put her in the most hidden spot possible."

Hannibal sent a sympathetic glance, filled with warmth and care, toward Charmaine and Penelope. "If you want, I can have her moved here, to our private graveyard, so you can visit her whenever you feel so obliged."

Sin looked at his wife, who looked as bland as ever. Not an emotion crossed her perfect face, not even the smallest shiver. Penelope, on the other hand, threw her crying self into the duke's arms and hugged him close as she whispered, "Thank you." The difference between the two sisters was almost ridiculous, his wife composed and cold as ice while her sister was a cuddly pot of sunshine.

It wasn't the first time he'd secretly wished for a little of Penelope's warmth and friendliness to rub off on Charmaine, and as always he felt like the worst cad ever to even consider it. Wasn't it the perfect and serene Charmaine he had fallen in love with? The Incomparable Queen of the *ton*? So why did he sit here wishing her to be something she wasn't?

He was so lost in his thoughts he didn't realize she was talking to him until she put a hand on his arm. Oddly enough, he felt caught with his hand in the cookie jar, and he blushed, grateful for her not being able to hear what he had been thinking.

"Could I have a word in private?" Charmaine's voice was as smooth as ever, but something in the way she grasped his arm told him this was important to her, and he nodded. They excused themselves from the rest of the Darling family, leaving the salon quickly, followed by his brother's and his uncle's teasing shouts about what they thought he and his wife were up to.

For a moment he wished the jokes were true. He found to his surprise that the thought of making love to his wife at this hour, in the middle of the day, was amazingly alluring. When they entered his study, he closed the door carefully behind them before turning the key with a lusty smile.

Why not give in to his urges for once, leave the ledger alone on the desk for an hour, and instead kiss his wife until he couldn't tell where he ended and she began.

Charmaine didn't notice his action nor his mood. She was too busy pacing and wringing her hands, too upset about something to be able to stand still.

He removed his jacket as he sat down on a corner of the desk, beckoning Charmaine with a finger to come closer. She looked at him with suspicion, and he couldn't blame her—he wasn't acting at all like his usual busy self.

"Come," he purred.

"No." She frowned at him from the other side of the room. "I'll stand here, thank you. I have something I must talk to you about, and I don't need the distraction."

So he was a distraction to her?

If he didn't kiss her soon, he thought he would swoon of fatigue. He needed to feel her body, her warmth, her breath. Just looking at her from the other side of the room wasn't enough. He wanted to know she belonged to him, that the woman he had loved for years was his to embrace whenever he wanted.

Sebastian's speculations about her being bored in their marriage had disturbed him, and he guessed he had to change a few things between them to keep her more satisfied. And if one of those things was making love to her in the middle of the day, so be it.

The sacrifices he made for her...

Charmaine, who was blissfully unaware of her husband's new unselfish stance toward her, continued with her walking and wringing. He managed to stay quiet and keep his patience for almost five minutes, an endurance worthy of a saint.

"I haven't got all day!" he barked in the end, not able to sit there and watch her luscious body walk past him one more time without reaching out and dragging her closer.

Startled, she jumped at the sound of his explosive voice and a light blush crept over her smooth cheeks. To soothe his harsh words he sent her an encouraging smile, which only rendered him a suspicious glance from her narrowing eyes.

"I-I'm sorry," she stuttered, something she normally never did, and he felt himself staring just as suspiciously back at her.

What was she up to? "Is there something wrong?"

She shook her head, then stopped and nodded. "Yes, to be truthful, there is. Something is terribly wrong, and I just don't know how to…"

"Yes?" he probed as her voice trailed off.

Again she started to tread to and fro, and he

couldn't stop a deep sigh. "What is it, Charmaine? You seem quite distraught about something. Tell me. I'm your husband. You can tell me anything."

She stopped and looked at him hesitantly, and again he felt that overwhelming urge to kiss her. She was just too alluring for him to listen to her. He could see her lips moving, but all he could think about was pressing his mouth gently against them, kissing her until she burnt for him just as much as he burnt for her.

"Promise me," she said as she walked up to him, and he woke up from his daydream, realizing he hadn't heard a word she'd said.

"Eh…"

"Promise me!"

"Of course."

She staggered against him, her relief obvious. "Thank you," she breathed, and for a second he drew back, wondering what it had all been about. Her worry was too obvious and her relief too large for this to be about something unimportant. But just as he was about to ask her and admit he hadn't heard a word, she threw her arms around his neck and did just what he had been fantasizing about—she kissed him.

All thoughts of her worries left him, and instead he kissed her back. Her response was immediate. He couldn't believe the heat she awoke inside him. Her eager response had him weak with need, and before she had a chance to change her mind he lifted her into his arms and carried her over to the small sofa.

She seemed in a frenzy as her trembling hands tried to unbutton his pants, and it made him almost breathless with desire. To see her need for him was the most exciting thing he'd ever experienced, and with a groan he ripped the pants open and lifted her skirts, tearing all the silky undergarments in his way until he finally could thrust deep inside her shivering body.

She screamed into his mouth as she came, and soon he followed her. The climax was better than ever, and afterwards he fell heavily down on top of her, unable to hold himself up.

"Thank you," she whispered again, and he chuckled, amused over her breathlessness.

"You are quite welcome, my dear."

She pushed lightly on his chest, without words letting him know he was becoming too heavy, and he rolled off her with a satisfied sigh.

"I didn't mean the lovemaking, although I am very much thankful for that too," she said with a small, shy smile as she stood and straightened her clothes. "I meant about you staying indoors for now."

He sat up in the sofa, frowning at her. "What are you talking about? I'm not staying indoors. I have loads of errands and visits to do."

"But you promised!" She staggered backwards as if she weren't able to stand by herself.

"I have promised you no such thing," he snorted, leaving the sofa for his desk and flinging open his ledgers.

"But you just did, before the…before…"

"Before what?" he teased, but she was too distraught to play with him.

"I told you about the danger, and you promised me to stay indoors. You said so just before I kissed you."

"What danger?" Her desperation was getting to him, and his frown deepened. "What are you talking about?"

She stared at him blankly. "I told you."

"Well, I wasn't listening. I was a bit preoccupied, staring at your kissable lips. What danger?"

Hesitantly she took a step back, and then another one. She stared at him with her unreadable eyes, and for some reason he was starting to feel a bit guilty for not having listened to her, as she had obviously been quite distressed—and still was.

"I'm listening now," he urged, but she didn't answer. "You can tell me now."

"N-no."

"Oh, come on. You have to tell me why you think I'm in danger. Is there someone out there who wants to get me?"

He chuckled again, too amused over the thought of her being this upset over nothing. He was a big man and quite able to protect himself from whatever danger she fantasized.

"You have to promise." Her voice was high-pitched and shaky, as if echoing the fear in her heart.

"No. Not until you tell me why."

"I can't tell you why!" she cried out.

"Then I won't stay indoors."

"Please, Sin. I *beg* you to reconsider."

"Tell me why, and I might."

"I can't."

Her voice was only a whisper, yet he heard her clearly, and with a sigh he opened one of the heavy ledgers, making sure she could see he was dismissing her. "If I'm not mistaken, we have had this conversation regarding another subject before, and just as I said then, I want to know why. If you're not able to show me enough respect to tell me, please leave. I have more important things to do, as you should be aware."

She didn't say one more word.

She just stood there silently, staring at him with those unreadable blue eyes before turning and leaving him alone in the study. Again he felt a sting of guilt, but he immediately erased the feeling.

So he hadn't listened to her. Why was she surprised? He was a man, after all, and men weren't known for their intellectual and spiritual conversations with women. That kind of talk you had with your male friends and relatives.

He ignored the little voice telling him his mother and grandmother probably would have killed him if they'd heard what he was thinking, not to mention what his sister would have done to him. Instead he forced himself to concentrate on the numbers he had abandoned earlier.

Five minutes later he put his pen down with a defeated sigh. It was no use. His head wasn't able to concentrate on figures. All he could think about was Charmaine and her fear that he might be in danger.

Why hadn't he listened to her?

He stood and crossed to the large window, looking out over the garden that was so lush in summer. Now it was clad in snow and painted a lovely and undisturbed canvas for his tired eyes and aching head.

He couldn't help feeling as if they'd never had a chance from the beginning, that their marriage was doomed before it began. Her trapping him into matrimony had indeed been a bad start, and refusing to tell him why hadn't exactly eased the tension between them. But then she had tried, he had to give her that, and he had a sinking feeling it was his own fault their marriage had become this farce.

He had fancied himself in love with her for so many years, secretly yearning for her from afar, but when she was dumped into his lap he just hadn't known what to do with her. He'd always hoped her cold and selfish air was just that—an air—and that she would be different when he got to know her. But to his frustration she had seemed even worse than Francesca had said for so many years, and he had started to loathe himself for falling so shallowly in love with her. All the shame he had felt over his own feelings he took out on her, not giving her any chance to come clean with him, or with herself, for that matter.

The month in Gretna Green had been an eye-opener, and he had met the Charmaine he had always dreamt about, but yet again he had managed to turn the budding romance into nothing when they returned home, putting his work ahead of his feelings for her, and keeping her as far away from his heart as possible.

And to no use.

He was too much in love with both the old and the new Charmaine to ever be able to let her go. And now, when she had tried to reach out to him, he had behaved worse than before, not listening to her at all, and humiliating her with his tasteless jokes.

He closed his eyes, leaning his forehead against the cold window. Sebastian had been right earlier when he said Sin ignored his wife. He had been doing that all his life, ever since he first laid eyes upon her and found her perfect.

What he should have done back then was to stop his hiding and instead told her just how adorable he found her. Maybe they still wouldn't have been an item, but at least he would have done the honest thing toward both of them.

Lost in his musings, eyes still shut, he never saw Lord Nester enter the garden, smiling cruelly as he saw Sin standing still in full view. Quietly his father-in-law lifted the gun he carried, aiming at his easy target.

The window broke as the bullet went through it, and Sin spun around as it hit him. With a groan of pain he fell out through the now windowless frame and down into the cold snow. With a shudder, his large body became still, and slowly a puddle of blood built under him, growing larger by the minute. Small snowflakes fell on him, trying to cover his unmoving body.

Lord Nester walked up to his victim and kicked him hard in the side, but Sin was gone and didn't make a sound.

"Now she's mine," the attacker hissed before hurrying back into the garden, his mad laughter echoing behind him.

When the servants came crashing through the door, Lord Nester was long gone, and later, when the Chester Park hunters went out with their dogs to search for the perpetrator, all footprints had disappeared under the newly fallen snow, and there was no scent left for the bloodhounds to catch.

It was as if the cold hand of a ghost had touched Chester Park.

Chapter Fourteen

Sitting silently in the same chair where she had spent the last four weeks, Charmaine stared teary-eyed at her husband. Heavy curtains on the windows effectively hid the fact that spring had arrived and that it was already a week into the month of March.

"Please wake up," she whispered, as she had so many times before, but as always he didn't stir, his breathing never changing its pace.

"It's a lovely day outside. Why don't you leave this room for a while?" Lady Newbury entered the room and laid a hand on Charmaine's shoulder before going to her son and putting a light hand on his cheek as she had done every day since the day he was shot.

Charmaine shook her head. "No."

"You should go out. Or at least do something else. Spend some time with your sister."

"No."

Lady Newbury sighed. "Who am I fooling? We have been sitting in here for a month now, you and me, and had the same conversation every day, and yet we both know that neither of us will leave."

Charmaine smiled, amused against her will. "Not until someone drags us out of here, at least."

"Poor George," Lady Newbury breathed. "He's been so supportive and strong in spite of what has happened, but this is really beginning to get to him. He said today it feels he's not only lost his son but also his wife. But I just can't leave Sinclair. What if he wakes up and needs me and I'm not here?"

Charmaine swallowed hard. "He thinks we've lost Sin?"

Lady Newbury nodded, dabbing at her eyes with a wrinkly handkerchief, one already soaked with hundreds of tears. "He's been so angry lately, and last night he lost his temper completely, shouting like a maniac, finally putting words to his anxiety. He's so afraid Sinclair will die that he can't even come in here and look at him in this condition."

"So that's why he's never been here?"

"It's too hard for him. He can't stand the thought of losing Sinclair, so instead he pretends everything is fine. The explosion was bound to happen sooner or later, and I'm glad it finally did. Now I can talk to him, share my feelings and listen to his."

Charmaine's gaze moved to her husband again, following every handsome line of his face with her eyes, and something cold grabbed her heart.

"Do *you* think he will…" She took a deep breath, too afraid to openly say what had tormented her since the shooting. "Do you think he will die?"

Lady Newbury sat down beside her, grasping her cold hands firmly. "No, I don't. You know what the good doctor said, that Sinclair wasn't that badly injured. The bullet barely grazed his temple, and even though he bled quite a lot at first, the coldness of the snow stopped the bleeding before it was too late."

"But?"

Lady Newbury let go of Charmaine's hand and lifted her handkerchief to wipe away the telling tears running down her cheeks. "But what if he doesn't wake up? What if he will continue to lie here like this for the rest of his life? Or worse, what if he wakes up as a different man? I've heard tales of how head injuries can change a man—and you should know, Charmaine, that it's never for the better."

The picture Lady Newbury painted was indeed awful, and Charmaine could understand the countess's agony. How could you ever decide what was better for your own child? To die or to a live a life in dire sickness?

Subconsciously Charmaine put a hand protectively against her belly as she thought of the small life growing inside of her. She had been shaken when she finally understood why she had been so tired lately, but the following nausea had offered her the truth. She was expecting Sin's baby.

Nobody knew about her condition, and she wasn't about to tell anyone, either, not even Penelope, who was the reason for her awakening to the fact she was pregnant. Her sister had just found out herself she was expecting, and constantly informed Charmaine about how she was feeling and what she had learnt about such things.

She knew Penelope probably would be quite vexed when she learnt Charmaine hadn't shared her secret, but she wanted Sin to be the first to know, and she would tell him as soon as he woke up.

If he woke up.

When he woke up, she corrected herself mentally, determined not to give in to the negative thoughts that kept disturbing her optimism.

"We can't give up now." She put an arm around

Lady Newbury's slender shoulders, offering her sympathy and extra strength. "We both know in our hearts that he will come back to us. He just needs his time to heal first."

Lady Newbury leaned her cheek against Charmaine's, patting the opposite cheek with her hand. "Thank you, my dear, for being here for Sinclair, but mostly for being here for me. I don't know how I ever would have gone through these last weeks without you. Really, I don't."

Charmaine felt the old lump in her throat as her mother-in-law's open affection washed over her. She wasn't used to someone showing her emotions, not real ones.

Her parents had both loved her, but it had been a different kind of love. Her stepfather had been obsessed with her, whilst her mother had been protective of her. Penelope loved her dearly, but if she was honest with herself Charmaine knew it was more because Penelope thought she was supposed to love her sister than actually loving her for the person she was.

Even though Sin didn't love her, she had now and then almost thought that maybe he did. But that still wasn't a true love. It was her wishing too hard for something until she almost could persuade herself that it was there.

But Lady Newbury was different.

Caroline Darling did care for her, for being the person she was. She hadn't had the strength to put up a façade while sitting at Sin's sickbed, and therefore her mother-in-law had met someone no one else ever had, the true Charmaine. And to Charmaine's surprise it seemed Lady Newbury liked that version of her very much.

The first week at Sin's bed they hadn't talked at all, only sat there, side by side, staring at his pale face, both secretly praying for his eyes to open and for the apparent agony to go away.

The second week, Sin had stopped looking as if he was in deep pain, and his new angelic look had them both so relieved they had almost smiled at each other. Almost.

The third week had started with them talking lightly about the weather and ending with Lady Newbury telling Charmaine every memory she had of Sin, from her pregnancy until the day he was shot. She couldn't have found a more interested audience anywhere.

When the fourth week arrived, they were completely at ease with each other, and even though Charmaine still kept to herself her stepfather's obsession with her and her fear that he was the one responsible for shooting Sin, there were no other barricades between them anymore.

"I wouldn't want to be anywhere else but here."

Lady Newbury nodded, teary-eyed. "In some strange way I'm glad this happened. Not that Sinclair got shot, mind you, but that I shared this with you and, in between all the tears and all the ripped handkerchiefs, got to know you."

Charmaine laughed softly. It was a hoarse and squeaky sound, but still it was a laugh. "I know exactly what you mean, and I must admit that I too am glad I got to share this with you. Thank you."

"No, my child, thank *you*. If you hadn't kept ignoring me while I treated you with all the contempt in the world, we would never have come this far. I was such a wreck…"

"Yes, you were."

Lady Newbury snorted with laughter. "You don't have to agree with me."

"You are a mother with a son who almost died. Of course I can overlook your rash behavior and lingering, nasty looks."

Lady Newbury shook her head. "Lord, just thinking about how I acted those first days makes me blush with mortification. I'm so sorry for letting my fears overcome me, but you were the only one there, and I was too full of weary feelings to be able to keep it all bottled up inside of me."

"I'm still glad you did. It gave us something to talk about when you had calmed down."

"That's true. I spent days trying to explain myself to you, without making any sense."

Charmaine laughed again. "You did appear a bit frantic, but in the end I caught the apology."

"She *apologized* to you?"

Sebastian walked into the bedroom, interrupting the intimate moment, and Charmaine immediately hid behind her mask to hide her true feelings from the one man who seemed able to see right through her.

"What about my apologizing got you so riled up?" Lady Newbury said with a roll of her eyes toward Charmaine.

Sebastian grinned mischievously as he sat down in the last empty chair. "You apologized. In my world, that's something so rare you can spend a lifetime waiting for it and never see it with your own eyes. You just hear tales from others who claim they know someone who knows someone who heard you utter the word 'Sorry.'"

"I beg your pardon," Lady Newbury huffed. "I do apologize now and then, but only when it's deserved."

"You've never apologized to me."

"Which says more about you than about me."

Sebastian's grin deepened. "*Touché*. I have to give you that. I must admit there haven't been many times when I honestly can say it wasn't my fault, or partly my fault, things happened."

"You are an imp, my son."

"So you keep saying." Sebastian leaned back in his chair, looking so much the blasé dandy that Charmaine had to bite her lip not to laugh at him. "But then everyone always keeps saying how much I remind them of you, so what does that make you, then?"

"You *look* like me, not act like me."

"I beg to differ." Sebastian's green eyes danced with mirth. "Even Charmaine here will have to agree with me, after sharing the same home with you for a couple of months, when I claim that you are not the proper and conceited matriarch you think you are."

"I *think* I am?" Lady Newbury gasped before Charmaine had a chance to come up with a witty reply to his disrespectful bickering. "You know as well as I do that I'm not so fond of people pretending to be something they are not, and yet you sit there claiming I am? Sebastian, that was low, even for you."

"*Even* for me?" He mimicked her earlier gasp. "How utterly rude of you to imply I'm going too far when you have the nerve to sit there pretending to like Charmaine, when she stands for everything you dislike, being the queen of disguise as she is."

"What are you talking about?" Lady Newbury sighed, not following her son's train of thought.

"Our Impeccable Queen here, who pretends she is the coldest, most heartless chit who ever walked across a Polite Society ballroom."

"Sebastian…"

He ignored his mother, instead leaning closer to Charmaine, nailing her with his green eyes that had lost all their previous mirth. A shiver ran down her spine as she met his probing gaze.

What was his game? What was it he was searching for? Desperately she strained every muscle she could to stay as serene as possible and keep her blue eyes cold and empty of emotion.

"Do you really think I'll fall for that, my dear sister-in-law? Haven't you realized I see through you?" Sebastian asked.

"Sebastian Darling!"

"Yes, Mother?"

"Stop harassing poor Charmaine. She's had the worst time of her life lately and doesn't need you bothering her with your antics."

"I don't harass. I asked one very simple question. Why are you pretending to be worse than you are?"

He wiggled pointedly with his eyebrows without letting his eyes leave Charmaine's face. Her back ached from the stress of trying to remain unmoved and seemingly untouched. His words reminded her entirely too much of the duchess's question at the beginning of Charmaine's marriage to Sin.

Why is a good girl like you pretending to be a bad girl?

Lady Newbury stood up and stepped in front of

Charmaine, effectively blocking her from Sebastian's probing eyes. "Stop it. She's not up for this right now. She needs her strength and her thoughts where they belong, with Sin. Not with his lunatic younger brother who seems to have lost his common sense."

"Ask her."

"Ask her what?"

Charmaine wanted to sigh with frustration. *Give up*, she thought. *Let it be. Just get out of here and leave me alone.*

But Sebastian was like a bloodhound who had found a trace. He knew he was on the right track, and he was not going to let his victim go. "Ask her why she's hiding her true self from everyone, including Sin."

"Sebastian..."

"Ask her!" he interrupted, and to Charmaine's utter horror Lady Newbury sighed, defeated, and sat down in the chair she had left moments ago.

"All right," she breathed, with another roll of her eyes. "Charmaine, I'm sorry for bothering you with this, but my son—the idiotic one, that is—thinks you are hiding yourself behind a mask..."

"Disguise," Sebastian corrected.

"Behind a disguise," Lady Newbury repeated, with her umpteenth roll of eyes as Sebastian gave her an approving nod. "And he would like to know why you are."

"Thank you."

Sebastian leaned forward and gave Lady Newbury a peck on the cheek before sitting back, crossing his arms and legs, and continuing to stare at Charmaine.

"Oh, for goodness' sake," his mother mumbled.

"The things I do for these children... The things I do..."

Again silence ruled the large bedroom as mother and son gazed expectantly at her, and Charmaine wanted to scream with frustration, since she couldn't simply throw them out of the room. But as always she backed down and hid behind her wall, as she had done so many times before in a desperate attempt to save herself from her father.

"You can start to talk now," Sebastian urged after a few minutes during which she hadn't said a word.

"May I enquire about what I am supposed to speak?" she asked, making sure to sound as haughtily polite as she possibly could.

"Now you are stalling." Sebastian flashed another amused grin.

"I'm not stalling."

"Yes, you are."

"No, I am not."

"Yes, you are."

"No, I a—" Charmaine shut her mouth, sending her obnoxious brother-in-law an annoyed glance.

"Why are you, my dear Charmaine, insisting on keeping up the appearance of being heartless and selfish, when we all know you are anything but? Your sister has been telling us this for years, but we never cared enough about you to find out the truth ourselves, not until you married one of us."

"Sebastian!" Lady Newbury glared aghast at her youngest son, but he merely shrugged.

"It's the truth. We didn't care about her."

"I know we didn't, and I don't disagree with you about it." Lady Newbury smiled apologetically toward

Charmaine. "But you don't have to be so straightforward about it, either, now, do you?"

"I don't mind straightforwardness," Charmaine admitted before she could stop herself and immediately Sebastian started to glow with satisfaction.

"See!" he beamed. "You are a Darling, whether you like it or not."

"What has me being a Darling to do with me being a cold, heartless chit?" She bit back another smile as Sebastian blushed slightly, not so comfortable with getting his own words thrown straight at him.

"Nothing, really." He squirmed. "It's just me sharing my opinion. And my opinion is that you should let the disguise go. Mother doesn't like dishonest people, and most of us are in full agreement. Uncle Charles is not, of course."

"Of course," Charmaine repeated meekly, starting to feel dizzy and quite overwhelmed. Not a unique feeling when it came to the Darling family's illogical logic.

"Uncle Charles has a tendency to like everybody. We don't know where he got such a treacherous attitude, but Grand-Papa swears Charles is his son and that there is no chance he could have been sired from another man's loins."

Charmaine shook her head, not knowing whether to laugh or cry. Having a discussion with a member of the Darling family was like banging your head against a stone wall, over and over and over again.

There was just no way to win, given the variety of rabbit trails they used in their arguments.

Penelope had told her so many anecdotes over the years, about different "discussions" she had overheard when at Chester Park, and to Charmaine they had sounded strange and yet so disturbingly attractive. This family's bluntness toward each other had seemed perfect. No lies, no hidden agendas. Just the truth, preferably used to hit hard on someone else's head.

"So now, when we finally have reached through the disguise, we will go back to the original question," Sebastian drawled. "Why are you pretending to be something you are not?"

With a deep sigh, Charmaine gave up. "Aren't we all pretending to be something we are not, in one way or another? I have a tendency to hide my emotions, and if that makes me seem like a heartless chit, so be it."

"But it's not who you are!" Lady Newbury grabbed Charmaine's cold hand in hers again. "You are such a sweet girl, with a heart of gold. Why have everyone think you are not? It doesn't make you any friends."

"But it saves me from attention I don't crave."

"From whom?" As always, Sebastian nailed the central question, and if this hadn't been such a stressful conversation to her she might have applauded him for his understanding. But just the thought of admitting to these two that her stepfather, curse his black heart, was in love with her and wanted her for his wife was too embarrassing to speak out loud. The mere thought of it made her squirm with discomfort.

"From unwanted suitors who don't take no for an answer," she replied instead, not a lie but not the whole truth either. Fortunately, both Lady Newbury and Sebastian seemed satisfied with the answer.

"Oh, my dear child," Lady Newbury breathed compassionately. "Of course you must have had your share of unwanted attention, considering the vast number of men constantly surrounding you. I remember a dear friend who made her debut the same year I did. She had a man who became completely obsessed with her. He followed her everywhere, even breaking into her home, stealing some of her things, including clothing. She turned into a shivering shadow of the once happy girl she had been, just because one man couldn't take no for an answer."

"How can anybody become so attracted to one woman that he would be unable to leave her alone?" Sebastian frowned, and Lady Newbury smiled toward him as only a mother could.

"And there we have the answer to the question of whether you have ever been in love."

Sebastian stared at her in confusion. "Whatever are you talking about? Of course I've been in love. I fall in love every week with some new alluring creature."

"Never been in love," Lady Newbury mouthed to Charmaine, ignoring her son's irritation.

"I have too been in love."

"No, you haven't."

"Stop that snorting, Mother. It doesn't suit you at all. And, by the way, how would you even know what I feel, when you can't read what's in my heart?"

"I know you. You are my son, and I carried you under my heart. There is nothing you can hide from me. Nothing!"

"I beg to differ…"

Charmaine looked at the arguing mother and son, and a warm feeling started to grow in her heart. All her life she had been surrounded by people who claimed to love and adore her, yet she had always felt unloved and on the outside. But these two, and the rest of their large, colorful family, handled her with the same warm contempt as they did all their family members, and somehow it made her feel like she belonged.

Like she was a part of the family.

Her own parents had always treated her as if she were special and put her on the highest pedestal they could find. They had constantly worshipped her, telling her again and again that they couldn't believe they had such a magnificent offspring.

But the Darlings didn't treat her differently, and she liked that immensely. She liked being liked. She liked being a part of something bigger.

But now and then she couldn't help wishing there were some place she could have some privacy, where she could be alone. She desperately needed peace and quiet and time to think things through.

During her childhood she had been constantly surrounded by her parents and the servants, and now as a married woman she was always surrounded by her husband's large family. And if she tried to hide in her bedroom there was always someone who sought her out, mostly Penelope.

Charmaine sighed heavily.

Penelope was the dearest sister and friend anyone could wish for, but—to be completely honest—she was a bit too intrusive now and then.

Or most of the time.

She looked at Sin where he lay still in the bed, and she sighed again. The sad truth was she would never be able to have the solitude she wanted. She was married to Sin, and he was the heir, the one destined to take over and run this monstrous house when his father and grandfather had passed on. As his wife, she would be expected to act as hostess and matriarch.

It was Sin's destiny, and she would of course stand by his side when that time came. But it could take years upon years. Hannibal was over seventy years old but in perfect health and would probably outlive most of them. At his demise it would be Sin's father, George, Lord Newbury, who was first in line to take over the dukedom and the responsibilities, not Sin.

But it was Sin who already had stepped forward, running the large estate perfectly even though he didn't have to. And Charmaine had to admit it vexed her a bit, the thought that it didn't have to be like this. Sin could back down if he wanted to, and they could have the life she desperately wanted. They could move to a smaller house, have a home of their own where she finally could find peace and not feel huddled all the time.

But it would never happen.

If Sin woke up again he would want to go back to where they had been before, with him politely ignoring her and her feeling alone and abandoned.

"He will wake up again."

Charmaine nodded, with a faint smile which must have shown how unbelieving she was, and Lady Newbury stared hard at her. "He *will* wake up again."

"If I were you, Charmaine, I would listen to her. She's his mother, and he would never dare to do something to vex her." Sebastian's eyes sparkled mischievously, and she couldn't help but giggle. His mother was right, he was an imp. A handsome, redheaded, wonderful imp, and she was so grateful he now was her brother, her friend, and her confidant.

"I know he will," Charmaine answered her mother-in-law, ignoring Sebastian's not-too-gentle bickering.

"It's the not knowing when he will wake that is the hardest to cope with. If I could know it will happen tomorrow, or next week, or even next month, it would be easier, because then we would all see an end to this. But as it is now, we can only sit here waiting, day in and day out."

"Which brings me to why I came here in the first place," Sebastian said to his mother. "Father wants your presence in the library. It was something about your plans for the upcoming Season which he disagrees with."

Lady Newbury sighed as she rose and stepped toward the door. "He is always disagreeing with me when it comes to the Season. If I didn't know better, I would think he doesn't want to attend."

"Of course he doesn't want to attend!" Sebastian looked just like his mother when he rolled his eyes toward her slender back. "London is so much better off-season. You know, when we aren't forced to go to balls, dinner parties, and boring music soirées every bloody night."

"No one is forcing you."

He snorted loudly enough that she stopped in the doorway and sent him a patronizing look that made his shoulders slump, and with a deep sigh he followed her meekly.

"All right, all right," he mumbled as he passed her, and Charmaine managed to keep herself from laughing until after the door closed behind them.

Those two were too much alike to ever avoid arguing about everything, but Charmaine had a feeling neither of them minded. They thrived in their constant battle with words and rolling eyes.

She sent a sympathetic thought to poor Lord Newbury, who had such a wayward family to keep up with. But then again, she didn't think he minded. He always looked at his wife and three children with more love than she had seen shown by any other man of his standing.

Sin had such wonderful loving parents, and she knew in her heart he would be just as wonderful and loving a parent toward their child. He would love their little boy or girl with all his heart, and never would he let the baby feel as unwanted and unappreciated as she always had.

She put a hand on her still-flat belly, longing for when it would grow and become larger and larger because of the baby growing bigger. Not able to withstand the longing, she stood and went to the large mirror, looking at herself from the side. She drew the dress closer to her body to see if there was a little bump. But no, she was as flat as ever.

Not able to resist the temptation, she rushed to the sofa and grabbed up a cushion and put it quickly under her dress, casting nervous glances toward the closed door all the while. Immediately she looked different, with a large swollen bump on her middle, and the lump in her throat grew larger as her heart rejoiced at what was to come. She was going to have a baby.

"Is this your subtle way of telling me I'm about to become a father?"

Charmaine stiffened and let the cushion drop to the floor. Slowly she turned, too afraid she had dreamt hearing the beloved voice. As her gaze fixed on the bed, she met the tired eyes of her husband.

Chapter Fifteen

"You're awake," she breathed, and he frowned slightly.

"Of course I'm awake."

"Are you really awake?"

"Charmaine, please stop that squeaking. My head hurts like hell. And yes, I am perfectly sure that I am awake. Oof!"

His arms automatically hugged her closer as she threw herself on him. Her eyes burnt as she dug her nose down deep into his neck, marveling over the sensational feeling of having him hold her again.

"My, my!" He chuckled. "One could think I've been asleep for days, not hours."

"One month."

She felt him tense slightly and knew it was better to blurt out the truth instead of letting him wonder. "You've been asleep for almost a month, ever since the day you were shot."

"What? I was shot?"

She sat up so she could look into his dark eyes. Confusion filled them as he dragged a hand through his hair.

"Yes, you were."

"By whom?"

She hesitated slightly before answering. "They don't know. Someone sneaked up outside your study and shot you through the window."

He sat up beside her, looking down at his hands. "Was I hurt?"

"Yes, you were shot in the head." She lifted her hand, caressing the small scar on his temple. "Right there."

His fingers moved over the scar, and she could see he had a hard time grasping the truth.

"Maybe I shouldn't have said something," she said, anxiety filling her heart. "Maybe I should have stayed quiet and let you come around slowly."

"No. I'm grateful that you did tell me. Now I have a chance to think this through a bit by myself before the storm comes down upon us."

She frowned at him. "The storm?"

He grinned, just as mischievously as his younger brother had a little while ago. "Mother."

Ah. His grin deepened as she smiled back toward him, and she threw herself into his arms again, not able to stand being so far from him now that he finally was awake.

"So are you?" he whispered softly into her ear.

"Am I what?"

"Pregnant?"

She felt him hold his breath as if her answer meant everything to him. "Yes."

Howling like a madman he rolled her down into the bed, putting himself on top of her, kissing her face wherever he could reach. She laughed as he howled again, and his apparent happiness sent shivers of delight through her heart.

It was so perfect.

This was how she had pictured it, the radiant joy he

would feel when enlightened about her wonderful news. A memory of how Francesca had been abandoned by her husband, the Duke of Hereford, after telling him about expecting his baby, came to Charmaine. Then it hadn't meant anything to her, but now, as she herself had had the pleasure to tell her own husband she was expecting their baby, she suddenly understood how utterly mortified Sin's sister must have been. To her it had been the best day ever, until her husband had thrown it all in her face.

She looked into Sin's shiningly happy eyes and felt the ice surrounding her frozen heart melt a little. In this moment of shared marital bliss everything was perfect, but she knew it soon would change. It always had before.

He would change.

It still hurt how he had cast her aside after their return to Chester Park. She was grateful for her old walls, which she immediately had put up again, saving herself from the pain she felt when he dissociated himself from her.

He kissed her again, this time on the mouth, and she couldn't hold back a grimace as his foul breath washed her face.

"Smells like flowers, I presume?" he grinned, and she wrinkled her nose a bit more.

"Rotten such."

"I think I do need to clean up a bit. But I'm starting to feel a bit weary, and I think I need to rest for a minute."

He lay back on the bed again, and she sat up, immediately starting to fuss over him, straightening his pillow, smoothing out the bedspread. He grabbed her hand and put it against his chest, on top of his steadily beating heart, before closing his eyes and slowly drifting back to sleep.

Breathlessly she sat there, waiting for him to do something or move slightly to show he was only sleeping, not back in his coma. But he merely lay there, breathing evenly, and in the end she couldn't stand it—she pinched him, hard.

"What?" he growled, turning over to his side, and she immediately scooted close to his back and put her arms around him.

"I just wanted to see if you were alive."

"That hurt!"

"I know. Sorry."

He grabbed her hands against his chest and let his thumbs caress her soft skin. "I will wake up again, I promise."

"You'd better."

He chuckled before drifting back into sleep, but even though the same fear came over her, she didn't pinch him again. Instead she waited a while before slipping out of the bed and sneaking out of the bedroom.

She had to stand still in the hallway for a few minutes before walking down to the library, where she found Lord and Lady Newbury in the midst of a heated argument regarding how necessary it was for them to partake in the social season of the *ton* which was to start in a mere month's time.

"Ah, Charmaine, thank you for arriving so perfectly," Lady Newbury breathed with relief as she joined them. "Tell my husband we have to go to London this year, too. Sebastian still needs us!"

Lord Newbury snorted loudly. "No, *you* need to be there for Sebastian. He definitely doesn't need you there. We all know how you tend to interfere, completely without common sense."

Lady Newbury gasped, outraged. "I. Beg. Your. Pardon! How can you say such a thing? I am your wife, and you love me. You should praise to the sky my ability to care for our children instead of showing this odd resistance to my being there for them."

"Emma Archer."

Charmaine stared, just as dumbfounded as Lady Newbury, at her father-in-law. Emma was one of her best friends. Or maybe calling her a best friend was a bit too much. They had used each other, back when Charmaine needed a shield against her suitors and her stepfather. Emma had needed the attention of Charmaine's surplus suitors. Charmaine knew she hadn't behaved too nicely toward Emma and their other friend, Lady Victoria Knightley, but she had been too uptight, too scared over what her stepfather might be up to. And too devastated over how her own life, including the choice of Lord Dane, was out of her hands.

"What about Emma?" Lady Newbury asked, but then a memory must have come to her, as she became fiery red and all her fighting spirit disappeared. "Oh."

"Exactly my point," Lord Newbury said with a smug smile. "I don't think I need to clarify myself more."

Lady Newbury shook her head. "No, you don't. But then again, the Emma situation was one slip. *One*. I will never do the same mistake twice."

"No, you will do others, just as embarrassing for Sebastian."

Charmaine looked from one spouse to the other, her mind racing. What had Lady Newbury done? Something embarrassing for Sebastian, she understood, but exactly what? That they had named it the Emma situation told her it had been something to talk about.

As far as Charmaine knew, Emma was still unmarried and still without a breath of scandal close to her name, so it couldn't have been something Sebastian did. Which left Lady Newbury.

In the end, she couldn't stand not knowing, and against her better judgment she cleared her throat and interrupted the discussion. "What happened?"

Lord and Lady Newbury stopped their arguing and looked at her blankly. "What 'what' happened?"

Charmaine closed her eyes briefly. "*What* is the Emma situation?"

"You don't know what she did?" Lord Newbury seemed quite pleased to impart the news. "I'll tell you what she did. My dear wife, whom most people think of as a sane and compassionate woman…"

"I *am* sane and compassionate."

"No, my love, you are not. Stop interrupting me."

"I am not interrupting you!"

Lord Newbury chuckled, shaking his head. "Maybe not, but you are certainly stalling the subject."

Lady Newbury opened her mouth, ready to disagree, but closed it again with an unappreciative snort her husband quite wisely chose to ignore.

"My sometimes sane and compassionate wife more or less forced the poor girl to ask Sebastian to escort her to last year's Green Park Picnic."

Charmaine frowned. "Which is not very good…why?"

"Your dear mother-in-law, the very one who sits there blushing, made the girl think Sebastian was in love with her but too shy to do anything about it."

"Oh."

"Exactly."

"And to make things even worse," Lady Newbury interjected, not able to let her husband tell the story by himself, "our dear daughter blurted it all out to the girl during the occasion, completely destroying the poor girl's heart."

"Now you are exaggerating a bit much, my dear," Lord Newbury interjected. "Emma wasn't the one in love with Sebastian. She thought he was in love with her."

Charmaine, who had spent most of her socializing time with Emma, knew the girl was deeply in love with Sebastian. Lady Newbury's little white lie must have been devastating for her. She tried to remember if Emma had said anything about it, but last year was all a blur to her. Her primary concern last season had been—other than her stepfather's unwanted attention—her feelings for Lord Dane, and the loss of him.

The thought of her loneliness then versus her happiness now brought back to her mind the real reason for her to have searched out her parents-in-law. "He's awake!" she squealed, and at first they just looked at her, dumbfounded. But as the truth hit them, Lord Newbury took a staggering step backwards, stumbling into a sofa, on which he sat down with a thud.

Tears sprung into his gray eyes, so much like Sin's.

"Are…are you sure?"

Lady Newbury's fingers grasped Charmaine's arm so hard she would probably have bruises. But she didn't mind, as the ecstatic joy in the mother's face was reward enough.

"He's sleeping again, but not in a coma, I assure you," she rushed to explain, as both parents paled visibly at the thought of losing him before having the chance of having him back. "He quickly became quite worn out, but he's been unconscious for a month, so it's not so strange."

"Was he…" Lady Newbury's voice trailed off, but Charmaine knew what she was thinking, as their earlier conversation was fresh in her mind.

"He was his usual self, although, I have to admit, a bit more smiling."

"Good Lord," Lord Newbury said, his eyes twinkling as he looked at his wife. "How will we ever be able to deal with this—a smiling Sinclair?"

"Oh, shush." His loving wife scowled at him but without her usual heat, before turning to Charmaine with a relieved sigh. "Thank you for telling us. Can I see him?"

It took Charmaine a second to realize that Lady Newbury was asking for her permission to see her son.

"Of course you can. He's sleeping, but it only takes a hard pinch to wake him up."

Lord Newbury grinned. "You know this because you've tried it?"

She smiled sheepishly. "He looked as if he were unconscious again, and I just wanted to make sure… He was most understanding about it, I assure you."

"Well, let's go and pinch him, my dear," Lord Newbury said to his happily smiling wife and held out his arm for her to take. Seconds later, Charmaine was alone in the library, staring absentmindedly at the door through which they'd disappeared.

He was awake.

She swallowed hard again as she sat down, unable to continue standing, as her legs kept wobbling. The truth had finally caught up with her. Her husband, who had been unconscious for a month after being shot by her stepfather, had come back to life. And so far he was without any direct changes regarding his sanity such as his mother had feared.

She knew Sin soon would forget to smile at her, again ignore her for his ledgers. She would go back to staying out of everyone's way, desperately trying to forget how wonderful life was when he forgot to distance himself from her.

She was deeply in love with him, and she knew there was no way she would ever be able to leave him. She needed to be near him, to look into his dark eyes and maybe one day see him look back at her with at least a bit of the love which filled her heart and soul.

Oh, she knew he cared for her. He was too good a man not to. She was his wife, after all, and he knew that as a good husband he had to cherish her. But he didn't love her, not the way she wanted him to. Not the way she needed him to.

And now she was carrying his baby. Automatically she put her hands against her belly, caressing the little life inside her. A little life which made it all worthwhile, all the sacrifices she had made until now and all the ones she would make until the day she died.

The sound of running steps woke her from her gloomy thoughts, and she had just enough time to remove her hands before Penelope came rushing through the door, looking ready to explode.

"Is it true?" she squealed when she saw Charmaine. "Did he wake up? Did he really?"

Charmaine nodded and had just time enough to brace herself before her sister threw herself around her neck and hugged her fiercely, tears streaming down her cheeks. It had always amazed her how different they were, even though they had the same parents.

Penelope lived with her heart on her sleeve and her every emotion visible. And if anyone happened to miss what she felt, she always made sure they knew anyway.

Charmaine, on the other hand, had learnt the hard way to hold all her emotions hidden and never let anyone know what really was on her mind. She had more times than she could remember said and done things that were contrary to her will, her personality, and her better judgment, but what once had been born out of desperation had in the end become reality for her.

"What did he say? Did he remember what happened to him? Did he see the shooter?"

Charmaine laughed. "If you let me go so I can breathe, I promise you I'll try to answer your questions."

"Oh." Penelope giggled, her cheeks reddening slightly. With an apologizing grimace she loosened her grip around her sister's neck. "I'm so sorry. It's just that, when I heard, I couldn't think about anything else but how wonderful this must be for you—your husband has woken up!"

"It's the best thing," Charmaine admitted, and new tears started to fill Penelope's eyes as she listened with a soft little smile. "He scared me half to death when he talked to me from out of nowhere, but when I understood he was awake…"

She shook her head, unable to find the words to describe her emotions, but for once Penelope was able to read between the lines and simply patted her hand with another soft smile. But the smile soon went away as her thoughts came back to what had happened.

"Did he remember anything?"

"No. I had to tell him that he had been shot. I think Lord Newbury will tell him the rest of it. I have, as you know, been staying at his side day and night and am not so sure about what has happened with the hunt for the perpetrator."

Charmaine waited silently for her sister to enlighten her, but Penelope was too caught up in her own thoughts to notice her sister's subtle plea for information.

"Who would want to kill Sin? He is the kindest, most unselfish person I know. And to be completely honest, there's just one person who has anything to gain with him dead, and that is Sebastian, being next in line to the dukedom. But we all know that he doesn't want the responsibility or the title. All he wants is his brother."

Father wants him dead.

Oh, how she wanted to spring out her secret to her sister, share the burden with her. But she was so used to saving Penelope from it all that the mere thought of having to tell her not only that he wasn't their father by blood but also the one who had shot Sin… It made her nauseous.

She had to tell Sin, though. There was no more escape from it. Somehow she had to tell her husband that she wasn't the person he thought her to be and that she carried a deadly secret.

What would he think of her?

What kind of daughter made her stepfather fall in love with her? She could easily picture the disdain and the contempt which would erase any love he might have for her. It wouldn't surprise her in the least. No, she was already expecting his change toward her.

She just had to figure out a way to handle life when he dissociated himself from her. Because he would. She had not only lied to him all through their marriage. She had also hidden her stepfather's plans from him and by so doing had taken away his chance to defend himself.

She could never forgive herself, so how would he ever be able to?

"It's so strange, the whole thing." Penelope didn't notice how absentminded Charmaine was, as she was too caught up in her own erratic thoughts. "Rake told me someone had seen a man run from Chester Park at the time of the shooting, and they think it was the bastard who shot Sin."

"What did he look like?" Charmaine's heart beat faster. Could she be this lucky? Could someone have seen Lord Nester?

Penelope shrugged, with a sad sigh. "Too far away for details, I'm afraid. But the guess is that it's an older or sickly man, as he didn't move as smoothly as a younger or stronger man does. Which, to see something good in all of it, at least leaves Sebastian out of it."

"Leaves me out of what?"

Sebastian strolled in, his usually impish grin much tighter, without the devil-may-care air he'd had earlier. As always, he poured himself down into a chair, looking the perfectly bored dandy.

"Killing Sin."

"Penny!" Charmaine stared angrily at her sister.

"Well, it was what we were talking about, wasn't it?"

"You think I was the one who tried to kill Sin?" Sebastian seemed more amused than ever, but Charmaine could sense the chord of uneasiness in him.

"No, of course not," she said and sent her sister another angry look. "We were talking about the man who was seen running away from Chester Park and came to the conclusion that it couldn't have been you, as he wasn't as young as you."

"But until then you thought it was me?"

"No, of course not," she repeated, her frustration clearly visible in her strained voice. "I've never heard of this until Penny told me about it minutes before you came into the room. No one thinks you killed your brother."

"*He is dead?*"

"No, no…" Charmaine took a deep, calming breath. "He isn't dead! Do you really think I would have told you about it like this if he *had* died?"

This time the mirth in his eyes was without a shadow, and she cursed herself silently for falling so easily for his bait.

"You are such an imp."

"I know." He grinned. "My mother keeps saying that, at least twenty times every day."

The thought of Lady Newbury and her nagging motherhood brought another thought to her mind, and she blushed slightly for forgetting to tell him immediately. "He's awake!"

Sebastian froze and stared at her with his unreadable green eyes. "Sin?"

"Yes. Your parents are there now."

"Is it true? Is he really awake?"

She nodded, and for once she didn't hide her emotions but let him see the compassion she felt in her heart. She saw tears glisten in his eyes, setting them to sparkling even more, like beautiful emeralds in the sun.

"Can I…"

She waved with her hand, dismissing him. "Go."

"Oh, my." Penelope stared at the empty doorway. "I've never seen anyone move that fast, especially not Sebastian, who has made it into a game to never hurry anywhere. It drives his mother insane, you know."

"They really *do* love them, don't they?"

"Who?"

"Lord and Lady Newbury. They really do love their children."

Penelope frowned slightly. "Yes, they do, as do the duke and the duchess. It's what parents do. Love their children."

"Ours didn't."

Charmaine couldn't believe she'd just said it out loud. Seeing the shock in Penelope's face, she realized her sister too was just as stunned over Charmaine's unusual straightforwardness regarding a subject they had never discussed.

"Mother loved us."

"Did she?" Charmaine whispered, almost waiting for the earth to crack beneath her silk-clad feet. But nothing happened. Airing the truth she had avoided for years appeared not to be something affecting the ground.

Penelope took her time answering, as if she desperately didn't want to answer the wrong thing, now, when they finally were facing their childhood.

"I like to think she loved me, that I was special to her in some way. But to be honest, she wasn't a person who was openly affectionate, and so I can't say I know she loved me because of things she said or did. But in my heart I know she did."

"She never told me she loved me, either." Charmaine felt like the worst daughter ever for admitting the truth. But this was Penelope—her sister. Who else would ever understand?

"She loved you more than anything." Penelope's smile was small and sad. "Definitely more than she loved me, I'd say."

This was the perfect time to stop the openness, to once again step behind the wall and let the conversation end, burying the subject forever. But, for the first time ever, Charmaine didn't want the walls back up. Ever since she'd heard about their mother's death she had kept wondering the same thing over and over again. And when she'd found out she was pregnant…

She had to talk about it. Because, in the end, she didn't want her child to ever wonder if it was loved. She wanted her child to take her love for granted. She wanted her child to never think twice whether her mother would be there for her or not.

She wanted her child to feel loved.

"Maybe she loved me in the beginning, I don't know. But in the end I think I was only a burden for her."

"Of course you weren't a burden to her. How could you have been?" Penelope snorted. "She was beyond proud of you, which you should be aware of. She was always with you, the proud mama, standing there basking in the admiration you received."

"But she wasn't with me because she wanted to be. She was with me because she had to be. Because she wanted to save me."

"Save you? From what? A hefty admirer?" Penelope snorted again. "Come on, Charmaine, you can't believe in such nonsense. She loved you."

"No, Penny, she loved *you*. The sweet, uncomplicated daughter who never brought her grief or forced her to go places and do things even though her body ached."

Penelope stood and came over to her sister, giving her a hard stare. "Now you listen to me. I was there. I saw Mother, and I tell you this—she was as proud as she could get. She loved standing there, watching you being surrounded by all those adoring men. I don't think she ever thought of it as a burden to go with you, because she was just too bloody proud of you."

Charmaine opened her mouth to defend herself and explain exactly why she thought of herself as a burden, but she closed it promptly as Rake came into the room, looking both relieved and exasperated.

"There you are!" He grinned as his gray eyes found his wife. "I've been searching for you everywhere, and everyone has had a different opinion of where you might have hidden. Not one of them thought you were here, though, which indeed is a bit strange, considering your quite open love of this room."

"Have you heard the news?" Penelope opened her arms to her husband, and without hesitation he pulled her closer to him, not caring about the audience.

A year ago, Charmaine would have laughed out loud if anyone even had hinted that Rake would turn into this softhearted, openly affectionate husband. He had been *the* libertine of his time and not good husband material at all, despite his status as one of society's most eligible bachelors. But in his and Penelope's case, true love had changed everything, and now they were the happiest couple imaginable, even outdoing the Duke and Duchess of Hereford, which in itself was an accomplishment worth noting.

Charmaine loved her sister with all her heart and knew her feelings were returned in full, even though it was hard to understand why, considering how she and their parents had treated Penelope all these years, leaving her on the outside. It had never been her choice to do so, but it had felt necessary so Penelope wouldn't suffer under the cruel thumb of their stepfather as she had.

Lady Nester had once hinted how relieved she was at her husband's obvious disinterest in his younger daughter and that she only wished she could tell Penelope this. But then Lady Nester would have had to openly admit what her husband was up to, and as she hadn't done so even to Charmaine, she would never have done so to anyone else. Instead she had patted her younger daughter on the cheek with her usual sad smile and continued with her quest to keep her husband as far away from her elder daughter as possible.

But Penny had found love and a welcoming home with the Darlings, and in the end had married the love of her life and secured her place in the family officially. But, as she thought about it, Charmaine realized so had she, when she married Sin.

She looked at Rake smiling tenderly toward his wife as he nodded in response to her earlier question, and Charmaine felt her heart skip a beat as she realized that she trusted this man completely. She knew without a doubt that he would step up for her, too, and do anything for her.

But more importantly—he would listen to her if she told him about Lord Nester and his plan to kill Sin.

Rake might seem the worst tease and most wicked scoundrel there was, but that was just the façade he used to hide his true self. Or, rather, that he *had* used to hide behind, as everything changed when he fell in love with Penelope and opened up a small door in the wall for her.

"Indeed I have. The whole castle is talking about it. If this isn't the best occasion for a vast celebration, I don't know what would be."

Rake looked up and met Charmaine's gaze and smiled just as tenderly toward her as he had toward his wife, his brotherly love washing over her.

Trust him, her heart coerced her mind, and with a deep and shaky breath she braced herself for what she was about to do. Before she had a chance to change her mind or even to think twice about it, she opened her mouth and let the truth free.

"It was Father who shot Sin."

Chapter Sixteen

The library was silent as a tomb as Rake and Penelope stared at her—she bewildered and he frowning.

"Are you sure?" Rake asked, slowly releasing his wife as he focused on Charmaine. "I mean, how could you know, if you weren't there when it happened?"

She took a deep breath. "Because he told me so."

"Sin told you Father shot him?" Penelope stared at her with large, scared eyes. "But you just said he didn't remember anything from the shooting."

Her sister's obvious disbelief was getting to her, and Charmaine felt herself withdraw behind her secure walls again. This had been a mistake. She should have stayed quiet. Of course no one would believe her. What had possessed her to think they would?

"He told you before, didn't he?" Rake said, surprising her with understanding the truth just as she was about to coax them into believing they had misunderstood her. "He told you what he was about to do."

She nodded slowly, her heart racing as she waited for his verdict, waited for him to start shouting at her for not telling them sooner, so they at least could have had a chance to stop the shooting before it happened.

But Rake did neither.

He just sat there, silently staring at her. Behind

him, Penelope leaned back on the sofa, her hands unconsciously picking at the needlework on a pillow, completely destroying the intricate stitches forever.

"I don't understand," she whispered out into the air without looking at her husband or her sister. "Can someone please enlighten me what we are talking about? What was it you knew, Charmaine? What is it you know?"

"Did you know that he was going to shoot Sin?" asked Rake.

She shook her head intensely, feeling a sudden need to clarify herself. Desperately she wanted to rise to her own defense in the matter and maybe be able to make him understand. "No, I did not. I-I was told about him wanting to kill Sin, but neither how nor when. If I had known t-that…"

Rake reached out and grabbed her cold hands in his, and the sudden show of compassion and humanity almost did her in. "It was all for you, wasn't it?"

She nodded again.

"How long has this been going on?"

"A few years."

His eyes turned as cold as ice. "How long? When you were a little girl, too?"

"N-no. It wasn't like t-that then. H-he was just too obsessed then, too proud, and too interfering. He wanted to dress me up like a doll, decide what I was to wear and how my hair was combed. M-mother didn't like that, and she…"

Her voice trailed off as the words eluded her and she took a deep, shaky breath before continuing stoically, speaking as fast as she could to get it all out as quickly as possible. "Mother made sure he never was alone with me. If she couldn't be with me, she had her maid there, one who wouldn't let him dismiss her. She was quite successful, as he stopped coming to my room for a while, until I grew up and became a woman, and he…"

She shook her head. She couldn't say it out loud, it was just too embarrassing for her.

"I understand." Rake's voice was like a velvety blanket, snuggling her crying heart, comforting her. "You don't have to continue if you don't want to. I just need to ask you one thing—did he ever touch you?"

Again she shook her head, knowing exactly what he was asking her now that she was an experienced married woman. "No, he didn't."

"But he wanted to?"

"Yes."

Rake's grip around her hands hardened. "I could kill him."

She laughed quietly, a sad little laughter that never reached her eyes. "Believe me, I wouldn't blame you if you did."

"He's your father, for goodness' sake! This is not how a father behaves toward his child."

"No, he's not."

Charmaine froze as both she and Rake turned to look at Penelope, who had been forgotten in her corner of the sofa. She looked back at them with large, terrified eyes.

"What?" Rake looked ready to burst, and Penelope made a small, uncomfortable grimace toward him.

"He isn't our father. Not really. He's just the man who happened to marry our mother. Our real father died before I was born."

Charmaine couldn't believe what she heard. Penelope knew? Had she been desperately trying to hide the truth from someone who had known it all along?

"H-how…" was all she managed, and Penelope shrugged slightly.

"He told me."

"When?"

"When he left me at Lord Bolton's. I asked him how he, as my father, could do that to me—leave me—and he told me then that he wasn't my biological father."

"Why didn't you tell me?"

"Why didn't *you* tell *me*?" Penelope repeated with an arched eyebrow, not looking too happy with her older sister.

Charmaine didn't know what to think. A part of her was furious with her sister for not telling her, but then again—just as Penelope pointed out—she hadn't said a word either.

"I would have told you immediately if I'd had the chance right after it happened," Penelope continued. "But we never met again after Father left me at Lord Bolton's, not until you already were married to Sin, and by then I had forgotten all about it. It wasn't important to me anymore. All that mattered to me then was Rake."

Rake began pacing as if he couldn't think straight when he was still. "But why kill Sin? Why now? You two have been married for a couple of months already. If he didn't want you married to someone else, he should have interfered much earlier, or tried to kill Sin much earlier. What possessed him to do such a vile act now?"

"Mother died," Charmaine said quietly, and he stopped in front of her, frowning down at her.

"What has Lady Nester's death to do with your father's urge to kill?"

This was almost too embarrassing, but she had to continue telling the truth, the whole truth, and nothing but the truth. "Because then he became free."

"Free?" Penelope repeated. "Free to do what?"

"Free to marry me."

"Oh, my God." Rake sat down on the sofa again, looking unusually dumbfounded, for him. "Why didn't that thought cross my mind? Of course he wants to marry you. He's not your biological father, he's your stepfather. To a man in love, marriage suddenly becomes the ultimate goal."

He held out an arm toward his wife, and she immediately scooted in under it, leaning her cheek against his chest. She smiled ruefully as he placed small, absentminded kisses on her forehead while he mentally processed the information he had been given.

Charmaine felt almost buoyant.

She looked at her cuddling sister and brother-in-law and could hardly keep a giddy giggle to herself. It was as if telling them had removed the burden from her tired shoulders. Now someone else knew, and the problem was not only hers to tackle.

Rake's immediate understanding had helped, of course. If he had been even the slightest bit accusing or upset over her choices, she might have turned her back on them and made the conversation end long before any real admissions were out.

But neither he nor Penelope had been accusing her

at all or throwing hard words at her. Oh, her sister had not been too pleased with her secrecy and unwillingness to share, but she still hadn't put any blame on Charmaine. That she had done all by herself.

Sin still has to know.

The little voice in her head echoed what she in her heart knew was true, but in a strange way it didn't feel as bad anymore to have to come clean with her husband. She had managed to tell Rake without him becoming angry as a bee that had had his honey stolen.

But would Sin be as understanding? She didn't know. Rake and Sin might be close relatives, but they still were as different as night and day. Where Rake was easy and fun, Sin was dark and brooding.

Rake lived life, while Sin controlled life.

But still, she had to tell him. And then she would have to tell all the others of the Darling family. And someone would become angry with her. Someone would accuse her of hiding the truth, and she would have to take that, because the truth was simple—she had been hiding.

Both the truth and herself.

"Why didn't you tell Sin about this?" Rake's dark, smooth voice broke the silence and interrupted her thoughts. "Why didn't you tell him about the threat?"

"I-I didn't know h-how."

"He's your husband, Charmaine. Your husband! You should just have opened your mouth and told him."

She felt her eyes burn, tears desperately trying to escape now that the accusing finally had begun. "It's not that easy."

"How can it not be easy? It might have saved him from getting shot! How long did you know about your father's plans before he shot Sin?"

"A couple of hours."

Rake looked as if he couldn't believe what he heard. "You knew it for a couple of hours and you still didn't tell him about it? Charmaine, for goodness' sake!"

"I did try," she cried out, too upset over his resentment to be able to stop. "I told him that there was danger and that he had to stay indoors, but he didn't listen to me. He never listens to me."

Rake stared silently at her before surprising her with a small grin. "I'm sorry. It's Sin we are talking about. He doesn't listen to anyone about anything, so why would he listen to you when you are trying to warn him."

Penelope released herself from her husband's grip and moved over to her sister's side and put her arms around her, offering her compassion and love. "I'm so sorry, Charmaine. I should have been there for you, when we were at home, but I was too busy ranting about what I was missing out on, and I never once considered what our stepfather's inattentiveness to me gave you on the opposite hand."

Charmaine hugged her closer. "It's not your fault, Penny, so don't blame yourself. It is I who have been behaving wrongly to awake such emotions in him. Had I been a better daughter, this would never have happened. But I was too caught up in myself to consider what it did to Father and his feelings."

"Now wait a minute!"

Both sisters looked up at Rake, who hovered above them, glaring as they sat hugging each other on the sofa. "How can you even think you are to blame for your father's unhealthy feelings toward you?"

Charmaine let go of Penelope and put her hands on her knees, as she did when she was trying to compose herself and not let her troubled inside rule what was on the outside. "It is someone's fault, and if it's not mine, who is then to blame? Father? He can't help what's in his heart."

"Of course he can." Rake seemed ready to explode with frustration. "He's the adult, and you were the child. It doesn't matter what you did or what you said, or what you say or do now, he will always be the father figure and should act as such. Fall in love with your stepdaughter? Bloody hell! It doesn't matter how you look at it, he's the one who has done wrong—not you. A father should be there for his daughter and carry her on his uplifted hands, making sure her life will be light and easy. Not drag her into hell."

Penelope sighed softly as she looked up at her handsome, avenging husband. "Isn't he just divine?"

Charmaine couldn't hold back a smile as Rake stared aghast at his admiring wife, and she agreed, "He sure is."

"He must be the most adorable man ever born. Doesn't he remind you of a knight in shining armor the way he stands there, declaring the wrongs of the world to us?"

"Indeed he does," Charmaine again agreed, and giggled, amazingly relieved to be able to do so, as Rake glared at her. "Just the armor missing, I'd say."

"Are you two insane?"

Penelope ignored her husband's unintelligent input to the discussion, instead turning toward Charmaine with an excited smile. "I know where there is some knight's armor! It's just outside the duke's private study. If Rake puts that on…"

"Bloody hell!"

Penelope pursed her lips as she looked up at her furious husband. "What's the matter with you? Where did all your chivalry go?"

"Out the door," he snarled. "Soon to be followed by the rest of me if you don't stop this nonsense and instead concentrate on what's important."

"You are important to me," Penelope gasped, and Rake immediately calmed down, his eyes turning darker and hotter.

"Penny…"

"Rake?"

"You know that I love you very much."

"And I you."

"And you know how much I love our discussions."

"Me too."

"But could you shut up for a second and let me talk things through with your sister. Please?"

Penelope rolled her eyes heavenward. "I *am* discussing things with my sister, thank you very much."

Rake closed his eyes and took a deep, strengthening breath. "Penny, my love. What your sister just told us is horrifying, and you just can't start talking about love and butterflies instead of…"

"Knights."

"Pardon?"

"I was talking about love and *knights,* not butterflies. Please do continue."

Rake made a big show of rolling his eyes, but Charmaine could tell he was laughing at his wife and the mysterious way her head worked. Penelope did live with her head in the clouds now and then, but this time it wasn't by accident. Charmaine knew all the nagging came from wanting to soothe the subject and give her some time to breathe and calm down, as well as to calm Rake down and lessen the intensity.

She sent Penelope a grateful look, which her sister accepted with a graceful bow of her head before beckoning her husband to continue.

"As I was saying before my once-so-dear wife rudely interrupted me, you have done nothing wrong, Charmaine. Believe me when I say that all the blame is your father's."

"But I am the one who made him fall in love with me, and therefore it's my responsibility to act upon it."

"Who said so? Your stepfather?"

"Yes."

"And how on earth can his wrongdoings be your responsibility? It's like saying it's my fault that my father couldn't sire any daughters."

Charmaine smiled politely at his joke. She didn't know what to think. Her stepfather had told her over and over again during the last several years that she was the one who had misused her looks and made him unwillingly fall in love with her. And when she thought how everyone else seemed to do the same thing, falling in love with her from across a ballroom just because she was beautiful, her stepfather's words actually made sense to her.

The only one who hadn't fallen for her looks was Sin. And Rake, of course. And the rest of the Darling men. But otherwise, most men had been staring at her with stars in their eyes while scribbling down their names on her dance card.

All those proposals to her, a girl with no great dowry or good connections, had all come because of men wanting her for what she looked like—Beautiful. Astonishing. Magnificent.

Rake went down on his knee in front of her and forced her to look straight at him. "You are now my sister, and I want you to know that I have come to love you most dearly for the sweet and caring person that you are. And you have, in your own way, shown me you love me back by trusting me with this—with your secret. All I ask of you, now, is that you let me decide what to do next. I want to release you from the responsibility of your stepfather's actions and for once give the man some resistance."

"Please, Charmaine," Penelope inplored, getting down on her knees beside her husband. "Both you and I have suffered in our different ways because of him. We deserve to be happy, you and I. We shouldn't be this afraid of opening up to others, and especially not so afraid of falling in love. You know how I struggled with my feelings for Rake, and I almost lost him because of being too insecure, thanks to Father never showing me I was worthy of his love or anyone else's love."

"What my longwinded wife is trying to tell you"—Rake grinned as he gave an amused glance at his wife—"is to let go. Leave your stepfather to me and get on with your life. You have a husband who just woke up from being unconscious for a month. Go and be with him. I will take care of your stepfather, and then you will never have to worry about him again. I promise."

Charmaine put a hand against her mouth as she felt her lips starting to tremble. Rake's warmth and gentle probing was becoming too much for her, and the pain in her throat and chest was spreading through her whole body, until she felt quite dizzy from the chaos of her emotions.

"I don't know how to let go," she managed to whisper, and Rake put his hand against her cheek with the most love-filled smile she had ever seen. But before he had a chance to answer, a voice was heard from behind them.

"You don't need to know how to. That's what family is for."

The threesome looked, startled, toward the door, where the duke and duchess stood with Lord and Lady Newbury. All four looked worn and heartbroken, and Lady Newbury was crying openly.

"Have you been eavesdropping?" Rake snarled, taken by surprise.

"If you don't want anyone to overhear your conversations, you should make sure you have closed the door completely before you start them." The duke left the doorway and walked briskly across the room, his hard eyes not once leaving Charmaine's face, and she shivered in response to the verbal lashing she knew she would get.

She knew how much Hannibal loved his family. He would never forgive her for endangering his grandson as she had. Rake had been right. She had known about her stepfather's plans for hours, and when Sin didn't listen to her she should have continued to the next person in line until she found someone willing to listen.

It was her fault. Her stepfather had been right. She was the only one to blame. It didn't matter what Rake said. Sin's parents and grandparents would never be as tolerant and forgiving regarding her role in what had happened as he had.

How could they be?

When the duke reached the sofa, he forced Rake and Penny, with a growl, to move aside before he sat down beside Charmaine. Before she had a chance to react, he grabbed her by the waist, hauled her up onto his knee, and forced her to lean her head against his shoulder.

His large hands, so much like Sin's, caressed her hair softly, and he bent his head down to rest his chin on the top of her blonde head. Her heart screamed with pain at being held just as she'd always pictured a devoted father would hold his beloved child. How she'd always wanted to be held.

With love.

"I'm so sorry," he whispered hoarsely. "Can you ever forgive me for not being there for you too? Anna and I knew how he mistreated Penny, and we did all we could to help her and strengthen her, but not once did we consider he could be mistreating you also."

Charmaine closed her eyes as the power of his words spread throughout her. Hannibal Darling, the mighty Duke of Berkeley, was crying openly for not being there for her, even though she had done nothing but wrong all her life.

"I never did anything, so why should you have?"

She felt his chest rumble as he laughed sadly, listening to her broken whisper. "You always did seem so sated and satisfied with your life, being The Incomparable Queen and the belle of the *ton,* and all. We all knew how Penny constantly was overlooked in favor of you, and we…"

His voice trailed off as he took a few deep breaths to calm himself before continuing. "*I never* thought twice about how it was for you. Penny tried to tell us, you know, always saying that you never wanted all the luxury he showered upon you, but we didn't believe her because you never looked anything but content about it. If we had known, we could have done more. We could have saved you."

He hugged her closer to his broad chest, and she could feel the even pounding of his heart against her cheek. Emotions she didn't know how to handle ranged throughout her heart and soul, and her breath came in gasps. The duke's kindness was too much.

Why didn't they realize she wasn't worth it?

Her heart ached so badly it must be ready to fly into pieces, crushed under the heaviness of the love bestowed upon her.

"Can you forgive me?" the duke whispered into her hair, his voice as broken as hers, and a strange sound came through her lips, a sound from the deepest shadows of her heart.

"Can you forgive *us*?" the duchess said as she squeezed herself down between her husband and Rake and put her arms around Charmaine and her husband, hugging both of them hard. "I promise you, Charmaine, you are safe here with us. No one wants to hurt you here. We are your family now, and all we want is for you to be happy. So please, please let us know the girl we have glimpsed now and then ever since you married Sinclair. Because that girl we adore. The fake queen we like too, but more out of awe than love."

"I don't think Lord Nester wanted to hurt her, though," Rake drawled from his side of the sofa. "That old goat probably would have stained his pants at the mere thought of being as close to Charmaine as you two are right now."

"Richard Darling!" The duchess let go of Charmaine and turned to stare at her youngest son. "That was extremely inappropriate of you to say, especially now. How rude can you be?"

"Oh, I don't know." Rake grinned, and Charmaine felt her throat slowly become less constricted and the heartache ease as he winked at her, showing her it was just a joke to lighten the situation for her. "I can try my very best to find out, if you want me to?"

"Richard, don't you dare!" his mother gasped, outraged, and then continued to lecture him about the manners of a well-behaved man.

Rake listened quietly to his ranting mother with an amused grin, which seemed to upset her even more, and now and then he would roll his eyes toward Charmaine, letting her know just how hilarious he thought the duchess was.

As always, he had amazed Charmaine with his remarkable insight about her, and she guessed it was because he too had been playing a part all these years. Everyone had always thought him the most infamous scoundrel and libertine of his time, which he never had denied, but he had turned out to be anything but.

The duke sighed deeply, loosening his firm grip of her. "And there all reason went out the door," he mumbled as he looked up at his dramatically lecturing wife from under his bushy, white eyebrows. "I love that woman more than life itself, but sometimes I must confess I find her quite daft. Those boys of ours walk all over her, and she couldn't enjoy it more."

With surprising strength for such an old man, he lifted her off his lap, putting her down on the spot his wife had left. "So, now that we have apologized to you for our ignorance, and you of course have accepted the excuse…"

His voice trailed off as he looked at her encouragingly, and she nodded quickly. "Of course."

"Good, good," he hummed, casting a quick glance at his wife, who was still occupied with her drama, before turning to Lord and Lady Newbury, beckoning them to come over and join him and Charmaine.

"We need to do some elaborate planning here," he informed them. "We have to come up with a scheme that will not only make Lord Nester and the threat he presents toward Sinclair go away forever, but will also allow Charmaine and Penelope to live the rest of their lives without having to constantly look over their shoulders, wondering what he might be up to."

Lady Newbury looked utterly calm and serene, just as Charmaine used to look whenever she felt the worst, and she couldn't help wondering what the good lady was up to now. Caroline Darling was a loving wife and a doting mother—a saint amongst the matrons of the *ton*. But under the peachy, motherly exterior she had a spine of indestructible stone, and Charmaine thought perhaps that if there was anyone she should fear in this room it was her mother-in-law.

Her father was Basil Sinclair, the Earl of Saxton, who was infamous for his cold intelligence and ruthless management of his department at the War Ministry. He was the king of the spies, and Charmaine had heard someone likening him to an octopus, his tentacles being everywhere, stirring every pot he could find.

Caroline was the apple that hadn't fallen too far from the tree. All things considered, she had connections to fear and envy.

"It would be best if he died," Lady Newbury chipped in, proving Charmaine's every thought about her right, and her husband frowned at her.

"So you think we should kill him? That's your grand plan? And who do you think should act upon this plan?"

"I said it would be best if he *died*, not that I was actually going to kill him. But I must admit it would be extremely satisfying to do so." Her small smile sent shivers down Charmaine's back, and the only thing she could think of was how utterly grateful she was that this woman was on her side.

"Well, *you* are not going to kill anyone," the duke bit out, and Lady Newbury groaned in disappointment.

"It seems I have to promise that I will not kill the man even though I think he deserves it. He is such an awful man, that Lord Nester. One daughter he ignores completely and has nothing against giving her away to a man he knows is a sadist, whilst obsessing about the other daughter and sending every suitor away to be able to keep her for himself."

"Such a charmer." Rake grinned as he joined in the fray against the duchess again. "Are you sure it's him you want to kill off? Why not get rid of old George, here, and seduce Lord Nester into marriage? Could be a ride you'd never forget."

"Now you make me shiver with disgust," Lady Newbury said with a grimace. "Just thinking about being anywhere closer than within a mile of that man makes me nauseous."

"Can you two just stop it?" the duchess hissed. "Even though I could stand here all day discussing various ways we could get rid of the bastard, we still have to come up with a plan that will work, and then move on it."

"Indeed we do," Lord Newbury agreed sternly. "We have to make sure the man never again can try to kill Sinclair, and we have to get him as far away from his daughters as possible. I've never encountered such selfishness before, and I'll tell you, I would never have guessed it was old Lord Nester, if no one had told me about all the things he's done. He seems such a good-natured and happy sort."

"Appearances can lie, which I think our dear daughter-in-law has made very clear to us all."

Charmaine felt her cheeks grow hot but didn't say anything. She was too guilty of the accusation herself, after all, having fooled the entire *ton* into believing she was another person. But she had an excuse—her stepfather's infatuation with her and her need to hide all emotions from him, as he tended to act out quite rashly if he thought himself threatened by another man.

Like Lord Dane.

"Killing is still out of the question?"

"Caroline, for goodness' sake!"

Lady Newbury sighed. "I just had to check."

"You are such a strange woman."

"And yet you married me." Lady Newbury started to sound a bit irritated with her nagging husband, and he grinned, looking just as mischievous as his younger son.

"I did, and during all these years I've never regretted it more than a day or two. Three at tops."

"I'm not very partial to you right now."

Lord Newbury lifted his wife's hand to his lips, putting a lingering peck on her knuckles. "Yes, you are, but you have always had a tendency to feel you have to make everyone think you're not. But sweetheart, no one believes a word you say when you try to convince them you loathe me. I'm just too adorable for them to believe you."

"Adorable?" The duchess snorted. "Since I am one of your oldest friends, I must say I feel I don't have to hesitate when it comes to telling you the truth, and in this matter the truth is that you are not."

"Not what?"

"Adorable."

"I am too. Have always been and will always be."

The duchess and Lady Newbury shared a look which told exactly how pathetic they found him, and then they turned their backs to him, promptly ignoring him. Not that he let that stop him from continuing to tease his wife.

"Last time I met Lady Easton, she told me all about how she still found me most attractive, and she informed me how lonely she felt when her husband was away hunting. Poor little thing. I feel so sorry for her, maybe I should pay her a visit now, and…"

"Don't you dare, you toad," his lovely wife hissed at him, her hands on her hips. "If you take one step toward Juliet Easton, I will make sure that you will suffer for it a long time. A long, *long* time."

Lord Newbury grinned wickedly toward his angry wife, obviously quite pleased with the way she responded to his teasing. "Still jealous, I see."

"I am not. I just don't like that woman."

"There's nothing wrong with Juliet."

Lady Newbury harrumphed angrily. "There's more wrong with her than right. She's a gossipy, vain snippet who thinks she's so much more than everyone else. Just look at the way she and her poor husband receive their guests every year at that annual ball they hold at the beginning of every season. Sitting on a platform in those throne-like chairs as if they're royalty, forcing everyone to walk past them and greet them. Not even Prinny acts that self-centered."

"Still jealous," Lord Newbury told his stepmother lightly, ignoring his wife's outraged gasp. "But who can blame her? It's me we're talking about, after all. I'm just too adorable."

"Wasn't it Juliet Easton who wanted to marry you when you tried to get rid of the betrothal to Caroline all these years ago?"

"Indeed it was. Such good taste."

"Rogue!" Lady Newbury hit her husband on the arm before again turning her back to him. She smiled in apology at Charmaine and Penelope.

"I'm so sorry, my girls, that you had to see that, but my husband has a tendency to love himself a bit too much now and then, and he always has to drag out the same memory of the same woman, just to rub my nose in it. I might have been a little jealous back then..."

"A little?"

Lady Newbury shot her husband a look that told him he could bury himself under the floor for all she cared, and returned to her interested audience. "That snippet, Lady Easton, decided she wanted George as her husband even though she knew he and I had been engaged since childhood."

"She didn't do anything until you told her you wanted out of the engagement so you could marry that vicar you were thinking yourself so much in love with."

"That has nothing to do with Juliet's brazen behavior. She was trying to be found in your bed. You can be glad I was there to stop her!"

"And that, dear audience, was the sole reason Caroline was found in my bedroom and had to marry me even though we both wanted nothing but out of the betrothal." Lord Newbury wiggled with his eyebrows at his wife, who threw her hands out in despair.

"I give up. Why try to reason with the unreasonable?"

The duke sighed, defeated. "They have been at it since the day they met. I don't know how many times I've cursed that infernal day my old friend King George thought it a splendid idea for his two close friends to join their families and had our children engaged to marry."

"You could have refused," Penelope said, her dazed eyes telling exactly how utterly romantic she found the subject.

"No, I couldn't. He was not only my close friend, but he was also my king. I had lost Georgiana a couple of years before, and at the time it felt safe to know that at least my oldest son would have his future known and safe. And as Basil was a close friend…"

"It was indeed a turbulent time, but it all ended quite well." Lord Newbury's face lost all its mirth. "How could I know that the woman I was engaged to was the love of my life?"

"How romantic," Penelope breathed, and they all laughed, knowing what a dreamy heart she possessed.

The door opened and Ivanoff came in, looking grimmer than ever. "Lord Nester is here for his older daughter."

"What?" the Darlings all shouted at once, and Charmaine suddenly felt the room spinning rapidly.

Her stepfather was there?

For her?

Whatever possessed the man to so calmly walk into the enemy's lair and claim his daughter? Did he think they wouldn't mind having their relative's would-be assassin under their roof?

But then, he didn't know they knew.

"I'm going to kill him," Lord Newbury growled and started toward the door, where Ivanoff stood looking a bit anxious.

"No, don't!" Charmaine called out, and to her surprise her father-in-law listened to her, halting reluctantly in the doorway.

"Are you trying to save him?" Lord Newbury said icily, and she shivered under his cold stare.

"Of course not," she breathed. "It's just that I think it's better to give in to him for now and let him meet me. Maybe I could fool him into telling me his plans, or at least have him openly confess that it was he who did the shooting."

Lord Newbury hesitated, clearly torn between her sensible suggestion and his desire to beat the cod to death.

"Charmaine's right." The duke ended his son's wavering. "We can't throw away this opportunity to get under the man's skin. If we handle this right, we might be able to find a way out of this, for all our sakes, but especially for Sinclair's."

Penelope grabbed Charmaine's hand, squeezing it tightly. "Are you sure you're up to it? Can you really face him, knowing he probably shot Sin?"

Charmaine sighed. "I don't know. But I have to try. If something good comes out of this for Sin, then it's all worth having to face him and pretend that I don't hate him."

"I couldn't."

Penelope looked so miserable that Charmaine had to put her arms around her and hug her close. As she felt her sister's shivering body against her own, she knew she had no choice.

She had to save them all from Lord Nester.

And if that meant giving in to his every whim, his every request—so be it. As long as she could find a way to make sure Penelope and Sin would never again suffer because of him…

She would woo him into believing she wanted him, and when an opportunity offered itself, she would throw all caution aside and do the only thing that would end this for forever.

She would kill her stepfather.

Chapter Seventeen

He stood by the fireplace in the lovely salon where the Darlings received their guests at Chester Park, staring in a calculating manner at all the precious little items decorating the room.

When Charmaine walked into the room alone, he met her with disbelief, as if he hadn't thought he would be granted his request to see her. But as he watched her move toward him, an ugly, oily smile took over from his uneasiness, and he rushed to meet her, his hands outstretched.

"Charmaine, my beloved! Seeing you like this is manna for my suffering heart. I have missed you so, and I couldn't stand the solitude any longer. I had to come, with a vain hope they would let you see me."

She forced herself not to shiver with disgust as his sweaty hands grabbed hers, dragging her closer to him so he could embrace her. She felt his lips against her neck, her hair, and her cheek, and she clenched her jaw hard so she wouldn't give away how repulsive she found him.

"Come, sit here," he urged her, reminding her of an eager puppy prancing with excitement. He dragged her to a sofa, where he sat as close to her as he could, his eyes not once leaving her face. "I had almost forgotten how astonishing you are, being separated from you as I have been. The Darlings don't understand the need I have to be with you, or the depths of my feelings."

"They think of you as my father." Charmaine tried to sound indifferent, and when Lord Nester laughed, highly amused, she knew she had succeeded. Or maybe he was just too excited to be with her again to care about how she sounded or what she said.

"I know," he snickered. "But soon they will be aware that I am so much more to you. It will be hard for them to understand, but they will have to live with the fact that you, my beloved, are the queen of my heart."

"They will never let me go."

He shrugged, indifferent, and lifted her hands to his lips, kissing her fingers gently and suckling on the fingertips with a growl of pleasure. She closed her eyes briefly, nearly overwhelmed by a wave of nausea, but managed to stay still.

She might have a hard time keeping her real self and her emotions from the Darling family, as their bluntness made it easier for her to be just who she was, but not with her stepfather. She was too used to pretending to be what he wanted her to be, suppressing all her true feelings. She didn't retreat even slightly when he gave up kissing her hands and instead leaned forward and started to place wet kisses on her neck and shoulder.

"Ah, you taste so sweet. I want nothing more than to remove all these clothes and finally make you mine. I am annoyed that *he* took your innocence from me, but I can live with that as long as I have you at my side for the rest of my life." His lips moved slowly up her chin, leaving a snail's trail behind, and she felt a cold shiver run down her spine. She closed her eyes, trying to stay calm, but a disgusted groan escaped her as his lips landed on hers.

"Oh, my beloved," he cried out as he put his hands against her cheeks, mistaking her revulsion for lust. "I knew you were going to enjoy this as much as I. We are made for each other, a match made in perfect heaven. Has he died yet, that ensnaring husband of yours, so you can come with me as mine forever?"

She shook her head, and he cursed harshly, releasing her face as he stood and banged his fist hard against the wall.

"I thought I did the job thoroughly enough. He looked dead when he lay there in the snow, blood all over. What is wrong with those Darlings? They're like cockroaches—impossible to get rid of!"

And there was the confession. She shuddered, knowing there was no turning back now. Had it not been her stepfather who had tried to kill Sin, she could have let him live. But not now, when she knew he was the shooter.

Now he had to die.

The Darlings had been all over her after deciding she had to be their pawn to get the information they sought. They had all been talking at the same time, their voices turning into a blur as they all had too many thoughts and too many plans about what she should say and what she should do.

She hadn't listened to any of them.

Instead she had put up her walls and made sure to soundproof them, too, so she could find the quiet, peaceful spot inside her where she could think of Sin and his kind, crooked smile that made her feel so good and made her want to hug him close and never let him go.

What would he say when all was said and done? Would he ever forgive her for what she had put him through? If she hadn't tripped him that day, he wouldn't now be lying in his bed, suffering from being shot.

His life would have been the same as before, and he could have stayed as he was. No wife who turned his life upside down and tore him away from what was important to him. No frustration and anger to wear him out emotionally. He would have stayed the calm and sane person he'd always been before her—before their marriage.

She thought about the baby growing inside her, and again the lump in her throat grew until she could hardly breathe. She was ready to die for Sin, if dying meant her stepfather died too. But killing Sin's baby…

She would try to stay alive. If she was thrown into prison for the murder of Lord Nester, at least Sin could get their child. It was a comforting thought, that Sin had both the Prince Regent and Lord Saxton on his side, backing him, if he needed help to gain custody of the baby, to rescue him or her from wherever Charmaine was held.

All she had to do was to keep the child alive and well until it was born.

One to die—one to live.

"I could try again," Lord Nester interrupted her thoughts. "And this time I could make sure he really is dead before leaving."

Her heart started to beat faster, and she tried to think of something to say, something to stop his evil plans and instead make hers possible. "You can't reach him. He's still unconscious, in bed."

He looked at her, his eyes unreadable as a

malicious smile played across his face. "But you can."

No. Good God, no.

"I can't," she whispered, and his eyes narrowed immediately.

"Why not?" He snorted, disdainful. "Because you still think yourself in love with him? Charmaine, my beloved, you are no more in love with him than I ever have been with your pathetic mother. He's just someone you had to stand for a while, and convincing yourself you are in love with him has merely served to make the whole thing more bearable for you.

He kneeled in front of her and grabbed her chin, forcing her to look at him. "You can kill him."

She shook her head, knowing she was stupid, because giving in to him would have made it easier for her, but she couldn't make herself agree to killing Sin. It was too far to go, even for a pretender like her.

Her stepfather sighed ruefully. "That makes it all harder, but all right, I'll take care of the killing. Or maybe we could just leave. Head out to the colonies and start over where no one knows who we are and where we come from. If I only had money..."

She lifted her gaze toward him, sensing an easier way out. Fleeing to the colonies with him? That would be the best solution for all her problems. Her stepfather would be as far away from Sin as she could take him, and Sin would in time be free to continue his life.

Was it seven years they waited before declaring a missing person dead? It was many years, but at least Sin would still be alive. He would still be on the young side of life and able to find himself a new wife. A young, happy girl who would love him for the person he was, and who wouldn't bring secrets and death into the relationship.

She ignored the mental stab of pain and looked up at her stepfather, not hiding her eagerness. "I can get money. Sin showed me where he keeps the money here at Chester Park, the money he uses to pay the laborers."

"My beloved!" Lord Nester squealed with joy. "What a grand idea. That would indeed be a perfect solution for our joint future. But is there enough money to keep us comfortable for the rest of our lives? I don't want to be forced to work. That's not acceptable for a gentleman such as myself."

Again she clenched her jaws so she wouldn't show how repulsive she found him. Of course he didn't want to work. All he wanted was to live the good life, eat good food, attend parties and assemblies, and indulge in extended gambling.

The money wouldn't last long.

For her child's sake she had to make sure there was more, more that was unbeknownst to her stepfather. Sin had given her access to the Darling family jewelry, and she could grab parts of the collection, hoping they someday would forgive her.

She couldn't let the child suffer.

"I think so," she mumbled, and he lightened up again, clapping his hands together.

"Oh, dearest Charmaine, this seems like my lucky day indeed. Here I thought I had lost you forever, but instead you have shown me your true feelings for me and made me the happiest man alive."

He leaned forward and kissed her lips softly.

"We have to leave soon. I have had some problems with my gambling lately. The cards haven't been with me, and I…"

His strained laughter echoed in the room. "Well, let's say I need to get as far away from here, and as soon, as possible."

Her thoughts raced through her mind. Every part of her screamed against leaving soon, leaving Sin. She wanted to spend more time with him, now that he had awakened. Collect as many memories of him as she could, enough to last for the rest of her life.

But at the same time, she knew there was no point in prolonging what was bound to happen whether she wanted it or not. She had to leave so Sin could live, so why not turn her back on her old life immediately and spare herself the agony of not wanting to put him and what they had together behind her?

"Is tonight soon enough?" she asked politely, and winced as Lord Nester excitedly squealed again.

"Tonight would be excellent. I'll go home, gather my things, and come back for you later, say, just after dinner? Everybody will be too busy with their port to realize you're missing for quite some time, hopefully not until breakfast tomorrow. Do you want me to come here, or do you prefer that we meet somewhere more secluded, like the old barn down the road?"

"The old barn would be fine."

"Wonderful, wonderful!"

Lord Nester shone like the sun in July, his happiness evident in every small movement he made. For him, this was a dream come true. The love of his life would be his at last.

To her it was a nightmare. A walk straight down to hell. But in the end it would be worth it. It had to be. Sin would be alive, and even though he would hate her forever, it would be a blessing to know he could at least be well enough to tell about it.

With one last lingering kiss on her hand, Lord Nester left her alone, and she couldn't hold back a whimper. Good God, how was she ever going to live a life in which he could touch her as much as he wanted? She almost threw up every time he came close to her. He made her feel too dirty to stand.

But she had to.

Somehow she would have to find the strength to let him close, let him make love to her. She couldn't escape it. He had too many times already told her how much he longed to conquer her body. He would probably be all over her as soon as they were alone, without the threat of someone walking in on them.

The door flew open with a crash, and soon the room was filled with Darling relatives. They were all there, every last one of them currently at Chester Park. The only ones missing were Francesca and her husband, as they were home at Pendragon with their triplets, and Sin, who was confined to his bed.

"We saw Nester's carriage leave. What did he say?" the duke asked as soon as he entered the room. "Did he confess he was the shooter?"

"Yes, Your Grace. He admitted as much."

"I will kill him!" Lady Newbury looked ready for war, and her husband pulled her close, embracing her soothingly. Or maybe he was just holding her closer so she wouldn't charge out through the door on a crusade she couldn't win. For such a small person, she was quite determined.

The duke pouted, disappointed. "I must admit I was nursing a silent hope it wasn't him. It's hard to grasp how our neighbor, a man who has known Sinclair most of his life, could cold-bloodedly try to kill him. I just can't understand how the man thinks."

"There's obviously something dreadfully wrong with him," the duchess agreed. "He has always been a good neighbor and a pleasant acquaintance. Other than his unhealthy appetite for gambling, he has always seemed a harmless and, I have to admit, quite uninteresting man."

"You never know what hides beneath the surface," Charles said, his usually warm, amiable face darkened because of this unexpected grief. "The good Lord does indeed work in mysterious ways."

"And behind every bend in the road, the unknown awaits you." Rake's wicked grin was quite inappropriate, considering the seriousness of the situation.

"Not to mention the infamous wolf who insists on hiding in a sheep's clothing," Sin's cousin Drake drawled in his normal, dandyish, bored voice.

"How unfashionable."

"Indeed." Drake's grin was just as wicked as Rake's, and giggles were heard throughout the room, releasing a bit of the tension.

"You two should be ashamed," the duchess hissed. "How can you laugh and joke when the rest of us are discussing these horrifying events?"

The duchess seemed unusually stressed over the situation. Normally she would be the one looking on the light side of everything, preferably with a little twist of drama.

"Mama, I have to admit I heartily disagree with you," Rake replied arrogantly, his ever-amused eyebrow raised high. "As long as I can laugh about it, I know there is something I can do about it. Lord Nester might be a dreadful sort of chap, but, rest assured, he's not untouchable."

"How?" Charmaine felt a small hope begin inside her. "H-how can you take care of him?"

Rake smiled sheepishly. "I don't know just yet. I haven't had the time to think this through thoroughly, but I promise you, Charmaine—I will. After all, it's *Lord Nester* we speak of. He will be no problem whatsoever for us. Trust me."

She smiled brightly to assure him she believed him, but in her heart she knew he was wrong. Because all these years they all had been wrong. They had all thought him harmless, yet he was anything but.

There was no way around it. She had to take care of this herself.

As if on cue, everybody started talking at once, discussing different solutions to solve the problem of Lord Nester. It was one outrageous idea after another, and when they started to consider if the old dungeons of Chester Park were secluded enough, she stopped listening to them.

They had no solution.

They had no way out.

This was a bunch of easygoing peers of the realm—how on earth would they ever be able to fight a war against an evil mind who would use every wile and deceptive trick he could think of?

"Don't." Penelope sat down beside her.

"I beg your pardon?" Charmaine mumbled her old mantra, the one that always took the edge off things, making it possible for her to sneak in behind her walls when she was caught off guard.

But this was Penelope, her sister, and she just snorted. "Oh, come on, Charmaine. You can't fool me. I know you. You are too serene and too calm. You are up to something, and I want to know what."

Charmaine laughed lightly, making sure she sounded as amused as possible. "Penny, my dear, *dear* little sister, I'm not up to anything. Frankly, I'm just so relieved to have all this out in the open and not have to do anything by myself."

"You are *definitely* up to something."

"Penny!"

Charmaine didn't know what to say. Penelope just stared at her with steel in her lovely violet eyes, something she had never done before. But Rake's love had given her strength to face any problem, including her evasive older sister.

"Why didn't you tell me? I could have helped you against him. I could have joined Mother in her unfailing quest to protect you."

Charmaine sighed heavily. "I don't know. When I was younger, I didn't mind his possessiveness, because I liked being in the center of every occasion. I was always admired wherever we went, and everyone, including Father, offered me anything I wanted. Back then, he wasn't in love with me, not as a man. He was just proud of me and enjoyed being the envied and admired father of an exceptional child."

"When did it all change?"

"The year I became sixteen years old. That was the year Mother let me join the social circle of our county and when I had my first admirers. I still remember how angry Father was when he received the first proposal for my hand in marriage. He behaved like a lunatic, throwing things around and screaming that I was *his*. Mother tried to talk to him, but it only made it worse, and in the end we all—including him—understood what sick feelings he had for me."

She took a deep breath to conquer the lump in her throat that made it almost impossible for her to continue talking. But she had to. If she were to leave tonight, she wanted Penelope to have the answers she sought.

"You still could have told me." Tears ran down Penelope's cheeks, and Charmaine's eyes started to ache in sympathy.

"I couldn't. Mother didn't want you to know what kind of man Father was. I think she was desperate for at least you to have a normal life."

"A lonely life."

"But you had a life, Penny. You had freedom to do whatever you wanted and to be with whomever you chose. I never had. You have friends. I don't because Father was too jealous to let anyone near me."

Penelope frowned slightly. "What about Emma and Victoria? I thought they were your friends."

Charmaine shrugged. "I wish. But no, they weren't. They were just using me, and I let them because Father relaxed when I was with them, and he could even let me leave his side for a while. I would have danced with the devil if it meant having enough space to breathe."

"It's so sad. Neither you nor Mother ever had a chance to live life as you wanted to because of his infatuation with you. Both of you throwing everything away just because he is too selfish to care about anyone but himself."

"Mother never had an easy time with him. It hurts that someone as goodhearted and kind as she was had to lose her freedom to such an awful man. She was worth so much more."

Penelope leaned back in the sofa, absentmindedly watching the Darlings, who were still deep in discussions regarding the removal of Lord Nester. "I wonder what our real father was like. Did Mother ever mention him to you?"

Charmaine shook her head. "No, never. It was Father who told me the truth so he could justify his love for me when I realized the true nature of his feelings."

"Why did you keep this to yourself for so long? Why didn't you tell someone?"

Charmaine mimicked the duchess's earlier move, throwing her hands out in despair. "Who? *Who* could I talk to? Mother forbade me to even hint about it to you, and I didn't know anyone else to trust. And even if I had wanted to tell someone else, Penny, I was never alone. There was always someone with me." She took a ragged breath to calm her racing heart. "I was *never* alone."

"I was always alone."

Charmaine's throat ached as she hugged her weeping sister. "I know. I'm so sorry."

"Sometimes I hated you so much."

"It's all right."

"I hated Mother, too, for not wanting me."

"She wanted you, more than you ever will know."

Penelope straightened her back, angrily wiping her tears away, ending the loving embrace.

"Maybe," she bit out. "But I would have preferred her telling me so while she still was alive, rather than to hear it from you now."

"I'm sorry," Charmaine repeated, her voice a mere

whisper, and Penelope laughed through her tears.

"Lord, how pathetic I am. Rake keeps telling me how my pregnancy makes me even more emotional than I usually am, and not in a good way."

Charmaine laughed too, amused against her will. "He's a good man, Rake. You are a lucky woman."

"I am," Penelope grinned, just as wickedly as her husband. "And he is one lucky man who has me."

"Indeed he is."

"Sin is a good man too."

"I know."

Penelope arched an eyebrow. "Do you? Do you really? Because from where I sit it seems you don't."

"I beg your pardon?" Charmaine glanced in surprise at her sister, who looked back with more stamina than she'd ever seen her show before.

"Because I can tell you are up to something, and I know that whatever it is you are planning, Sin's not a part of it."

Charmaine gaped, too dumbstruck to manage to hide behind her composed face, and Penelope snorted triumphantly.

"I knew it!" she cried out, but before Charmaine had a chance to respond, the Darlings came over, chattering excitedly.

"We have thought of a perfect plan," Rake informed his wife and sister-in-law excitedly, but he was interrupted by Harry's loud harrumph.

"*I* thought of a perfect plan." He glared at his younger brother, who shrugged indifferently and, with a wave of his hand, let Harry explain. "You see, I have this old friend, Lachlan Macquarie. I met him through the army. He is now the governor of New South Wales, and even though he has these strange thoughts of emancipation I still think he would make sure Lord Nester would never get any special treatment, and he would keep the man there until his death."

"Australia?" Penelope gasped. "You are going to send Father to Australia?"

"Why not?" her beloved husband asked. "We can't get him any farther away than the other side of earth."

"I still think killing him would be the best solution," Lady Newbury muttered, but no one paid any attention to her, as they all had discarded her bloody plans some time ago.

Charmaine stared at Harry, trying to grasp what he had said. Send her stepfather to Australia? That would indeed be a solution, but then again, it wasn't until forever.

She knew her stepfather.

He would be back in England sooner or later, and to live under the constant threat of his return would be more than she could stand. How would she ever be able to keep Sin safe if she didn't know where his would-be assassin was? And what said her stepfather wouldn't use her children against her?

No, it was not a good plan. But she was not going to tell the gloating Darlings that. Instead, she smiled and nodded and congratulated them all for solving her problem. And all the time she waited impatiently for the right moment to excuse herself and sneak off.

Penelope kept staring at her with narrowed eyes, but she didn't say anything. Charmaine could only guess her sister was waiting for a better time, thinking she had all the time in the world. Penelope couldn't know Charmaine more or less already had left Chester

Park behind her. In her mind there was no other way to go.

She had no other option.

Her mind was made up. She had to leave them all behind and only bring a few things with her in a small bag. Too much baggage would only slow her down. There had to be seamstresses in the colonies, as the visitors they'd had from overseas all had been clad in just as fine garments as she had. She could have new clothes made for her, which would satisfy her stepfather's need to show her off and make everyone envious of his beautiful daughter. No, not daughter—wife.

Another wave of nausea washed over her, but she had made up her mind, and somehow she was going to see this through. It wasn't forever. She just had to stand his touch until they were settled on the other side of the Atlantic, for her child's sake.

And then he had to die.

Without looking back, she left as soon as she could, using the excuse of making sure Sin was all right. Of course they let her go, their compassion following her as she left.

She went straight up to her room, where she packed as much clothing as possible into the small bag she had chosen. She took only practical dresses, ones to keep her warm during the weeks or months it would take for them to travel by ship across the Atlantic Ocean.

After collecting her thickest coat, she hesitated at the door connecting her room to Sin's, wanting desperately to go to him and for one last time feel his strong, protective arms embrace her.

But she couldn't.

If she did, she would never be able to make herself leave him. Not now when he was awake and looked at her with his dark, inscrutable eyes. But she couldn't leave him without explaining herself, either.

Determined, she slipped unnoticed down the stairs and into Sin's office, where she quickly collected the money from the hidden drawer where he kept it. It was more money than she had been aware of, and she knew without doubt her stepfather would exclaim over it.

Behind Sin's study there was a secret room which held all the most important documents and all the family jewelry. Feeling like the worst cad ever, she picked a few necklaces with large stones that would be easy to remove and sell separately.

After hiding her loot in the pockets of her dress and coat, she sat down at Sin's desk and took a piece of paper and the pen he had left lying by the inkwell. For the longest time she sat there silently, staring blankly at the white paper, not knowing what to write to make him understand why she did this, why she left him for her stepfather.

She wanted him to live happily, have a better life than the one he had now. Somehow she had to make sure he tried to start anew and not chase after her or the child she carried. The latter would be the hardest—the baby was, after all, his heir, and as such too important to let go.

An unwanted wife was not.

In the end, she simply scribbled down what was in her heart, knowing there was no need for her to think twice about what she said. All she needed was for him to know she wanted him to be happy.

My dear husband,

I can't find words enough to tell you how grateful I am that you have awakened and in such good health. My relief eased many tied knots inside of me, and I know now that stress lured me into believing I carried your child.

I can never forgive myself for being the reason why you were shot and almost killed. You are such a wonderful, special man and deserve more than a wife who can't show you how highly she thinks of you. Promise me you will find a good, loveable woman who will fill your heart with love and laughter as I never could.

For the first time in my life I will do the right thing and make sure that you and Penny are safe forever.

I set you free.

Your wife,

Charmaine

Without reading her note again, she put it down on the desk, making sure Sin would find it as soon as he came into the room. With one last lingering look at the heavy ledgers he held in such high esteem, she left the room silently, heading toward the old barn and a future she didn't want.

Outside, it poured rain, and she hurried down the long driveway until she reached the old barn, where a dark carriage awaited her. Without a word she let the driver help her up, and as soon as she sat down on the bench, the carriage started to roll down the road, away from Chester Park.

Away from Sin.

Chapter Eighteen

March was definitely not the best month to visit Southampton, Charmaine thought as she stood at the dock, staring up at the tall clipper that was to take them to their new home in America.

"It's so cold I think my nose is about to fall off," a woman standing next to her said, her eyes sparkling with mirth, and Charmaine smiled politely.

"I do agree. I hope they have good heating aboard the ship, or I think we'll have two unbearable months ahead of us as we cross the Atlantic."

"The captain admitted that in the worst case scenario it will take three months. All depending on the weather and how much ice still is floating in the sea."

Three months stuck in a small cabin on a ship with a lovesick Lord Nester? Charmaine felt a stroke of panic. How was she going to survive this?

It had been only one day since she left Chester Park in the dark of night, but she had already regretted, too many times, her decision to leave with Lord Nester for the colonies. If it hadn't been for the accident, she knew he would have used her already, over and over again. But to her luck a wheel had broken while they were stopped briefly in Sandhurst collecting some items Lord Nester had stored there and didn't want to leave behind.

The driver had scratched his head, not really able

to explain how the wheel had been able to break when they stood still, but she didn't care. The relief she felt over getting out from the confined space of the carriage was almost overwhelming. And to make things even better, they soon learnt there was no possibility to fix the wheel for at least two days, which left only the stagecoach if they were to get to Southampton in time, as the ship would sail the next evening.

As the stagecoach was scheduled to leave early the next morning, Lord Nester eagerly went to the inn to rent a suite for himself and his daughter.

"This is the last time you go under that flag," he had whispered to her excitedly. "Next time, when we can be sure no one who knows us will be around, you'll be known as my wife. But don't you think you'll get any sleep tonight, my precious. I've waited too long for you to let you spend the night sleeping."

His leering eyes had told her exactly what his plans were, and she had swallowed hard to avoid throwing up all over him again. She felt so nauseous she almost missed his sullen face when he returned from speaking with the innkeeper.

"What a stroke of bad luck," he whined. "The inn is full to the brim because of the pre-season races at Ascot, and all the innkeeper could offer was a place for you in the room where his serving wenches sleep when they work late. I have to stay in the carriage, as there is no room for me."

"Oh, that's awful," she breathed, hoping she sounded at least a little disappointed. She must have succeeded, as he'd seemed satisfied with her meager response.

"Soon it will be only you and I. We must simply

wait until we reach our secluded cabin on the ship."

That night Charmaine had slept like a baby, feeling oddly secure in the unknown bed in an unknown room. In the morning, after a quick breakfast, they had boarded the crowded stagecoach. It had taken them all day to reach Southampton, and it was with great relief Charmaine accepted the driver's hand getting out of the carriage, having spent ten long hours bumping into the other passengers.

Darkness had already fallen when they finally reached the docks and found the tall ship still there, awaiting their arrival onboard. A small crowd of people looked up at the ship, shivering in the cold and staring at the rickety gangplank in disbelief. It was as if they couldn't believe the thing would carry their weight, much less their luggage.

Lord Nester shouted for help but was ignored by the sailors, who much preferred flirting with the harbor harlots to carrying the obnoxious man's heavy bags.

"I can't believe such rudeness," he gasped, outraged. "Don't they know who I am? I'm their superior. Superior! If it weren't for me, they wouldn't have anything to pay those ugly whores with."

He guffawed angrily as he bent down and lifted the smallest of his bags, missing the black looks from the sailors who had overheard him. Charmaine sighed. This wasn't going to be a smooth ride across the Atlantic.

"My wife packs too much and makes me carry it around," she heard Lord Nester whine to a lady close to his own age. With pursed lips the woman sent Charmaine a disgusted look, and she felt her heart sink.

This was no new start for her.

This was a large kick backwards to her old life, the

life before Sin. Before the Darlings. Before being saved.

And there was nothing she could do about it. She knew because she had already lived that same life before. A part of her cried, *"No, I don't want to go back to being that cold person again—always envied, never liked."* But the rest of her sighed with dejection, knowing there was no way she could change the first impression once it was set.

Her father was once again going to play the role of the jovial and likable peer, and she was to act as the cold, spoiled, self-centered beauty. The only difference from before was that she would be acting as his wife instead of his daughter.

At least she wouldn't have to endure all the lovesick men this time. That was something, she presumed.

One of the sailors, a slender man, strolled through the crowd, and her eyes narrowed suspiciously as she watched him move. There was something familiar about the man which made her look twice. Something about him made her wonder if she didn't know him.

But she didn't know any sailors.

Her breath caught in her throat as the man lifted his head and looked straight at her with his laughing eyes.

Drake Darling.

He winked at her as he moved amongst the crowd, circling slowly so he would pass her where she stood on the edge. But when he came up to her, he didn't stop. Instead he pursed his lips to silence her, urging her with a small nod to look backwards as he followed the footsteps of her stepfather.

What was Drake doing here? As far as she knew,

he had been with the rest of the family after her father's visit at Chester Park yesterday. He had not mentioned going away, especially not to Southampton. She would have remembered, as it would have endangered her own plans.

But, somewhere between last night's dinner and now, Drake had left the coziness of Chester Park and followed her to Southampton.

Not only followed her, she realized—he had been there before them, standing with the sailors and flirting with the women of suspicious occupation. She frowned slightly as she looked back toward the rest of the group of men, this time looking more closely at them. They seemed to have no cares in the world as they bandied words with the ladies. They were too far away for her to see them clearly, but as she watched them more closely she soon discovered familiarities in the way they moved, and she gasped.

She could hardly believe her eyes when she realized they were none other than Rake, Sebastian, and James, Rake's twin brother. Three of the most fashionable gentlemen of her acquaintance, who never wore anything but the most excellently sewn clothes and who ruled the *ton* with their wickedness and their amused grins.

And yet here they were, dressed in dirty old clothes, looking exactly as the filthy and brawny sailors they pretended to be.

They seemed unaware of what was happening over by the ship, but they didn't fool her, not now when she knew who they were. Especially as Rake winked at her and sent her one of his amused grins, telling her without words that they were there for her.

And that was the truth.

These four men were there for her. They cared enough about her to follow her across the country and dress themselves in dirty sailors' outfits just to be there for her.

How had they known?

She had thought she'd deceived them all, that no one had understood what was about to happen. But obviously she hadn't. They had figured it all out and beat her to it.

The only thing was—what were they going to do now? They obviously hadn't planned to storm in and openly take her back to her family. That would ruin her reputation and create quite the scandal. Especially as she was there under the assumption she was Lord Nester's wife and not his daughter.

They had something else in mind, and she felt her heart sink as she watched Drake move closer to her stepfather. There was nothing they could do, nothing they could say, that would make that man give her up. He had wanted her too long and would not surrender peacefully now that he had her in his hands.

The Darling men were, after all, just a bunch of gentlemen, unused to the way of the world outside their secure little social circle. The only one who had a little experience from anything else but the *ton* was James, but what could one man's time in the army help in this situation?

"You, there," the fashionable lady Lord Nester had spoken to called out to Drake as he passed her. "Go and relieve the gentleman of his burden."

"Not my job," Drake scoffed, and Charmaine was impressed at how different from his normal dandyish self he sounded.

The good lady gasped, and her large bosom nearly made the small buttons of her coat fly off. "How dare you, you infidel! Don't you know who I am?"

Drake looked at her over his shoulder as he continued toward his prey, his eyes cold and uninterested. "No."

The lady gasped again, grabbing her walking-stick in her hand as she followed him, impolitely pushing aside the people standing in her path.

"I am the Countess of Linley and..." She shoved two men harshly aside, their angry voices following her as she moved closer to Drake. "And I'm not used to being met with this rudeness! Stand still when I talk to you!"

Drake stopped just as he reached Lord Nester, and Charmaine held her breath as her stepfather looked at the sailor with interest, clearly amused over the little drama playing out in front of him.

"What?" Drake sighed as Lady Linley stopped in front of him.

She immediately threw out her finger, poking him hard as she spoke. "This is unacceptable. You, a simple sailor, are not to treat me this way. When I talk, you stop and listen. And you will be polite toward me. Do you hear?"

Drake shrugged indifferently. "Whatever..."

Lady Linley leaned forward, her nose almost touching his. "Whatever what?"

He frowned at her before shrugging again. "Bloody hell, lady, you sure are one deranged aristocrat."

"Deranged?" Lady Linley gasped, even more outraged than earlier, but this time she caught Drake by surprise and pushed him hard in the chest. Unprepared for the assault, he tumbled backward and landed with a loud *oof* on top of Lord Nester's bag.

The crowd gasped unanimously and moved closer, so that Charmaine lost sight of Drake at her father's feet. Everyone stared at the scenario by the gangplank, and no one was looking at her where she stood with her bag. Without a sound, Rake and James came up to her and dragged her and her bag a little distance away with them.

"Give me your coat," Rake urged, and she hastened to do as asked. He gave her a quick, reassuring smile, which felt oddly comforting, before throwing the coat further to Sebastian, who immediately left them again, walking back toward the ship.

A shrill whistle effectively silenced the mumbling crowd, and a tall, bearded man, who without doubt was the captain, came down the creaking gangplank. His dictatorial voice soon had the people scurrying around, gathering their luggage before boarding the ship.

Lady Linley's voice was just as shrill as the captain's whistle as she grabbed his arm and washed the poor man's ears with complaints about Drake's behavior. Charmaine couldn't hear what she said or what the captain answered as she and Rake briskly walked across the dock toward an anonymous carriage that awaited them, but the countess seemed satisfied with the answer received.

Under Lady Linley's supervision, the captain had a few sailors carry the disinclined Drake aside, away from what was left of the gawking crowd. Without looking twice at Drake, Lady Linley grabbed Lord Nester's arm, forcing him to walk her up the gangplank.

Her stepfather looked like an owl as he tried to look back toward the crowd, obviously searching for her face, seeming more and more distressed when he couldn't find her. If it hadn't been for the lady's firm grip of his arm, he probably would have bolted down the gangplank again, but he was too used to acting the nice gentleman to leave Lady Linley in a disrespectful way.

When they had reached the top of the gangplank and were about to enter the ship, Lord Nester's face changed from anxious to relieved, and without further owl-like movements he disappeared beyond the gunwale.

"H-how…" Charmaine stuttered, and Rake pointed toward the boat.

"Look."

To Charmaine's surprise a shape dressed in her lovely coat walked gracefully up the gangplank, and she leaned back in her seat, not believing her eyes.

"H-how…" she stuttered again, and this time Rake chuckled, clearly amused over her inability to think.

"We paid a woman who is travelling with her husband and five children in steerage to put on your coat and keep it on until the ship had sailed far enough to not turn back. You saw it yourself—your father now believes you are on the ship."

Charmaine shook her head. "But he will find out, I promise you. As soon as he can get rid of Lady Linley, he will go and search for me to take me to the…"

Rake's smile was filled with compassion as he put an arm around her shivering back. "Don't you fret, my dear, we have it all under control. I know Lady Linley. She is a *very* strong-willed woman, and it's unlikely she will budge easily or let your father leave her too soon, especially not with this upset. By the time he finds out you are not on the ship, it will be too late for him to do anything about it. The captain won't turn the ship around to come and get you, and he will have to jump into the water and swim back if he doesn't want to wait until he's in New York and buy a bed on another ship back."

"But he has money—he can pay the captain to turn the ship around."

"With what money?"

Drake climbed into the carriage and removed his dirty jacket with a sigh of utter satisfaction. "That one was so dirty I think it could have stood by itself."

"As long as he bought the play, you can be as dirty as you like."

"Oh, he bought it, all right. The man was so angry with me for my disrespectful behavior toward Lady Linley and especially toward himself, he completely forgot he had all the money in his bag."

Drake removed a packet he had hidden under his jacket and opened it, showing them the money filling it to its brim.

"That's Sin's money," Charmaine gasped, and the two men laughed.

"Do you really think we would have let that bastard leave with our money?" Rake chuckled again. "To be fair, a large chunk of it is missing, but as it has all gone to a good cause, we don't think Sin will fret too much about the loss."

"W-what…" Charmaine was still stuttering, unable to think straight. "Where did the money go?"

"Well, we had to pay our coat-wearing lady. She

and her family will now have a great start in their new life across the ocean. Money easily earned, for her, although we warned her it might get a little ugly when Lord Nester discovers she isn't his daughter."

"Wife."

Rake lifted an eyebrow toward his nephew, but didn't let the input get him off his track. He clearly liked telling the story, and both James and Drake were starting to look a bit impatient.

"Of course. Wife. And then we had to give the captain some coins, too, so he wouldn't be willing to turn the ship around."

"Of course," Charmaine repeated numbly, still not able to fully grasp what had happened.

"And then there is Lady Linley's part."

Charmaine sat up straight, staring at Rake with disbelief. "Lady Linley was paid? B-but... How did you manage to..."

Drake grinned mischievously, looking more boyish than ever, taking over the storytelling—to his uncle's frustration. "Oh, we have known Lady Linley for quite some time, and she loves to pretend being wealthier than she really is. So when we noticed her among the passengers, we took the liberty of offering her a deal she simply couldn't refuse."

"I can't believe this..."

"Do you know, Charmaine, when you look as flabbergasted as you do right now, you are not as beautiful as you usually are."

She couldn't help herself. They were acting too smug, and before she had a chance to change her mind she rolled her eyes. A lot.

Their laughter was liberating. She could feel some

of the tension leave her as she shared their amusement over her honest reaction.

"Oh, Charmaine." Drake grinned. "Promise me you'll never hide from us again. We do like you more when you're human than when you're a goddess."

"Oh, stop it!" She waved her hand toward him, not wanting to hear him rant about her looks, but he just laughed at her. Loving disrespect: the Darling solution to how life worked out best.

"Anyway," Rake continued, with a glare toward his nephew, who was trying to stare starry-eyed at Charmaine. "Don't mind the clown. He just can't help it."

What a family, she thought tenderly. Not one bone of respect toward each other, and yet they were all secure in the knowledge of how loved they were.

A quiet knock on the carriage door interrupted the strange conversation. James let Sebastian in before calling out to the driver it was time to leave.

"No need to stick around," he explained to Charmaine, and she clutched her hands hard together as she stared at him, wanting to believe him.

"You can relax now," Rake said gently, as always sensing when she was disturbed. "He will not come after you again."

"You are wrong," she said hoarsely. "He won't give up. In six months' time he will be back to finish what he started, and nothing can save Sin then. Nothing."

"You are so wrong, sister dear," Sebastian drawled. "Your dear stepfather will not be coming back. You see, we have made sure he will not have any means when he arrives. He will have to work his way to a ticket, and I promise you, he will fail. He is not the working kind of man. He will try something reckless, like gambling, rather than living on what money he has left. I promise you, he will sooner end up as a drunk than succeed in saving for the ticket back."

She shook her head, not knowing how to stress the matter. She knew her stepfather—he would be back.

"No, he won't." Drake seemed able to read her mind, but nothing surprised her anymore when it came to him. Had he removed his clothes and told her that he was instead a woman she would only nod in light acceptance.

"It's true, what Drake says." Rake smiled. "We left your father with enough money to start over in New York but with less than what a ticket costs."

"But you can't promise me he won't come back. You can't. He might be on the other side of the Atlantic, but still... Someday he will stand outside Chester Park again, and then Sin's life will end."

"He won't come back."

"You can't know that!" Her distressed tone brought her even more compassionate looks from the four gentlemen.

"But what if I told you we can?" Rake stretched his legs out in front of him, rendering him angry glares from his twin, who sat in the opposite seat. "You see, we have not only paid the steerage woman, the captain, and Lady Linley. We also made sure to send a man with the ship whose only job is to follow Lord Nester for a year and report back to us what the dear man is up to. If Lord Nester tries to return to England, our man will do his best to stop him, without revealing himself. Would your father by some strange stroke of luck or unexpected wit manage to buy himself a return ticket, our man will make sure we are informed about it and will continue to follow your father until he is sure we can take over the job of rendering him innocuous."

Charmaine bit her lip as she tried to make sense of what Drake had told her. "B-but what if the man loses Father? What if he manages to slip away and boards a ship undetected? Then he could be halfway across the Atlantic before your man hears about it."

"Will not happen."

Drake's conviction was quite catching, but Charmaine still didn't believe it could end this easily. Her life had been so awful during the last few years, turning her into such a horrendous person. The mere thought the solution could be this simple made her feel strangely humiliated.

"Your man might not fulfill his part."

"He will."

She shook her head. "You can't be sure."

"I can and I am."

She sighed deeply with frustration. "You can't trust a random man to do what you have paid him to do when you have no way of making sure he fulfills his part."

Drake shrugged indifferently. "That's why we sent a man we do trust. This is not just about you, Charmaine. This is about your sister, too, who we happen to hold in very high esteem, which I thought you were aware of."

She nodded curtly. Of course she knew how much they adored Penelope. It had been her sister's salvation and something Charmaine in secret had envied.

Drake's unreadable eyes pinned her to the carriage

wall, and she felt the warmth of a faint blush on her cheeks when he smiled wryly as if he had read her mind again and seen how petty her true feelings were. What was it with these Darling men who made her wonder if she was made of glass?

"You both are now part of our family," Drake said smoothly. "But you are not the only reason we do this. You see, my dear, this is also about Sin—our Sin. There is no chance we will send someone we can't trust, as this is about Sin's life, which will hopefully be a long and prosperous one."

She hadn't thought about it like that. Of course the Darlings didn't want their beloved Sin to live with a death threat over his head.

"Do you remember Hereford's valet, that odd man called Bear?" James kicked Rake's legs aside while gazing inquiringly at Charmaine.

She ignored Rake's groan beside her. "As a matter of fact, I do. He's that giant of a man who looks like a Viking, isn't he?"

"Exactly." James nodded slightly, his light gray eyes looking almost silver in the dim light of the lamp. "Hereford met him in France during the war and trusts him completely. He is on the ship and will follow your stepfather closely, making sure Lord Nester stays as far away from England as possible."

It had taken a while for the carriage to make its way through the crowds gathered to see the ship off, and now, as she glanced out through the small window, she could still see the ship hovering over the dock. Sailors were lifting the heavy ropes that kept the ship attached to land, while more sailors were preparing the sails high up in the masts.

The ship was leaving, and with it her stepfather.

Could it be true? Was her stepfather leaving England—and her—forever?

The men were almost obnoxiously cheerfully as the carriage rumbled farther and farther away from Southampton and its docks. They kept bragging to each other how well their plan had worked out.

But Charmaine was too tired to listen. Too drowsy to pretend amusement or even attention, she leaned her head against the cold wall, her thoughts spinning as fast as the wheels beneath her.

What would happen now? She knew she would have to face Sin and tell him the truth, the truth he had been asking for since they first were married. Her heart ached at the mere thought of his losing what little warmth he felt for her, but she had no choice.

No more lies.

She hadn't done anything but tell lies to everyone, including herself, during the last few years, and she'd had enough. She wanted to start over and become a new person—a new Charmaine. She could only hope Sin wouldn't mind her transforming into the real her. Although, as she thought of it, he had never cared for her fake person, so why would it bother him if she became someone else?

"Good Lord, Charmaine!" Rake's amused voice interrupted her pitiful thoughts, and opening her eyes she found him grinning at her.

"I beg your pardon?" Without thinking she blurted out her standard response when she didn't know what to say, something that made Rake, Sebastian, and Drake squeal like little girls, while James, as always, looked blasé and withdrawn. She frowned toward them, irritated. "What?"

"Do you know you *snore*?"

She stared at them with disbelief. "I do not."

"Oh, yes, you do. Who would ever have guessed that? The Incomparable Queen of the *ton* snores."

Why did he sound so stunned?

Snoring wasn't so uncommon. Her stepfather had snored every night during her childhood, sometimes so loudly it felt as if the roof was about to lift from the echoes twirling in every corner of Harveyfield. Her mother had more times than she could remember looked like a hollow ghost at the breakfast table after listening to him all night. And they didn't even share a bedroom.

Sitting up straight, she glared at Rake, who still was chuckling, and tried to look as formidable as she could. "I. Do. Not. Snore."

"Yes. You. Do."

"Nobody has ever told me before that I snore, and so I don't believe you. I definitely don't snore."

"We'll just have to ask Sin," Sebastian told the other men. "He will tell her the truth. He always tells the truth."

Rake sighed. "Yes, he does. The bore."

Drake looked eagerly at Charmaine. "Can't you make him stop being so very boorish? Couldn't you just tell him to lighten up and realize there is more to life than ledgers and responsibility?"

"Is there?" Rake drawled, and his nephews grinned in response.

James rolled his eyes. "Could you three cease your merriment? What's wrong with taking things from the serious point of view? We can't all go around laughing and dancing our way through life. Someone has to make sure we *can* live a carefree and joyful life, and unfortunately that has fallen in Sin's lap."

"He doesn't think it's unfortunate, though," Sebastian said, and it was quite clear that he had no understanding of how anyone could think responsibilities weren't tedious. "He thrives when locked into that dungeon of his so he can lean over those old dusty books, calculating his little numbers."

"Maybe things will change now," James said with a small but unbelievably tender smile, and she stared breathlessly at his handsome face, welcoming this unusual show of affection from him. "Surviving a lethal wound does something to a man, and one tends to look differently at life." James never showed his emotions. This was unprecedented. Penelope had once told Charmaine he had been a different man before his time in France, more open and easygoing. War changed men forever, and both James and Sin's cousin Raleigh were living evidence of this, two quiet, sad men withdrawing themselves from the rest of the family's fun-loving high spirits most of the time.

"I hope so," Sebastian breathed, sounding like a little child wishing for a star, and they all laughed lightly.

Oh, they were such a strange family, Charmaine thought as she looked at the four men surrounding her. Before she had married Sin, she had always looked upon the Darling family with envy, as they seemed to care so deeply for each other. Most men of her acquaintance were prone to look down at women, patronizing them, almost treating female relatives as if they were enemies and not family members.

But not the Darlings.

When Penelope with light steps used to leave Harveyfield for Chester Park, Charmaine would sit in her bedroom window, watching how eagerly her sister almost ran toward the castle. More times than she could count had she wished she too would be included in the invitations to join the colorful family, but it never happened.

Oh, she had been to Chester Park many times, but always on public occasions and with her parents. And, as always when her parents were with her, she closed herself from anyone trying to befriend her, knowing her father disliked it when she gave her attention to anyone but him.

No wonder everyone found her cold and uninteresting. If it hadn't been for her looks, she probably would be a social pariah by now, not wanted by anyone but Lord Nester.

But now she was a part of the Darling family, as they, without any remorse, had taken her into their midst and promptly treated her like one of their own. No one seemed to think twice about how bad her marriage was or how it had started.

Even Sin, though filled with anger and resentment, had treated her as one of them, not once mentioning she didn't belong.

All he had wanted to know was *why*.

"Why didn't you tell us?"

She stared at Sebastian in confusion at first, not able to grasp what he asked her, as she had been too lost in her own thoughts. "I beg your pardon?"

"Why didn't you tell us?" he repeated with a hint of exaggeration, and she blushed in response.

Indeed, why. It seemed to be the one most important question.

"You could have told us about your stepfather. We would have understood." Drake's voice was alluring, softer than velvet. "Or at least we would have tried to."

She gazed dizzily at him. Why, indeed. Why hadn't she told them the truth from the beginning? It would probably not have made things easier for her, but at least she wouldn't have felt so alone and incapable of handling the situation.

And she wouldn't have alienated Sin.

Rake snorted and gave Charmaine a chance to gather her composure. "And what would that have gained her? It's not as easy for everyone to open up as you seem to think it is. If you are used to keeping things to yourself, it soon becomes hard even to admit you need a nap. Something I thought you knew all about, my dear nephew, who has more secrets than anyone else."

"Maybe," Drake admitted slowly. "But that's different, you know. Me working in secret for Basil is not the same as her being used by her stepfather."

"I beg your pardon!" Charmaine gasped, not knowing which was more startling, that he would think her stepfather had used her or that Drake so lightly revealed working for the War Ministry.

"You do say that a lot." Drake grinned and looked as dandyish as ever despite the worn and dirty sailor clothes he still wore instead of one of his colorful and fashionable ensembles that had made him and his friends infamous.

"I know," she admitted, and he grinned even more mischievously at her, almost as impish as his cousin

Sebastian.

"I don't mind, though. You may keep on saying it as much as you want."

"Oh, I may, may I?"

"Uh-hum." He held his hand in front of his face and pretended to be interested in his perfectly cut nails. "I'm a gentleman, and a gentleman never fights lost causes."

"She *does* say that a lot." Sebastian flashed his impish grin. "I'm in complete agreement, dear cousin. Better let it be and dive deeper into the more delicate subjects. Did the sick bastard ever come to your bedroom?"

"Ian!"

"What?" Sebastian looked innocently at James. "I just asked. She doesn't have to answer if she doesn't want to. No pressure."

"No pressure, indeed."

"Uncle Rake, you don't have to sound so disdainful. I'm only curious. Aren't you?"

All four men turned their heads, and Charmaine bit back a smile. Oh, yes, they were. But she wasn't about to give in to them. Not yet at least. Instead, she looked straight at Drake, who met her gaze innocently.

"So you're a spy?"

Chapter Nineteen

"Yes, Drake is a spy," Sin admitted as they strolled through the Chester Park maze, enjoying the warmth of the early spring sun this crisp day in March. "He said as much to you?"

"Not really. He blurted it out when talking about something else, and when I asked him directly he denied it completely."

"He's a handful."

She laughed lightly, so at ease walking with him through the narrow path which branched out now and then to confuse the wanderer about where to turn next. "I have to agree with you there. It's so strange no one in the *ton* sees through his disguise, that the slender, exquisitely fashionable dandy, who seems he might break in two if you breathe too hard upon him, in fact is a hard-hearted, intelligent spy."

Sin's dark eyes were serious as he stopped and looked down at her. "You should know better than anybody how little the people of the *ton* really see."

"True." She blushed. "Most people of our acquaintance only see what they want to see, and it doesn't matter if it is a spy dressed up as a dandy or…or a beauty trying to cover a dark secret."

"Why didn't you tell me?" Sin echoed Drake's question as he started to walk again, and she groaned inwardly, too used to feeling uncomfortable with the answer to that. But then it dawned upon her he already knew all there was to know. Her secret was set free. "I...I didn't...know...how to," she admitted, still almost fearful to tell him too much too early. But then again, maybe it was better to just say everything straight out for once and deal with his reactions then and there and have it done with.

"Do you find me that hard to talk to?"

There was a definite tone of hurt in his voice, and she silently cursed herself for causing it. "Of course not. I was just so used to keeping everything to myself that I just didn't know how to start."

He nodded and patted her hand on his arm absentmindedly as he left the path they had been on, instead moving down another path, and then another. As he seemed to know where they were heading, she allowed herself to be led, staring down at her feet while wishing he would turn and kiss her.

It had been a week since he woke from his coma and she went on her little trip to Southampton. One endless week, during which she'd had her whole life turned upside down and finally been freed of her darkest nightmare—her stepfather. They had all been there, all the Darlings, asking her questions and more questions until she was ready to burst from having to explain herself over and over again. They were just too genuinely interested in what had occurred right under their noses to be able to stop inquiring.

It wasn't as if they held her actions against her. No, their fascination circled mostly around how she had managed to endure the sick infatuation that had kept her nailed to the wall. Penelope sat patiently beside her, stoically supporting her as she re-lived the horror of their stepfather in telling it over and over again.

Charmaine knew Penelope was hurt by how she had been excluded from what had happened, but there was nothing she could do about that now. It had, after all, been their mother's choice.

But Sin hadn't said one word when she told him the truth, the day after their return from Southampton. She had told him everything about her childhood, how obsessively proud her stepfather had been of her, and how he had slowly built walls around her until she was unreachable by others.

She had not softened anything when she came to the part when Lord Nester had realized she was a grown woman and fallen desperately in love with her. The possessiveness from her youth had turned into a jealousy that had made it impossible for her to say or do anything without him watching her.

Not even when she came to the end of her story, telling him about why she'd tripped him into marriage, why she'd left him to save him and why she'd lied about not being pregnant, did he flinch. He just watched her face with his dark, unreadable eyes as he listened, not once taking his attention from her. In the end it had felt as if she were crawling in front of him, silently begging him to accept her for what she was.

But he never said a word.

When she had finished, he turned his back to her and fell asleep, or pretended to at least. And the next day he had acted as though nothing out of the ordinary had happened, and she knew she had lost him. Whatever it was they'd had was gone.

The lump in her throat had ached and ached, so much she thought her neck would break. But she was unable to get rid of that lump.

As they entered the clearing in the midst of the maze, she at first didn't notice the small gazebo standing in the middle of a small pond. Not until Sin walked over the bridge and held open the small door for her to enter did she realize it was there.

"What an enchanted place," she breathed, impressed, and Sin sent her a slow grin over his shoulder as he closed the door behind them.

"It is. It was my great-great-grandfather who had the maze built, to trick the woman he loved into marrying him."

She sat down on the bench that followed the circular walls, and he joined her, stretching his long legs out in front of him. He was such a large, handsome man, and she knew half the young women of the *ton* were in love with him.

She had never considered him as a possible husband, but then again, she had never considered anyone else, either. The only one who had ever made her think about a joint future was Lord Dane, and look what a mess he had turned out to be.

Sin wasn't as fashionably blasé or arrogantly witty as most of the men of the *ton*, including his own relatives. Instead, he preferred the quiet life in Berkshire, managing the family estate rather than dancing his nights away in London.

She adored him for it.

He was the most unselfish man she knew. To him, heritage and family were all that mattered, and she knew he would do anything he could to make sure his family had a smooth, worry-free life. She found his serious approach to life refreshing, and his willingness to bow to the heavy machinery of an estate as large as theirs was impressive.

He wasn't afraid of responsibilities, and to her, who had grown up in a house where no one really cared about anything but themselves, it was highly attractive.

Sinclair Darling, the Earl of Chilton, was a man you could trust with your life, and she loved him more than she had ever thought she could love anyone. Somehow he had dug a hole in her wall and succeeded with something no one else had done—he had found the way to her heart.

"My ancestor, whose name was Dominic, was secretly in love with a young woman and wanted nothing more than to marry her."

Sin's soft voice interrupted her thoughts, and she looked at his strong, manly profile as he stared out through a small window toward the entrance to the maze.

"What was her name?"

"Maria, but everyone called her Merry, as she was born with the sun in her heart and a smile which I've heard was to die for."

"But there was no sun in her heart for Dominic?"

Sin shook his head. "No. He had once, quite by mistake, offended her publicly, and she couldn't find it in her heart to forgive him."

"She must have loved him very much."

"Probably." Sin grinned. "She was a woman, and women do tend to act in mysterious ways when it's a matter of the heart."

"Oh, shush." Charmaine put on her best offended look and slapped him lightly on the arm. He chuckled softly in response as he took her slender hand in his big, warm ones.

All the giddiness left her with a pouf, and she felt almost breathless as she stared into his dark eyes. Slowly he lifted her hand and placed a chaste kiss in the palm before softly closing her fingers around it, savoring the kiss for her.

"Dominic was a man of action," Sin continued softly, without letting go of her hand, and Charmaine almost couldn't hear what he said as her heart pounded so hard, so loudly. "And when he couldn't persuade Merry into marrying him, he instead went to her father and asked for her hand."

"The cur!" Charmaine gasped. "How could he go over her head like that when she already had refused him?"

"That was exactly what Merry thought, and when her father proudly announced to her that he had promised Dominic her hand in marriage, she was furious."

Sin absentmindedly stroked the soft skin on the inside of her wrist with his thumb, and she had an almost undeniable urge to kiss him.

To prevent herself from doing something she would regret, she released her hand from his and stood, pretending to look out the window. She felt his gaze, but she didn't care if he wondered what was the matter. She just couldn't stand being that close to him and not be able to show him exactly how much she cared for him.

Somehow she couldn't help but feel sorry for the young woman, Merry, who was put in such an awkward position, married to a man she secretly loved but didn't know if he loved her back. The likeness to her own situation was quite strong, and she had no problem understanding the frustration Merry must have felt.

"Why didn't he just tell her that he loved her? I'm sure she would have felt it much easier to forgive him if she had only known her feelings for him were returned in full."

"Who knows? Maybe he didn't think it would help, that there was no possible chance for her to love him back. Or maybe he just didn't know how to tell her."

Charmaine snorted with disbelief. "How could he not know how to tell her? How hard can it be to say those three small words?"

"I love you."

Her heart skipped a beat as she turned to stare at his serious face.

"I beg your pardon?" she whispered hoarsely, not believing what she had just heard him say, and he looked back at her, arching an amused eyebrow in that very Darling way which she suddenly decided she disliked immensely.

"Weren't those the three small words Dominic should have told Merry? I love you?"

Her heart sank like a stone as a wave of disappointment hit her. For one small moment she had thought he had acknowledged his love for her, and although she was quite aware he was not in love with her, her heart had leapt with joy.

"Y-yes," she stuttered and sat on the bench across from him, her old lump in the throat growing unmercifully again.

"Anyway," Sin continued, stretching his legs even farther across the small floor until his feet almost touched hers and looking deliciously comfortable and huggable, "Merry wasn't too pleased about the engagement, and during the time leading up to the wedding she did absolutely everything she could think of that would make him want to end the engagement. It was rumored, though never confirmed, that she even dressed in men's clothes and stopped his carriage to rob him and some friends of his."

"She did?" Charmaine was impressed. That was a young woman she would have loved to meet. Such spirit and gumption was worth admiring, because it was something she had never possessed herself. She was a survivor, but she would rather follow the stream than fight it.

"It is said so. Dominic was furious with her, not for robbing them but for putting herself in a position where she could have been killed."

"Poor Dominic."

"Indeed. But in the end everything turned out well, and they lived happily until they both died of old age."

She looked at his feet so close to hers, and she touched one of them lightly with her own foot, in an awkward show of affection. "Do you think we will live happily until we die?"

"I hope so."

She smiled nervously toward him. "I hope we will be happy."

"Well, then, I guess I can guarantee you we will, because if we both want to be happy there is no way we cannot be, is there?" he asked with a wry smile, and she sank back, feeling oddly sad.

Who was she fooling?

There was no way she ever would be happy if Sin didn't love her. She would again be caught pretending to be something she wasn't, and in this case it meant she would have to spend the rest of her life repressing her feelings for him.

She couldn't do that. Not anymore. She was free now, free from her stepfather and his almighty shadow. This was about the rest of her life, so why should she sit back and pretend she wouldn't mind a loveless marriage?

Merry wouldn't have stayed quiet, she thought with a mental smile. She would have fought for what she believed in, and Charmaine wanted to believe in a marriage filled with love. But if she declared her love for him, could she take it if he rejected her, or even pitied her?

Probably not. But then again, she didn't want to live the rest of her life in a loveless marriage, pretending to be satisfied. She harrumphed nervously, and he looked at her with an inquiring eyebrow raised.

"Yes?"

She took a deep breath. "I love you."

His smile faded away as he stared at her, his eyes dark in a face frozen in silent shock, and she knew this was her one and only moment to ever be able to persuade him into loving her back.

"I really do," she continued quickly while she still hadn't lost all her gumption. "I love you so much, and I j-just don't know how to live without you."

She swallowed as he stared at her without any reaction whatsoever. She knew she was about to lose him forever. Lose her happiness forever.

She stood and took the few steps necessary to stand directly in front of him. Breathlessly she kneeled, grasping his unmoving hands in hers.

"Do you think it is possible for you to love me back? I would be…" She blinked to get rid of the pain in her eyes. "It would mean everything for me to know if you just loved me a little. So could you? Could you please love me a tiny bit?"

He was silent for so long she almost stood up and left him, but just as she had decided to admit defeat he shook his head slowly. "No, I can't."

Her heart broke into thousands of pieces and only old habit made her capable of forcing a smile onto her face. "Well, one can't ask for everything, I guess."

But when she tried to move back to get away from him, he clasped her hands with one of his and forced her to stay, sighing deeply as he put his other hand against her cheek. To her surprise, she saw tears in his eyes, and a small flicker of hope started to dance inside her.

"How could I ever be able to love you only a little when you mean everything in the world to me?" His voice broke, and with a faint whimper she threw herself into his waiting arms, hugging him desperately closer to her until she could feel the steady beat of his heart against hers.

"I love you," she whispered, her voice raw with emotion, but she just couldn't stay silent anymore. She wanted to chant the words to him, to the world, over and over again until she had no voice left.

"I love you too."

The tenderness in his voice went straight to her heart, and tears filled her eyes, but she didn't care. Slowly that lump in her throat grew smaller and smaller with every sob, until it disappeared altogether, leaving only a wonderful feeling of peace.

His warm, safe hands caressed her hair, and she sighed in her happiness, amazed at how protected and at home she felt. Nothing scared her anymore. Nothing. She was exactly where she wanted to be, in Sin's arms.

"I never thought you would love me."

His quiet admission surprised her, and she leaned back so she could look into his eyes.

"Why?"

"Because you are you and I'm just me. I'm nothing special. In fact, I'm a bit of a bore. But you... You are the Incomparable Queen. The most beautiful woman any of us has ever seen or ever will see."

"That is the most stupid thing I've ever heard."

He chuckled as she snorted straight out, and before she had a chance to react he grabbed her waist and hauled her up onto his knee. She gave a sigh of contentment as he put his arms around her again and gave her a peck on the nose.

"You are one disrespectful woman."

"I am? Oh, I'm sorry, I didn't mean to. It's just that I don't find it so impressive about me being beautiful or the Incomparable Queen."

"Don't apologize, my dearest. I don't mind the disrespectfulness. I must admit I rather like it."

"I love you, Sin."

"And I love you, Charmaine."

"Do you really?"

He nodded. "Yes, I do. I have for the longest of times."

"You have?" She remembered what her father had said about Sin staring at her, and she frowned slightly. "For how long?"

"For many years."

"But you never said anything. You never even looked at me, as far as I can remember."

"I know. I didn't want you to know how I felt."

She snorted again. "That's ludicrous."

His eyes laughed at her obvious curiosity. "It might be, but I never thought it possible for you to love me back, so I tried to spare my heart from sorrow."

"But if you had given me a chance…"

"When? You were always surrounded by too many suitors to even notice me. I did ask you to dance now and then, but I don't think you even noticed it was me you were dancing with. You just stared out into space, moving as if you were a puppet."

"I was." And it was the truth. She hadn't had a chance to think for herself. Her stepfather had sent her dancing with one man after another to make sure he would get the satisfaction of denying them when they came proposing. Denying them in her name.

"I know that now. Only the Lord knows how much I would like to kill that man. I promise you, Charmaine, I have never hated a man so much as I hate your stepfather. It sickens me we let him escape, that we gave him a chance to start over somewhere else."

She put her hand against his cheek and smiled tenderly toward him. "Don't let him get to you. Please. I'm so sick and tired of him ruining my life, and now I just want to be happy. With you."

The kiss he gave her made her whimper with need of him, and he grinned as he heard the faint sound. "Do you know how hard it was for me to leave you every night?"

"Why did you leave me? All I wanted was to be with you."

He blushed slightly, seeming uncomfortable. "Because I was so close to telling you how much I loved you every time we made love. I just couldn't keep my hands off you—still can't, if you notice—and I was so scared you would find out how pathetic I really am when it comes to you, I just couldn't stay. But I wanted to. Desperately."

"Don't ever leave me again."

His arrogant smile made her warm all over. "Oh, I can promise you that. Don't you think I will ever let you out of my bed again. We can turn your bedroom into a dressing room. Lord knows you have dresses enough to fill it."

"I beg your pardon. I don't have that many dresses."

"You soon will, I guess. Especially as we are heading to London and the Season soon, where you will shine on my arm and show every last gossip how much you love your husband."

"Oh I will, will I?" She laughed over his silliness, but deep inside she knew this was important to him. "Well, I guess I couldn't hide the love I feel for you anyway, so all right. I'll give the matrons something to talk about."

His hand played with a blonde strand of hair that had slipped out from her bun, and she waited patiently for him to come out with what it was on his mind.

"I'm not overly fond of the Season," he finally let out. "I must admit I would rather spend those months at home here at Chester Park than stumbling around in a ballroom."

"Me too."

"I know how much you love those assemblies, and

for you I will go anyway. I promise you I'll take you to every last one you want to attend."

It was quite obvious he hadn't listened to her, but she didn't mind. She rather liked the notion of him coming to London with her just to please her. She didn't like the Season at all. There were too many people, and it was too crowded. But at the same time, she wouldn't mind going with Sin. Just the thought of being presented as Lady Chilton to all her old acquaintances made her warm all over.

She was so proud of him, and proud that he was her husband. Her man. She wanted the *ton* to know how much she loved him, and she definitely wanted them to know how much he loved her.

"I guess the Season will be better when I have you with me and can fondle you whenever I am so minded," he said, his dark eyes burning for her. With a sigh she threw her arms around his neck again and kissed him with all her love.

Slowly he put her down on the floor, and as his hands transformed her into an emotional being she knew she couldn't be happier than she was at that moment. Somehow all her wishes had come true, and she was happy. She was loved. She loved.

Life couldn't get any better than this.

Epilogue

September, 1815

Sin,

I bring glorious news to you. The devil is dead. As I've told you before, he has been gambling extensively and lost more than he has to more men than he should. Unfortunately for him, he didn't pay the wrong men back, and yesterday he was attacked, and killed.

I hope this news gives your lovely wife and her just-as-lovely sister relief. He will never come back to haunt them as he has tried to do ever since we arrived here in June. It was becoming quite difficult to keep him here, and his death has eased my life considerably.

Hereford says you two are expecting a little one, and I can only say it saddens me, as I will probably not be able to get back in time for the blessed event.

After I received the death certificate, I buried Lord Nester here in the colonies and made sure his grave is unmarked, just as you requested.

If all fares well, I'll see you at Christmas.
Bear.

A word about the author...

Mother of kids.
Writer of romance.
Addict of coffee.
jenniferwenn.com